# in her veins

## EMMY ELLIS

*This book is a work of fiction. Names, places, events, and characters are fictitious or are used fictitiously, a product of the author's imagination. Any similarities to actual events, or persons, living or dead, are purely coincidental.*

# Chapter One

*S*hut. The. Fuck. Up.

Did you hear what I said? I'm not playing games today. No messing. Sick of you piss-arsing about with my mind, making me do things I don't want to do. Yes, you heard me. I don't want to do them. Only reason I do is to get rid of you. Makes me feel better when I do what you say. And then everything goes calm, like it should be. Like I'm normal and the same as everyone else. That's all I've ever wanted, anyway.

I got rid of them and I'll get rid of you. It's all about choosing the right moment. I'll make it on my own without you, you'll see.

*Are you laughing? You are, aren't you?*

*Right, that's it. You've pissed me off. I'm an adult now, and no one can make me do anything I don't want to. Go on, get lost. Get out.*

*Fuck. Off.*

# Chapter Two

**M**other sat on the sofa opposite me, her skirt bunched to the waist, legs splayed open. A needle dangled from the vein on her inner thigh. She'd nodded out again, the liquid drug careening through her body, reaching every avenue of every vein.

She'd be nice when she woke up, tell me to go to the shops and get some sweets. I couldn't wait. Hunger twisted my guts—I last ate in school at lunchtime.

I never bought sweets, though. I'd buy a sausage roll or a sandwich—eat half, save the rest for the morning. No breakfast cereal in our house, see. Not much of anything.

Mother stirred. A smile broke out on her face and, with eyes still closed, she reached for and removed the needle. The syringe wasn't empty; she'd blacked out before her thumb had finished the squeeze.

"All right, sugar?" she said.

Mother smiled again, displaying chipped, stained teeth. Moving her greasy hair from her eyes, she stood, straightened her skirt, and almost floated towards her purse on the sideboard.

"Want some sweets?"

I removed my thumb from my mouth—the pad shrivelled from my sucking—uncurled myself from under my blanket and stood before her.

She handed me five pounds. "Don't come back for an hour, okay? Bob's due."

I took the money and left the house. My arms, bare in a sleeveless, thin dress, sprang goose bumps. I shivered. A car drew up to the kerb, headlights blinding. I rubbed my eyes then dazedly watched Bob getting out of his car.

"Hey, Carmel. Isn't it our special night tonight?" He winked.

I shook my head and, with knees together, hugged myself to banish the cold.

"It's not Thursday yet, is it?" My small voice carried nowhere.

"You're a smart cookie for a kid, Carmel. You're right, it isn't Thursday. I was just kidding."

I sighed. Bob rapped on the front door, its surface scarred from years of neglect. He pushed down the handle and let himself in, smiling back at his *favourite little girl*. He shut the door.

Head bowed, I made my way to the shop. Hunger should have spurred me onwards, but I dawdled to waste minutes.

The shop's overhead heaters blasted my skin as I went inside, and I stood in the warmth until I'd defrosted, only to be chilled again by the open refrigerator while deciding what to buy. Bacon sandwich with lettuce, or a ham and tomato? They'd been reduced in price—I could buy two.

My stomach growled. I grabbed two packets of sandwiches and walked down each aisle, not wanting to leave the warmth of the shop. I paused to watch a shelf stacker place packets of dainty teacakes on a rack. I looked at the sandwiches and thought about putting one back and buying some of those cakes. My sluggish mind tried to total the cost, but I sighed and gave up.

The shelf stacker finished her task. I followed her to the next aisle. She filled a shelf with reduced-price bread, down from eighty-five pence to twenty. I had enough to buy a whole loaf. I could only have two pounds out of the five Mother had given me. If I took less than three pounds home it meant my nose would bleed, my face blacken. She was good at that kind of thing, punishment.

The clock behind the counter indicated another forty minutes needed to pass before I could return home. I paid for the sandwiches, the uncut loaf of bread, and loitered beneath the heater over the door for one last blast of comfort.

Outside, a drizzle of rain fell, a fine mist that wetted quicker than a downpour. Huddling against the shop wall, close to the door so that heat warmed me when it opened, I sat on my haunches under the protection of the canopy. I ripped at the loaf; its dryness stuck in my throat, and my gums clogged with the crust. I waited.

People passed by in their thick, warm coats, droplets of rain on their shoulders, drips from umbrellas. They ignored me, the shivering child with breadcrumbs around her mouth, filthy fingernails bitten to the quick.

Time plodded on. The clock on the village hall showed fifteen minutes before home time, so I gathered my food in the carrier bag and stepped out from the canopy, nose numb, toes unfeeling. Rain drenched me. My mind wandered.

"I need a new coat, Mam."

"Yeah, well, I need me smack, so you'll have to wait. No smack, no customers. No customers, no smack and no coat, see? Go fuck yourself for a new coat. Pinch one from school or something."

I didn't want to have to do that, but the harsh weather would force me to. Maybe the lost property box would have a pretty pink coat with cream fur around the hood, or perhaps a sparkly purple one with matching gloves attached through the arms with elastic. On the other hand, maybe it wouldn't have any coats at all.

I rounded the corner. Bob's taillights greeted me, and I wished Thursday was here already. Running full pelt, I dashed indoors, the meagre heat in the house not much different from outside.

Still clutching the carrier bag, I scooped my dirty blanket from the floor, wrapped it around myself, and trudged upstairs to my room. On my bed, I counted.

Forty-seven hours until Thursday. The one day a week I felt special, where I was allowed a bath, had my hair done nice, and wore the pretty dress with the ribbons. Where I was sometimes told to sniff the powder through a rolled up ten pound note, got hugs from Bob, and had my picture taken. To me it was Heaven.

Because on Thursdays I felt loved.

Looking back, it wasn't all bad. I must have been happy at some point. I think. Like at school with the other kids. Normal. I felt normal with them most of the time. The same as, you know? We all had to wait in line, all had to sit on the square of carpet at registration time. Everyone was treated like everyone else. Or so I thought.

I went to stay for tea at another child's house for the first time once and noticed the difference between my life and hers. Belinda Abbott sat on the table next to mine in class, the only table in the room shaped like a fifty pence piece. I didn't know it then, but that table was for the *problem* children. You know, those with hassles at home, or the kids with learning difficulties. So, there was a difference even then, wasn't there? Singled out. Again. But—I felt special being at that table, so it doesn't count in the long list of things I now consider to be the points in my life that marked me out as *strange*.

The first difference? Belinda's mam collected us from school. My mam didn't bother. She'd considered me well able to walk the two miles to and from school since the age of four.

"Hello, darlings," Belinda's mam said. She hugged Belinda first and then me. I remember feeling awkward in her embrace, as if I didn't belong, and heat flared on my cheeks. "Are we ready then?"

Belinda took my right hand, and her mam took my left. My palm was sweaty with self-consciousness, and I wondered if Belinda's mam would snatch her hand from mine. She didn't. She held it all the way to her house. I watched carefully to see if she wiped her palm on her coat or washed her hands at the sink in the kitchen once she let my hand go like Mrs. Draper, our teacher, did once. She didn't.

I knew I smelt, could smell myself, so it made sense other people would smell me too. What a kid—grubby-faced every day except Thursday. Belinda's mam didn't seem to notice, or if she did, she hid her feelings well.

"What would you like for your tea?" she asked and crouched on in front of the open freezer door.

I sidled up behind her and jumped back in shock. Food filled every one of the shelves. Boxes containing amazing stuff like chicken curry and pizzas blared at me in glorious colour. I blinked. Belinda's mam shifted the contents to the side to see better into the depths, and I caught a glimpse of Bird's Eye fish fingers. We only had the cheap kind at home.

"Spaghetti Bolognese," said Belinda.

Her mam turned to me. "Is that what you'd like, Carmel, or d'you fancy something different?"

Not only did I get to choose what I wanted, but I could have something different to Belinda. Her mam was willing to cook twice? Too much to take in. Warm liquid trickled down my legs. I looked at the pristine floor tiles. They shone; they weren't covered in dirt or stains. Well, I'd be lying if I said that. I'd stained them. A pool of piss the colour of apple juice grew bigger the more my bladder released. Tears stung the backs of my eyes, and I fisted them away and stared at the mess I'd made. I sensed Belinda's mam watching me.

"Whoopsie doo, love. Looks like you had a little accident. Belinda, would you go upstairs and fetch me some of your knickers, socks, and a skirt?"

Relief flooded through me as Belinda first skipped out of the kitchen then bounded up the stairs. Still staring at the floor tiles, I winced—the cold from the open freezer nipped at my damp legs. Piss discoloured my socks.

"Well, now, Carmel. Belinda will get you some clean clothes, and you can have a wash in the bathroom before you put them on. Actually, Belinda has some clothes you can take home with you, if you like. That's if your mother won't mind you having them. Do you think she'd mind?"

I nodded. Mam would go mad. She'd go on about not being a charity case, that she'd rather I wore my scraggy clothes than take any given by do-gooders. It was okay to steal a coat from school, but to accept clothes as a gift…

"Oh, well, never mind."

Belinda's mam shut the freezer door and crouched in front of me, apparently oblivious to the piddle that crept ominously close to her hosiery-clad knees.

"Carmel. Is everything okay at home?"

Although a slim woman, fat laced her jowls. She looked like the school hamster when it packed its cheeks with food. Belinda told me her mam worked in the new women's clothes shop in town while Belinda attended school. A fashionable mam. My mam didn't dress like her. I couldn't see Belinda's mam wearing short skirts that showed off her knickers and tops that barely covered her bra.

Belinda scooted into the kitchen, saved me from answering. "I got me pink jeans, me red knickers, and me purple sparkly socks, Mam. Carmel, d'you like me sparkly socks? I do, they're my favourite, but you can borrow them, all right?"

I turned from Belinda's mam to my friend. My throat clogged like it had with that loaf of bread. "All right," I said.

"Right." Belinda's mam stood, two round patches of piss on the knees of her tights. "Belinda, you take Carmel upstairs and show her where the bathroom is, and I'll get along and make the dinner. Carmel, you didn't say what you'd like for your tea."

"I'll have the same as Belinda. Thank you, Belinda's mam."

She laughed. "Oh, Carmel. You can't call me that. My name's Margaret, but you can call me Margo."

She ruffled my hair, and her fingers snagged on my unruly mop. I took the clothes Belinda held out, and she said, "Here y'are. Come on, let's go and play upstairs. We can dress up if you like. You wanna do that?"

I smiled for a second. That smile faded; I took a step, and urine squelched in my shoes. Heat filled my cheeks again, and I followed my friend out of the kitchen. I'm not sure, but

Belinda's mam made a funny noise. I think she might have been crying.

⁂

I put the toilet seat down in the bathroom and sat on it, the coldness of my damp clothes uncomfortable, and glanced round, eyes wide. So many toiletries; surely they couldn't use that many? Dozens of bottles of bubble bath and shower gel stood along the bath edge against the tiled wall. Three corner shelves held shampoo, conditioner, and body creams. The windowsill, well, I could hardly see it for the amount of different perfumes. Large thin bottles, small fat ones. Round, oval, even star-shaped—all posh, all calling out for me to smell them.

I kicked off my shoes and peeled off my socks. The shoes *thunked*, and the socks splatted on the floor. My knickers almost fell down (the waistband had lost its elasticity), and I placed them beside my socks along with my skirt. I needed to find something to wash with.

Stacks of freshly laundered face cloths sat folded neatly on a wicker hamper. All shades of pink to match the bathroom colour scheme. I chose a cerise cloth and brought it to my nose, inhaling the wonderful smell of washing powder. Anger flared in my gut. Ripped squares from old towels, complete with hanging threads, served as washcloths at home. Ours smelled of damp not roses. Ours felt slimy not fluffy.

I turned to the seashell-shaped sink and marvelled at the gold taps. The porcelain shone as if polished. I leant forward and looked at myself in the taps; my nose appeared huge, my face skewed and odd. Putting in the plug, I turned on the hot water and waited until the sink half-filled. I pretended to be a princess living in a posh castle. The pretty pink soap smelt so lovely that I had the urge to put it in my pocket and take it home.

"Carmel, luv?" Belinda's mam knocked on the bathroom door.

"Yes?"

"I have a carrier bag here for your wet clothes. I'll leave it just outside the door, all right?"

"Okay," I said.

I waited until Margo's footsteps receded before plunging the face cloth into the water and rolling the soap in my palms so much my hands whitened with foam. The water turned milky. I wished, after the soap's perfume rose with the steam, that I was having a bath. As I soaped my legs, the stench of urine and my everyday aroma jumped up and slapped me in the face. It smelt worse here somehow, as though being in such clean and pristine surroundings made the whiff of me more obvious.

The washcloth soft on my legs, I wiped off the soap. I wanted to experience the feel of that warm cloth on my skin time and time again.

"Carmel. Hurry up. You've been ages," Belinda called.

"Okay," I said.

After washing, I dressed in Belinda's clothes and sat on the toilet seat to pull on the sparkly purple socks.

I felt well posh.

"You put on the white one, and I'll put on the pink one. We'll be queens, and those teddies there are the people. D'you wanna wear some of my mam's shoes? I wear them all the time, and they clip-clop just like they do on me mam when she walks me to school or we go to the shops."

Belinda held two long, frilly petticoats that must have once been the underskirts of a wedding dress. I took the white one and stepped into it. It reached to my armpits and dragged on the floor.

"Roll the waist bit over loads of times, and then I'll tie one of me belts round you so it don't fall off."

I did as she said, creating a big fat sausage around my waist. Belinda cinched a silver belt around me to top off the ensemble, and I walked over to her full-length mirror. I looked ridiculous, but right then I felt just like the queens we pretended to be.

"What's your queen name going to be?" Belinda asked.

I thought for a moment and spied a row of porcelain dolls on a shelf above Belinda's bed. Those dolls looked so pretty in their frilly gowns, their faces so perfect, rosy cheeked. "Queen Dolly."

"Queen Dolly. Right." Belinda stepped into her long skirt. "Well I'm going to be Queen Scarlet. She's the best queen of them all."

With those words, the game lost its appeal.

For just once in my life, *I* wanted to be the best queen of them all.

# Chapter Three

"Get yourself in the bath quick sharp, Carmel. Bob'll be here soon, and you're fucking filthy." Mam, dressed in her evening attire, looked reasonably presentable, if a little brassy.

Her blonde hair, washed and styled, hung loose. Her short black skirt and white blouse reminded me of a waitress in the posh café in town. She'd shaved her legs—a slight nick on her knee bled—and she slid her feet into pointy black stiletto shoes.

"Well, what are you standing there for? Bloody gawping at me like you haven't just been told to do something. I tell you, Carmel, if you play me up tonight and act dumb I'll bleedin' brain you. Look at last week. Jesus. Making out you didn't know what Bob wanted you to do. You've been doing it long enough now to know the ropes." She glanced my way, and her penetrating, brown-eyed stare had anger burning inside me. Why wasn't she like Belinda's mam? Why wasn't Belinda's mam like mine?

Standing from the grubby sofa, she teetered for a second in her high heels then righted herself. "Well, go on. Don't just stand there. Get in the bath while I have me medicine."

I turned from her and left the room, slinking upstairs.

"And don't forget to put that dress on!" she screeched. "Didn't stand there ironing it for nothing. You crease it, and your arse is dust."

"Okay," I said.

Our bathroom—what can I say? One bar of shitty white soap, the surface marred with ravines from lack of use. No bubble bath, and only one bottle of shampoo. Thoughts of Belinda's bathroom filled my mind, and I frowned, trying to comprehend why our homes were so different.

Too young to understand, see. Too small to realise the real reason for the differences.

We didn't have any family that visited, or anyone we went to see. All I knew was our small, shabby little house and everything that went on in it. Why would I query my life pre-Belinda when I had nothing to compare it to? Fuck, I watched TV, but to me, those people weren't real. Mam said they were all actors and nobody really lived like that. Mam said people who worked in shops and offices weren't our kind. We should mix with our own. But who *were* our own? Were they Bob and Pete and Frank and…?

A grey ring circled the inside of our bath. I had to fill the bath to the ring and not go past it. Usually, the water sloshed above the ring with my weight once I got in, and if I managed to stay in there long enough, the ring got soggy and I smudged it. If I tried *really* hard and used my fingernails, I scraped letters of the alphabet into the ring to pass the time and pretended I was a teacher writing on a blackboard. The whole class would listen to me, find what I had to say interesting. I remember thinking I might try to be a teacher when I grew up.

Mam'd had a bath before me, her water still there, so I undressed and climbed in. The ring had been soaking for some time, so I eased back in the dirty water and, using the handle of Mam's Bic razor, I scraped out letters. It must have taken some time—the bath water got cold—and Mam shouted, "Get the fuck out of that bath, Carmel. *Now.*"

I hastily washed with the odourless soap and rinsed my body. Pulling the plug out and wrapping the chain around the tap as many times as I could—I had a thing about doing that—I stepped out of the bath. Mam had used the only towel we owned. Its cold dampness and the sharp chill in the room slapped my skin, and I took a quick intake of breath. Dry. Must get dry.

Before leaving the bathroom to run into Mam's room and put on my dress, I turned to look at my handiwork on the bath ring.

QUEEN DOLLY.

"Carmel! *My favourite little girl.*" Bob swept me into a hug.

I lit up inside. Only on Thursdays, though. Any other night he came round, unease settled in my gut, and I never understood why. His demeanour seemed different on Thursdays. He looked at me kindly, spoke to me nicely. Every other evening I was plain Carmel, the kid who had to get out of the house and out of the way for an hour or two.

We stood in the middle of the living room. The rough brown carpet grazed the soles of my feet. I hung my head while he hugged me. Grit and dirt nestled between my toes, and I remember thinking: *I must make sure they're clean before any pictures are taken.* Mam had smacked the living daylights out of me that time when the pictures had showed a smudge of jam on my cheek.

Bob held a bag. He drew away from me. "Carmel. I've got something for you. I think you're good enough now to wear a new, different outfit, don't you?"

A new outfit? But I loved my pretty dress.

"Answer him, Carmel," Mam said. "You're a damn rude kid."

Mam's medicine obviously hadn't worked yet, or she hadn't had time to take it. Or maybe she hadn't taken enough. She got like that sometimes, where her body must have screamed, "More H. Give me more H, Annette." It would depend how many Harrys or Freds had been to the house—they determined Mam's medicine and her mood. And my treatment.

"I'll love the new outfit, Bob," I said.

Bob stared at me, his eyes glassy — like the dolls' eyes at Belinda's. "Yes," he finally said. "It'll look good in the pictures." He held the bag out to me. "Get it out, then. Take a look."

He smiled.

I smiled.

I sat on the edge of the couch and opened the bag. Material wasn't in it. Well, not the material of another pretty dress, anyway. My first close-up glimpse of leather. And silver chains, the links larger than any necklace I'd seen. I reached into the bag, grasped the outfit, and pulled it out.

Mam barked out a brittle laugh. "I thought you were joking when you said you'd be buying that, Bob. Fucking hell, you're priceless. How did you get one to fit a kid?"

Straps. Straps linked with silver chains.

Ugly.

I didn't want to wear it.

"Someone made it for me. Get extra money for these kinds of pictures, Annette."

"Good," she said. "I want to make the rest of this place nice like the back room."

"Take her out the back and show her how to put it on. I'll get the camera from the car." Bob left the living room.

I couldn't shift my gaze from the outfit.

"What are you standing there like that for, Carmel? You heard him. Out the back with you. I'll help you put on your new clothes."

Mam laughed again, a spiteful sound that jarred my nerves.

The back room was *posh*, or so Mam said, and I'd believed that until I'd gone to Belinda's house. Posh to Mam obviously wasn't the same as reality. Red, painted walls. Black silk curtains that matched the sheets. I know now that that room was gaudy and trashy and all the things people associate with prostitutes. A red fluffy carpet covered the floor—no dirt there.

"Get out of that dress, Carmel, and hurry up about it. Bob hasn't got much time tonight—gotta be somewhere else by nine."

I took off my dress, put it on the bed, and stood naked.

"Right. Let's have a look at this thing." Mam held the outfit in front of her, turning it this way and that, obviously trying to work out which way up it went. To me it looked like a web of dog leashes. "Ah, here we go. Come over here."

I took the few steps needed to reach Mam, and she bent to my level, still holding up the leather. "Put both your feet inside these loops."

The cold chains moved up my legs, and I shivered. Two more loops for my arms, a rough twist of my body from Mam so I faced away from her, and the metal's jangle told me she'd secured the outfit.

"Turn round and face me, kid."

Bob came into the room at that moment, stopping in the doorway to stare at me. I used to think of Mam and Bob and all the other men as old when I was small, but now I know they were in their twenties at this point in my life. Still young themselves, perhaps they didn't realise the wrongs they committed. Or maybe they didn't care.

Bob wasn't a good-looking man. Made me wonder if that's why he came round to our house—no other female would give him a second glance. His cheeks, pitted with scars, possibly from chickenpox, gave him a ruddy complexion. He reminded me of a burns victim. And his nose…how was it possible to have one so big and hooked? I used to wonder if it was a fake one stuck on with glue, but I pulled it once and it didn't come off. A bird of prey, that's what he was. His dark hair—always greasy—hung long and lank about his shoulders. Sometimes he wore it in a low ponytail, and I'd think he looked like a girl. I remember he wore a tan suede jacket, the pockets fat and filled with Mam's medicine and all manner of things to do with it.

He smiled, one I didn't like, and said, "Well, my favourite little girl. You look so pretty."

I didn't feel pretty. I smiled anyway.

"Looks better than we thought she would, eh, Bob? Think of the fucking money." Mam's laugh—she laughed a lot that night—made me want to cry.

"Best get down to business then." Bob flipped his dark fringe off his forehead.

At his words, I moved to get on the bed, the chains a melody of sound as I walked.

"No. Not on the bed tonight, Carmel."

That Thursday night it took a long time for me to get to sleep. I licked my sore lips to soothe them.

My new outfit hadn't made me feel special— not like the pretty dress had. I didn't mind having my photos taken and Bob hugging me if I wore that dress, but that new outfit—no, I didn't feel special anymore. Didn't feel loved.

Didn't feel anything.

Afterwards, alone in the back room, I walked to the full-length mirror to see exactly how I could be so pretty in such a thing. I decided I didn't look very nice at all, but if it meant Mam could earn enough money to make the rest of the house posh like Belinda's then I'd wear the outfit again and again.

I scrutinised my features. I owned hair and eyes and a mouth, everything Belinda had. Apart from my raggedy clothes and shoes, my tangled hair, to a stranger, I could *possibly* have resembled any other kid, one of a crowd. But as an adult now and seeing the same kinds of kids running riot in the street—I don't think so. People must have known I wasn't cared for properly.

And no one did a thing about it.

At school the next day, Belinda said, "Will you be allowed at my house again after school? I reckon my mam will say yes, and we can play queens again. Or if you don't want to play queens we can do jigsaws and stuff."

Friday. Mam would treat herself to extra medicine. She wouldn't even notice I wasn't there. "Yes. I can come to your house."

I would be Queen Dolly and wash myself with the pretty soap when I visited the bathroom. I thought I might even cop a spray from one of the perfumes on the windowsill. If I got really brave, I could shit my knickers. Maybe I'd get a bath then.

Smell clean. I just wanted to smell clean.

# Chapter Four

L ike Mam, Belinda's dad always seemed angry. Deep ravines lined his forehead even if he wasn't pissed off. I didn't like it when he came home from work. Belinda's mam changed upon his arrival. She didn't smile much, and a frown wrecked her brow too. My tummy always tightened at the sound of his key in the lock, and I awaited the change in atmosphere. Belinda didn't seem to notice and carried on as usual.

This one day we sat in the living room. He walked in and slapped his briefcase down so hard on the coffee table that I jumped. My heart thudded, and I really thought he was angry because I was there. Belinda and I had been making jigsaws at the little table, and the pieces bounced in the air and scattered on the carpet.

"Aw, Dad." Belinda sighed and picked up the pieces.

I followed suit.

Belinda's dad left the room, the acrid smell of his aftershave lingering in his wake. Murmured conversation filtered through from the kitchen, but I couldn't make out what they said.

Belinda interrupted my concentration. "You haven't got a dad, have you, Carmel?"

I hadn't thought about it much before that. "Nah, just a mam."

"Reckon it might be nice to just have a mam," she said. She threw puzzle pieces into the jigsaw box. "What's it like with just you and your mam?"

I put a piece of jigsaw away. "It's all right."

"My dad said you got lots of uncles. I haven't got an uncle. Got some aunties, though."

*Uncles?*

"Nah. I haven't got any uncles. Just me mam."

"Well, my dad said…"

Belinda's dad walked into the room with a small white dessert bowl, slammed it on the table, and said, "Your dad says you talk too much. Your dad says you can both have some sweets before dinner if you shut up."

My tummy clenched, not at what he'd said, but his tone. However, the possibility of sweets soon made the discomfort fade. Belinda's dad—I never did learn his name, but secretly christened him Arsey—opened his briefcase and pulled out a large bag of Bassett's Liquorice Allsorts. Belinda ripped open the bag and filled the bowl. Arsey left the room again, and we both feasted on the sweets.

Dinnertime came, and the four of us sat around the big dining room table. I sat opposite Arsey. A little uncomfortable, I hung my head and pretended he wasn't staring at me. That night we had tuna and pasta bake. I'd never had pasta before. The cream-coloured sauce looked so appetising that my mouth watered. Filled with sweets or not, determination to clean my plate took over me. Belinda fussed with her food and poked it around with her fork.

"Stop messing about, Belinda," Arsey said.

I chanced a peek at him. His face was frightening and hard, cheekbones standing out like the pole under a tent.

"How many sweets did you have?" he asked.

Belinda didn't answer. Arsey scraped his chair back and stomped into the living room.

"Margaret! Come in here a moment, please."

Belinda's mam quietly sighed and left the dining room. I strained to listen.

"That fucking scabby kid's eaten all the sweets," Arsey said.

"Oh. Well, I think…it's just that Belinda's the one who isn't eating her dinner so—"

"Sticking up for the scab-bag, are we?"

"No, I—"

"I don't want her here anymore. Teaching Belinda to be greedy. Besides, she stinks. How am I supposed to enjoy my meal with that stench? Her mother's a bloody tart, and God knows what state their house is in. And you're happy for our child to be friends with *that*?"

"Well I…I feel sorry for her. I didn't think it would hurt for Belinda to make friends with someone less fortunate than herself. Learn some compassion."

"If she had learned some compassion I wouldn't mind, but all she's been taught is to hog a whole bowl of sweets and is now currently wasting her dinner. Dinner I've provided by working hard, while you…"

I gobbled the rest of my meal and got up from the table.

"See you at school tomorrow, Belinda."

"You going home?"

"Yes."

"Oh, all right, then."

Belinda's mam and Arsey didn't see me walk into the living room, move past them, and out of the front door.

Story of my life. Unnoticed.

⊗⊛⊗

I let myself indoors. Mam was sprawled out, asleep on the sofa. Her mouth hung open, and I recalled one of Bob's sayings. *Shut your trap, looks like you're catching flies.*

The towelling material of Mam's formerly peach dressing gown, now grey from filth, swamped her skinny frame. Her bare feet hung over the side of the sofa, ankles standing out like mountains. Raised veins, river-blue, snaked over the tops of each foot. Between her toes, small holes topped by scabs shouted her addiction. Heroin had certainly ravaged any beauty she'd previously had; the skin beside her eyes— earthquake cracks. I imagined being an ant and walking on her face, finding those wrinkles and wondering how I would get across their width to the other side. Far from the usual greasy look, Mam's hair appeared cotton-wool dry. Perhaps she'd dyed it one time too many?

She stirred, snapped her mouth closed, and nestled her head in a more comfortable position against the filthy, ragged cushion beneath it. She mumbled in her sleep, and I tiptoed past her to the kitchen. I needed a drink of water to wash away the taste of bile on my tongue, which had risen on hearing Arsey's words.

Rinsing a cloudy glass under the tap and filling it, I gulped the water and told myself I would never go to Belinda's house again. Though I loved it there (I could forget who I was and pretend I was Belinda's sister), I knew that today had been my last. I'd use my grubby white blanket as a petticoat and be Queen Dolly in my own room—tie the corners together to make sure it didn't fall off.

Belinda's mam had said I was less fortunate. What did that mean? Arsey had said I'd taught Belinda greed. I knew what the word greedy meant, but it wasn't me who had been so. Belinda had eaten far more sweets than I had, said she wouldn't get told off for eating the whole bowl because I was there. She assured me her dad wouldn't tell her off in front of me. And he hadn't.

I sighed and placed the empty glass in the washing-up bowl. It balanced precariously on top of other dirty crockery: tea-stained mugs, plates encrusted with tomato sauce. The air smelt like vinegar, so Mam must have been to the chip shop for her tea. Though the pasta at Belinda's had been nice, chips from the chippy would have gone down a treat. We rarely ate those. Think it was only on our birthdays that we did.

Birthdays.

We'd been at school for three weeks since the Christmas holidays ended. The date that day—what was it? Well, the week before we'd put January fifteenth at the top of our letters to Santa, thanking him for our presents. I thanked him for the book I got that had a sticker inside proclaiming it belonged to Shorefield Library. I frowned at that, because didn't the book belong to me?

I counted the days on my fingers. Five days since the Santa letter day. January twentieth.

My sixth birthday.

I left the kitchen and tottered into the living room and up the stairs. Maybe there would be a present on my bed? Perhaps the birthday fairy had forgotten that morning, or had been running late and couldn't get to our house in time before I left for school.

My room smelt musty—dust and dried piss. One candy-striped bed sheet hung at the window on a piece of string, shabby with holes worn in the fabric. The blackness of the evening peeked through two of those holes that were close together and brought to mind the goblin's eyes in the book our teacher read to us at school. My bed sheet was as I'd left it, a tangled mess, my white blanket a ball.

No present. Maybe I'd got the day wrong?

I grabbed my blanket and raced downstairs. Mam still lay asleep, so I curled up on the chair and tucked the blanket all around me and stared at her through the pattern of holes. Thoughts of wrapped gifts and birthday cakes filled my mind. I didn't get excited at the prospect of having a cake, I somehow knew that wouldn't be in the cards, but, young as I was, I knew I got a present on my birthday, on the end of my bed for when I woke up on the day.

My eyelids grew heavy, and the last image I remember was of pulling pink ribbon from a brightly coloured box and having a mam that didn't look like mine singing happy birthday.

"Wake the hell up, you stinky little cow."

I snapped my eyes open to see a mam that was definitely mine, staring down at me. She'd snatched my blanket away, dumped it on the chair arm. Cold air bit my skin.

"What you doing going to sleep? You know you've got to wake me by seven. Bob's coming to collect some money. I got a new bloke starting tonight. I'm not even fucking dressed. Silly little bitch."

Her fist against my temple sent pain from one ear into the other. I scrambled off the chair, blinked, and clutched my blanket to my chest. We stared at one another. Spittle dribbled down one side of Mam's chin, and her cheeks blazed red with fury. Her breaths slowed. What I thought of as hatred in her eyes softened somewhat, and she flopped sideways and landed in the chair I'd just vacated.

Sobs jolted her slim frame. She bunched her eyes shut, and tears sprouted from them, slithering down her cheeks, their journey ending at her jaw line. It seemed I stared at her for a long time until her cries stopped.

With eyes still closed she said, "The birthday fairy came this morning. She forgot to leave your present on your bed and she put it in the bin."

My heart leapt.

"Go and get it out, Carmel," Mam said, her voice low.

I turned from her and left the house, walking down the small alley between our house and the next. Two metal dustbins stood side by side. I lifted the lid of the bin with our house number, forty-four, on it. A doll lay on the top of household refuse. A porcelain doll, just like Belinda's.

Except a diagonal crack ran across my doll's face, and she'd lost an eye. Baked bean sauce dirtied her yellow hair, and a wet teabag stained her dress; a piece of potato skin stuck to the ivory frill around the neck.

But—she was *my* dolly, and I loved her already. I would fix her face and wash her dress, clean her hair and brush it nice.

I named that doll Nelson.

# Chapter Five

A nd so my relationship with Nelson began. I hugged her to my chest, dirt and all, and made my way back inside. Mam stuffed a newspaper and magazine down the back of the sofa—her attempt at tidying up. Her dressing gown flapped open and revealed sagging tits. Nothing I hadn't seen before.

"Thank you for the doll, Mam."

"Go to my room and get my fucking dress. Hurry up."

I held Nelson's hand and ran upstairs.

"We'll be going out in a minute, Nelson. We can't go to the shop because Mam hasn't had her medicine so she won't remember to give me any money. But we'll go for a walk, all right?"

*All right, Carmel. That sounds lovely.*

"It will be lovely, Nelson. I'll show you all the places I go to, and on Thursday you can watch me have my pictures taken."

*Can I have my picture taken too?*

I stood on my tiptoes and took down Mam's dress on its hanger from the front of her scarred wooden wardrobe. "Oh, I don't know, Nelson. I'll have to ask Bob. If he comes round before we go out, I'll see what he says."

*Okay, Carmel. I like having you as a friend. Will you be my best friend for ever and ever?*

"I will, Nelson. So long as you'll be mine."

*I'll be your best friend. I like you. I think you're wonderful and pretty and fun and everything.*

I held Nelson in one hand and Mam's dress as high as I could with the other to prevent it from dragging on the floor.

Downstairs, Mam snatched it from me, flung off her dressing gown and said, "You best take care of that doll, Carmel. Not every kid gets a doll like that." She stepped into her dress. The sequins sewn onto the shoulders…how they twinkled in the light from the bare ceiling bulb. "You named the doll yet? Every doll's gotta have a name."

"Her name's Nelson," I said.

Mam laughed so long and hard as she zipped up the front of her dress that I thought she'd explode. She coughed, and her eyes watered, mascara from the previous day making black tears run down her cheeks. Cheeks that matched the colour of her red dress.

"Now look what you made me do," she said. "Fucking near made me choke myself." Mam swiped her palms over her face. "Nelson, eh? The Admiral? Why did you call your doll that?"

"Because she's only got one eye."

"And how the hell do *you* know about that geezer?"

"I learned about him at school."

*Your mam's mean, Carmel.*

I squeezed Nelson's hand to let her know she should be quiet.

Mam placed her hands on bony hips, leaned her weight on one leg. "Jeez. When I was your age I never learned nothing like that. You wanna know why Nelson's only got one eye?"

"Because he lost it having a fight. Mrs. Draper said—"

Mam's mouth formed a tight, thin line, and she narrowed her eyes. "Not *that* Nelson, you silly bitch. The *doll*."

I nodded, wanting to know.

"Because I poked her fucking eye out and smacked her face against the wall. Wanna know why I did that?"

I blinked and nodded again.

"Because you didn't come home on your birthday and eat chips with me. Because you're an ungrateful little cow, aren't you?"

Nod number three.

Mam stared at me briefly then flounced off into the kitchen shouting, "Make sure you stay out until nine tonight. Got two coming round back to back. Pinch a coat from school yet, kid?"

"No, Mam."

"You'll be cold out there, then."

I stood, unable to move my feet, and heard one of the kitchen drawers open. The sound of Mam's make-up being tossed on the worktop filtered into the living room, a sign she was readying herself for the night ahead.

*Why don't you put your cardigans on, Carmel? You won't be cold if you wear both.*

I turned, walked up to my room, and grabbed them from the small heap of dirty clothing on the floor.

"You sit there, Nelson." I bent the doll's legs and sat her against the wall at the head end of my bed. No pretty pillowcase covered my flat and stained pillow, but Nelson didn't mind. I put my cardigans on. They smelt of dirt. The scent of Belinda's clothes came to mind, and I paused, thinking for a tiny while.

It wasn't fair. Really wasn't fair how life treated people differently. My childish mind only saw the things I dearly wanted—scented soap, nice clothes, a clean and tidy house. I had none of them, and Belinda had them all. I closed my eyes and bunched them shut, flared my nostrils, and breathed in the odour of my room—the stench of a rotting, wasted life.

Bile twisted in my guts, and I imagined it to be a whirlpool like I'd seen on TV. I squeezed my eyes tighter. *Mustn't let the tears escape.* The inside of my nose stung from the effort, and a sob that sounded like a cough barked from my mouth.

*I won't cry. I won't…*

I remember thinking that. Remember it all.

The blast of Mam's hairdryer barged into my thoughts. She must have wet her hair at the kitchen sink.

A click sounded, indicating the electricity meter had shut off—not enough money in it again. The house darkened. Night noises from our street sneaked through the crack in my bedroom window. Kids shrieked, and cars drove past, their wet tyres slashing through puddles. I widened my eyes to adjust to the darkness and patted my bed for Nelson. I grasped her hand and left my room with her dangling by my side.

"Carmel? *Carmel.* Get your arse down here. *Quickly.*"

I scooted downstairs, my senses guiding me to the kitchen.

"Yes, Mam?"

"Here. Go and get someone to swap all this change for a fifty pence piece. I'm fucking sick of that electric meter running out so quickly. Just when I'm doing my bloody hair and the men are due round soon."

I stretched out my hand, and somehow, in the darkness, Mam found my palm, depositing a jingle of coins.

"Get a fucking move on," she said. "Ask the snotty bitch next door, and if she hasn't got one ask the dirty old bloke at the end of the row."

I groped my way to the front door, reached up, and thumbed the latch so I could get back indoors. Cold air snapped at my nose and cheeks, and I walked down our short pathway then up next door's. Snotty's front door had been painted recently—a posh dark red. I glanced over at ours, scored with deep gouges and peeling brown paint. Shame soared through me. I balled my hand into a fist and rapped on Snotty's door.

A light snapped on in her hallway, and a black, human shape loomed behind the netted window.

"Who is it?"

"Carmel." I heard her sigh even through the wood.

"What do you want?"

"Need to change some money for fifty p for the meter."

Her shadow moved, and the light snapped off. I stood for a moment, wondering whether to knock again, then turned and walked to the end of our row, to the old man's house. His door wasn't wood but UPVC, with a posh silver handle. Two glass panes held stained glass, like those in a church—clear glass with a tulip pattern in each centre; a green stem and a red flower. I pressed my finger on the bell pad.

The outside light, shaped like a black iron lantern, popped on. Muffled whistling from inside the house grew louder as the old man neared his front door. The silver handle moved downwards, and the door opened.

"Well, hello, Carmel. How're you diddling, my dear?"

"I'm okay, Mr Lawton. Me mam sent me to ask if you can change this money for a fifty p." I held up my coin-filled palm.

Mr Lawton stepped back, and his right arm disappeared behind the door. I knew he was reaching for the old gravy tin he kept on a shelf.

Bringing the tin to his waist, he flipped open the lid. "Well, I'm sure to have a fifty p in here. Got to keep a stock of them for *my* meter, see. Let's have a look, shall we?"

The coins tinkled as he moved them around. Mr Lawton's eyes narrowed behind his thick glasses. Mam said he was a dirty old man, but he looked nice and clean to me. Finding fifty p, he brought it out of the box and held it out.

"Got one. Here you go." He handed me the coin but made no move to take what I held out to him. He closed the tin lid and placed it back on his shelf. "Now, then, you have a nice night, won't you, my dear?" He moved to close the door.

"Mr Lawton?"

"Yes?"

"You forgot to take my money."

"So I did," he said. "Well, if I forgot it means it wasn't much on my mind, so I can't need it too badly. What say you keep those coins, buy some sweets at the shop?"

I nodded. "Thanks, Mr Lawton."

"Have a nice night now, Carmel."

I turned, waved, and skipped down the path, the coins clutched in one fist and Nelson's arm in the other. At our front door, I pulled down my sock and hid the loose change inside, nestling them underneath my foot so they didn't make a noise. I stepped inside.

"Took you long enough." Mam stood in the hallway in front of the cupboard under the stairs. The electricity meter was housed in there among old shoes and all manner of junk. I jumped as I'd expected her to still be in the kitchen.

"Snotty didn't have one so I had to ask Mr Lawton," I said.

"Ask you in to cop a feel, did he?"

*Cop a feel? Mr Lawton?*

"No, he didn't, Mam."

I closed the door, walked to Mam, and handed her the fifty p.

"Must be mellowing in his old age." She handed back the money. "Get in that cupboard and feed the meter. And hurry up about it. I haven't got all bleedin' night."

The cupboard belched out the smell of dirty feet and staleness. I crouched, sat Nelson beside the door opening, and climbed into the cupboard. The stiletto heel of a shoe dug into my right knee. I clamped my lips together to stop a squeal.

The electricity meter sat on the back wall, and in my haste to get to it and put the coin in, I dropped it amongst the mountain of junk.

My heart thudded. I swear Mam's breath touched the back of my neck, and I scrabbled about to find the coin. I had to be quick, else her temper would snap—Mam turned so nasty without her medicine. I patted around and dug my hand between her boots and shoes. The hook of a coat hanger snagged on the sleeve of my cardigan, and I flapped my arm to get it off. It wouldn't budge.

"Haven't you done it yet?" Mam's voice may as well have belonged to a demon—that's how it sounded to me.

*Should I tell her I've dropped the coin?*

I rooted around in the debris. "Not yet." Vomit filled my throat, and I swallowed it back. My palms grew sweaty.

*Come on. Where are you? Please let me find you. Please.*

"Carmel! Put. The. Fucking. Coin. In. The. Meter."

Mam would have been gritting her teeth.

A lump filled in my throat. "I've dropped it."

"You've *what*?"

Mam's fist landed smack in the centre of my back. She hoisted me so quickly from the cupboard that the back of my head cracked against the doorframe. I clamped my jaw and closed my eyes to shut out the pain as it spread over my skull. After lifting me into the air, Mam threw me down next to Nelson, the doll's foot digging into the base of my spine. The wire coat hanger, still attached to my sleeve, jangled against the wall. Without looking at it, I took it off and dropped it on the floor.

My eyes had adjusted to the dimness enough for me to see anger in Mam's eyes—the streetlight outside our front door shone through the glass and illuminated her features. She was a sinister dragon. At least, that's how I saw her.

She lunged into the cupboard, grabbed a shoe, and threw it at me. It smacked into the side of my head, and before I had a chance to register the pain, more items from the cupboard rained down on me. With each new throw, each new pain that sprung on my body, Mam said, "You're stupid. You can't even do that one simple thing. *One small thing* like putting a fucking coin in the meter and you go and cock it up."

Anger abated somewhat, Mam swooped down on hands and knees and patted around in the cupboard. She must have found the coin, because it tinkled into the slot. Mam turned the silver key handle, the coin plunked into the belly of the meter, and the electricity flicked back on.

I must have looked a sight: a young girl sitting on the floor, crying and rubbing her painful body, snot dribbling from her nose, face possibly ruddy and streaked with tears.

"Get up," Mam snapped. She looked angrier than I'd seen her before—brow all furrowed and features twisted in spite. Her pursed mouth, open slightly, showed the blackness of her front teeth— the legacy of heroin. "Get the fuck out of here. And when you come back, make sure I don't see you. I don't want to see your shitty little face until the morning."

A sob hitched in my throat. Without taking my gaze from Mam's, I reached behind me for Nelson and stood up.

"What the fuck are you staring at? Get out. *Get out.*"

One last glimpse at Mam's angry face, and I switched the direction of my gaze to her bunched fists. From past experience, I knew if I didn't get away from her right then, she'd strike me with them. I turned, stumbled over scattered shoes, and fled down the hallway, skidding on the cheap linoleum and banging my shoulder on the front door. Grappling with the lock while holding Nelson and shaking proved difficult. Mam's footsteps bounded behind me, and I managed to open the door and slip through it just in time, only to bump into the chest of her first customer that night.

"Henry," Mam said, her voice on the other end of the scale to what it had just been—sweet, polite, breathy.

I ran to the end of our street without looking back and didn't stop until I was safely around the corner.

*Carmel. Your mam's a monster.*

"I know, Nelson."

*Your mam's house is smelly and dirty and a nasty place to be.*

"I know."

*Your mam doesn't love you like she's supposed to.*

I didn't answer. Instead, I brought Nelson to eye level and looked at her poor, cracked face.

*Your mam is wicked, Carmel. She hurt me and she hurts you.*

I sniffed and inhaled deeply. Then ran to the park.

# Chapter Six

*I*t's not as easy as that. I have to wait until the right time. I can't just get them when you tell me to. What? Do you seriously think I can just walk up to them and do it? You make it sound like I can turn it on and off like a switch but I can't. I just can't.

Last time was all right. Last time it happened...well, the opportunity arose and it all worked out, didn't it? No one around. No one to see. No one to point the finger.

I beg your pardon? Oh, come on! I'm not going to listen to you anymore today. You're just being silly.

*I mean it. Go away. I don't want to hear your voice right now.*

*Do you want me to smash you to pieces?*

*No? Well then.*

*Shut. Up.*

# Chapter Seven

Though the darkening sky should have prevented kids from going to the park, it didn't. Streetlights and a giant circle of trees surrounded the play apparatus set up in the centre of a large field. We could play until our mams called us in. Well, other kids' mams called them in, but I went home when instinct told me the men had left our house.

"Wanna go to the park, Nelson?"

*Yes. Will you push me on a swing?*

"Yep."

I traipsed over the field, grasping Nelson's hand all the way. As I neared the central park area, I squinted to make out who played there. I smiled. Belinda climbed the side ladder of the monkey bars, grabbed the first overhead bar, and swung down. She swayed her body to gain momentum and moved one hand at a time to further bars until she'd made it to the other end. Her long hair danced from side to side, and she clambered down the other ladder and back to solid ground. No other children were out tonight. I wasn't surprised. The cold chill of the wind ensured the sensible kids stayed indoors.

"Belinda!"

She turned towards me. "Carmel. Hiya!"

I came abreast of her, and she said, "My mam and dad are shouting, so I came out to play. My dad said you're not allowed round my house no more. I'm well sad about it. How come you left so fast?"

"Needed to get home. It's my birthday today, and my mam had a present for me." I clutched Nelson's hand but kept her dangling behind me.

"Whatcha get?" Belinda's beautiful blonde hair looked so pretty with its curls—much like Nelson's would once I had a chance to brush it and make it nice.

"I got a doll just like yours. Wanna see?"

"Go on, then."

I brought Nelson from behind me and held her up. A dark stain ruined the back of the doll's dress. When Mam next slept, I'd wash it.

Belinda laughed. "That's not like my dolls. That's old and broken and really, really horrible."

I frowned and turned Nelson to face me. She *was* maybe a little tatty, but she looked all right to me. "She is not horrible. *You* are."

"I am not."

"Are too."

We stared at one another for a long time, our breaths ragged with anger. Belinda's cheeks stained red, as did the tips of her pierced ears. Her bottom lip stuck out, and her eyes brightened with unshed tears. She curled a lock of hair around her fingers and stuck the thumb of her other hand into her mouth.

Her eyes narrowed, and she smiled around her thumb. "My dad thed you sthink. I reckon he's right because you got a sthinky old doll and a sthinky old house and a sthinky old mam."

I blinked, squeezed Nelson's hand. Raised my arm. I swung my dolly in the air and struck Belinda's face with it. She removed the thumb from her mouth and wailed, her mouth gaping. Her tonsils waggled. She stopped abruptly, swiped the back of her hand across her nose, and sniffed.

"Aw, I *hate* you, Carmel." She stamped her foot and spat at me, spittle landing on my cheek.

I cuffed it with the sleeve of my cardigan — wasn't the first time I'd been spat on. She turned and ran out of the play area and onto the opposite field.

I gave chase.

I can't explain the exhilaration that coursed through me. Though angry, I sensed elation and something I can't define — freedom? A release of inner turmoil? The uneven ground proved no obstacle. I flew across the grass as if wings of vengeance lent me speed. Belinda didn't fare so well, her chubby, well-fed legs unable to carry her steadily. She stumbled, falling to the ground on hands and knees. The ends of her pretty long hair flung forward and rested on a patch of soggy mud. Now her hair was soiled like Nelson's.

Coming up behind her, I wanted to kick her on the arse, but she turned and sat on the grass, facing me.

"Carmel. I'm sorry," she said, concentrating on her hands nestled in her lap.

She fiddled with her fingers, wringing an unseen cloth. I didn't answer, and she glanced up at me, widening her eyes, just like Jerry's on the cartoons when Tom caught up with him. Maybe I looked like Mam just did back home, a big old scary dragon? I pursed my lips in anger at the thought of being like Mam.

"Say sorry to Nelson, then, and I'll be your friend again," I said.

Belinda pouted and stared at the dark sky as if in thought. She stood and planted her hands, complete with sausage-like fingers, on her hips. "I'm not talking to a doll. Not one that looks like that, anyway. Scabby old thing." Her nostrils flared, and she took four steps backwards. "Scabby, just like you." She laughed then poked out her tongue and turned, running towards the edge of the playing field.

Anger blackened my already tainted soul by covering me in its shroud, whispering into my ear that Belinda was a bad, bad girl. Tears threatened. A quick glance at Nelson had my ire rising to a new level. No one called my doll scabby. No one.

*Go get her, Carmel. Get her and hit her for being so mean.*

Belinda had a head start on me, but my legs were whippet thin and my agility and fitness so much better. Dodging slaps from Mam and running out of the house to safety was commonplace for me. I caught up to Belinda within seconds, heard her laboured breathing as she struggled to keep running.

Three large circular chunks of concrete stood a few metres ahead of us at the edge of the field. They must have been used to anchor something into the ground. A long, rusty metal spike protruded from the centre of each one. Council men had perhaps pulled them up and forgotten to take them away. I registered them in my mind and continued chasing after Belinda.

A few feet away from the concrete, I caught up to her and shoved her shoulders. She squealed and stumbled, her hands windmilling beside her. Slow motion took over my sight, and I clutched Nelson. My breath sounded loud, as if amplified on speakers set in the tree branches. My heart battered wildly, and Belinda fell forward...forward...

She hit the concrete and screamed—a horrific sound that fascinated me for a second—and I turned Nelson to watch with me as one of the metal spikes poked through the back of Belinda's skull. I turned round in a full circle, noting the still-deserted park. The trees—conspirators now, witnesses to what I'd done—loomed majestically around the edge of the field, a complete circle of wood and foliage. Black in the darkness, their leaves rustled as the wind sifted through them— laughter. I reckoned they laughed at what had happened. The stars winked, and Mr Moon gave one nod of his noble head, his smile wider than any time before.

Satisfied only nature had been a spectator, I returned my attention to the scene on the ground. I bent Nelson's legs into a sitting position and placed her against one of the other concrete chunks to watch me. I stood at Belinda's feet, taking in her splayed body. Arms akimbo, legs slightly parted, head fixed on the spike, my former friend made no sound. Her hair around the spike changed from blonde to red; those long tresses spread out, shrouding the concrete upon which her face rested.

Straddling her, I knelt and hooked my arms under hers, clasping my hands across her chest. And pulled. Pulled so hard I had to grit my teeth. Animalistic noises growled in my throat with the effort. Moments passed. I panted, thought of all the wrongs done to me, and with one last yank Belinda's head popped free of the spike. The force of the pull flung me backwards. I let go of Belinda, and she fell forwards, face scraping the spike but landing on the concrete lump next to it.

*Turn her over, Carmel.*

I stood, moved beside Belinda, and tugged at the side of her sweater, turning her onto her back. Her body thunked onto my shoes, and I freed my feet from her weight.

Twisted and broken, she rested much like Nelson had in the metal rubbish bin. Though Belinda's face was bloody and messy, I saw she'd lost an eye—the spike had driven right through it—and when she'd fallen forward again the spike must have carved a diagonal slash across her face. Her mouth a grimace, she reminded me of all things horrific.

*I want a cuddle, Carmel.*

I picked Nelson up and hugged her to me; she felt good in my arms. I looked at Belinda again and idly wondered where her eye had gone, stared at the gory cavity it had once sat in. Her knees, dirty where she'd fallen on the mud... Her calves at odd angles... The buckle on one of her shoes, obliterated from sight by a chunk of mud and grass, wasn't in keeping with the Belinda I knew, usually so clean and tidy.

*You still got that fifty p in change, Carmel?*

"Yes."

*Can you show me the shop you told me about? Get some sweets?*

"Yes."

*You don't want to worry about her. She was nasty and called us scabby.*

I took one last look at Belinda, turned away, and ran back across the playing field, through the park, and out the other side. The sense that the trees and Mr Moon, the stars, and the night birds all observed my journey invaded my mind, but I shoved them away, uneasy now that *something* had seen the accident. I held Nelson's hand and slowed to a walk once we reached the pathway that led to the shop.

"Shop's along here, Nelson."

*What sweets will you get?*

"Dunno until we get there."

We walked in silence for a time.

*You don't need nasty friends like her.*

"I know."

*Besides, look who's scabby now.*

"Yes."

I inhaled two deep breaths, and a giddy laugh bulged in my throat then spilled out of my lips like vomit.

"Nelson?"

*Yes, Carmel?*

"I didn't get to push you on the swing."

*That's okay. Maybe next time?*

"Okay."

I loved our local shop. I spent so much time there—you know, keeping warm, wasting minutes—that the staff knew me by name. If a new person started working there and I came up to the counter, one of the others would say, "And this is Carmel. She's one of our best customers." I'd beam inside but allow only a small smile. I really was quite a shy little kid. Now I had Nelson to introduce to *them*, and it made me feel important, like they appeared to me.

Shivers juddered my body more than usual, and the shop's warmth toasted my frozen fingers. I stretched them from the claw-like position they'd been in from clutching Nelson and knelt to the side of the doorway, retrieving the coins from inside my sock. The overhead heater blasted the back of my neck. I wished we had heating like that at home to make the air less frigid, more comforting.

Money and doll in hand, I walked the shop aisles to see if anything had been cut in price. Nothing had. I walked to the counter and gazed at the shelves behind, laden with huge jars of sweets. Lemon drops, Barley Sugar Twists, Sherbet Pips. So many different things to choose from. My head ached.

The smell of newspapers, bread, and tobacco filled my nostrils, and I closed my eyes to breathe in the many scents.

"Well, hello there, Carmel. And how are you this evening?"

I opened my eyes and smiled a little. Mr Hemmings, the shop owner, propped his elbows on the counter and leaned towards me, his chubby face and double chin hidden by a full, brown beard. His eyes always seemed to sparkle, and he winked like the stars had at the park.

"I'm okay."

Mr Hemmings frowned. "What have you done to your hand?"

*My hand?*

I looked down. A streak of blood smeared the back of it. "Nothing. Probably just scratched it or something."

"Here. Spit on that and give it a wipe, eh?"

Mr Hemmings held out a clean, pressed handkerchief. Crisply white, it looked to me like it had just come out of the packet. I didn't want to spit on it, wipe blood and get it all dirty. With Nelson cradled in my arm, I cleaned myself then held the handkerchief out to Mr Hemmings.

He stood upright and clasped his hands across his barrel chest, resting them on the top of his protruding gut. "No, no. You can keep that. Plenty more of them upstairs in my flat." He smiled, showing long front teeth much like a rabbit's. "So, what have you got there?"

I stuffed the hanky in my cardigan pocket and held Nelson up. "This is Nelson. She's my new dolly. Mam got her for my birthday today."

"And isn't that a big girl you are now? And Nelson. What a lovely name for such a beautiful dolly."

I smiled, so wide. "She's my best friend."

"I'm sure she is. I'd like to have a best friend like Nelson. Well, now, as it's your birthday, would you like to choose some sweets from the jars?"

I nodded and held out the loose change. "Mr Lawton let me have these."

I pondered on what I should buy. Rainbow sherbet and a lollipop to dip with, or the lemon drops? Maybe even fifty little sweets? I stared at the penny sweets, arranged in rows of small tubs on the counter.

"That's kind of Mr Lawton then, isn't it? Have you decided what you'll have?" Mr Hemmings smiled again and drummed his still-clasped fingers against the backs of his hands.

"There are lots of sweets. I don't know what to have."

He laughed, a rich bellow, and placed his palms on the counter. "What are you choosing between? What are your favourite things?"

I bit my bottom lip and thought about it.

*Fifty penny sweets and the sherbet and lollipop.*

"Well, I want fifty penny sweets, because then I get to choose all different ones. But I like sherbet and lollipops, too, and I dunno what to pick."

The shopkeeper reached under the counter, brought out two small white paper bags, and placed one by the cash register. The other he snapped open and began putting in one of each penny sweet. My mind panicked. I hadn't said what I wanted for sure, and now he'd filled the bag—way over fifty sweets—and I didn't have enough money to pay for all of them. Next, he opened the second bag and turned to reach for the pink jar of sherbet. Placing the open bag on his scales, he poured the delicious granules into it. The weighing needle moved past the quarter pound mark. My heart thudded. The purchases would cost much more than fifty p. The urge to run grabbed me, but instead I remained still and squeezed Nelson's arm.

"What colour lollipop would you like?"

Did I want the sherbet and lollipop, or the penny sweets? I didn't know, I just didn't know, and the indecision gnawed at my belly. Warm liquid snuck down the insides of my legs, and fiery heat streaked over my cheeks. I hoped Mr Hemmings wouldn't notice.

"I'd like a pink lolly to match the sherbet, please."

"Pink it is, then."

He reached again to the shelf behind him and took down the jar of lollies, digging his hand inside and fumbling around in search of my lollipop.

"There we go. One pink lolly."

He handed it to me, as well as the bag of sherbet and the bag of penny sweets.

"Fifty pence please, young lady." Mr Hemmings held his hand palm upwards, and I reached up to the counter and placed my sweaty coins in his hand.

"I'll have the sherbet and lollipop," I said. I wanted the penny sweets so badly, but the sherbet held more appeal. It lasted such a long time.

"There's upset I am, then, Carmel. Mr Lawton's money bought the sherbet and lolly, and my present was the sweets. Won't you take the sweets as a birthday present from me? After all, you're my best customer, aren't you?"

My tummy flip-flopped. I grinned so hard my eyes shut, and even though the piss on my legs had begun to dry and itch, I didn't care. Didn't care.

"Thanks, Mr Hemmings."

He laughed again—such a wonderful sound. "That's quite all right, young Carmel. It isn't every day you have a birthday, is it? Do you want a small carrier bag for your things there? Quite a handful you've got, what with holding the pretty Nelson too."

I decided in that moment that I loved Mr Hemmings. Really loved him.

"Yes, please."

Purchases in the carrier bag, he handed it over the counter to me. "Now then. You go along that aisle there," he pointed to where the newspaper stand stood, "and you pick yourself a nice magazine to read. You can sit on the stool behind the counter with me—only because it's your birthday, mind—and read it until it's time for you to go home."

This time I held the piss inside.

# Chapter Eight

I pushed down the handle, and the front door opened—the men had gone. I stepped into the hallway and imagined heat blaring down on me like in Mr Hemmings' shop. A shiver scampered over my skin; goose bumps jumped up to say 'Boo!', and I hunched my shoulders. With Nelson pressed safely against my chest, I crept up each step on silent feet. Mam mustn't hear me.

I made it to my room without incident, hid my sweets under the bed, and climbed onto it with my clothes on. Too cold to get undressed, I pulled the ratty sheet and my blanket over my head and breathed out through my mouth to warm my cocoon.

I shifted to get more comfortable, and the stench of dried pee from my socks and knickers wafted around under the covers. I'd have a strip wash in the morning. Even if the unscented soap didn't make me smell nice it would clean away the odour. I thought of the pretty pink soap at Belinda's again. I tried to recall the name stamped across the top of it and frowned in concentration. *Camay*—that was it. I'd buy some *Camay* when I grew up, so many bars I'd fill a whole shelf with them.

I didn't analyse the *accident*, only thought that I wouldn't be going to Belinda's anymore, would never use the fluffy face cloth or wear the petticoats again. Still, I'd yet to try out my own petticoat. I'd wrap my blanket around me tomorrow and see how it looked. Nelson could have a tea towel around her, and we'd be queens together. This time, though, *I'd* be the best queen of them all, me being older and bigger than Nelson.

Saturday tomorrow. Mam would take her medicine and nod out for most of the morning, maybe wake and send me to the shop for some bread or milk. Saturday afternoons and evenings, business increased. Afternoons, I stayed indoors.

Maybe Mam's class of customers or the acts she performed weren't as sordid as those in the evening, but either way, I didn't mind. I'd stay in my room and play queens, and afterwards, I'd have a little sleep to catch up on all I'd lost during the previous week.

I woke to the sound of Mam screeching up the stairs.

"Carmel! Get your arse out of bed *now*. I need you to run to the shop and get some milk. I've fucking run out and I haven't got any for my cup of tea."

Rubbing the crust of sleep from my eyes, I grabbed Nelson and ran onto the landing. I'd wash when I got back. Maybe I'd clean Nelson's dress and hair too.

Mam stood at the bottom of the stairs, the anger from the night before gone. She didn't look as kind as she did when she'd had her medicine, but it at least seemed like I wouldn't get hit. A cigarette dangled from her bottom lip. She held the banister rail with one hand, the other palm flat against the opposite wall. She said, "Be quick, kid.

You know what I'm like without my cuppa first thing in the morning."

I walked downstairs. She slapped a fiver in my hand. I curled my fingers around it and ducked under her arm and into the hallway, reaching up to the lock. I snagged the latch and opened the door.

"You got a big bruise on the side of your face, Carmel. Just shows you what dropping a coin will do, doesn't it?"

I stepped outside onto the path. My bottom lip quivered, and I pressed it against the top one to still it. Mam's laughter drifted after me, and I shut the front door and ran as fast as I could to the shop. The carton of milk cold against my fingers, I dashed to the counter and paid for it, said a hurried hello to Sharon, the Saturday assistant, then raced back home. I pressed Nelson's cheek to mine once I got back into our hallway, kissed her forehead, and went into the kitchen.

"Christ. Devil on your tail?" Mam asked.

I re-boiled the kettle, slopping hot water over the worktop as I poured it into her cup. Mam sat at the small kitchen table and smoked, waiting for me to make her tea.

She sucked on the cigarette and blew the smoke out with force. "What you up to today, kid?"

"Nothing much."

"Not going to your friend's house to play? I mean, you spend so much time with her you may as well live there. I'm obviously not good enough for you. Ungrateful little cow. To think I kept you when I could have aborted your arse and led the kind of life I wanted. Kept you, though, didn't I? And look what it got me. A scutty little kid who gets in my way all the time."

I didn't reply. There wasn't any need to. Mam obviously wanted to rant. She did that a lot. I shut out her voice and squeezed the tea bag against the side of the cup, imagining it was her head, and as the tea infused into the boiled water, I fancied it was Mam's blood.

With so much time on my hands, I thought too much. What else was there for me to do? I didn't have my mind stimulated by Mam. She wasn't one to spend time with me, wanting to nurture me and help me grow into a well-balanced adult. I knew early on I'd only have myself to rely on. Still, hope grew inside me, a pretty flower in the soil, even if that soil *was* badly fertilised. I had my dreams and desires. They kept me going.

I added milk and two sugars to her teacup. Her voice droned on in the background, and I remember while I stirred that tea and created a small whirlpool in the cup that the most vivid memory I'd take with me into adulthood was the damp air that smelled of dust and piss. I'd never forget it—it followed me every second, latching onto my clothing, a leech on skin. Of course, I'd remember Thursdays, too, but who wouldn't?

I carried Mam's tea to her, and she thanked me by blowing a stream of smoke in my face. My eyes watered, and I coughed. Her raucous laughter reverberated inside my head, and I thought of what we'd learned at school on Friday. I imagined I sailed on choppy seas and Mam was Scylla, grasping all those men, creating an eddy in my ocean so vast it became Charybdis. I'd get sucked into that whirlpool and be devoured if I let it happen. Tempting, so enticing to allow the waters to wash me away, drown me in its vitriolic swirls, fill my lungs with its badness and carry me away dead…dead…

I stood still, for some reason unable to move away from Mam.

"What are you staring at, dumb kid? Piss off out of my face."

As always, Dragons came to mind, what with Mam taking another drag of her cigarette and exhaling through her nostrils. She was a dragon all right. Big and scary—only lashings of verbal abuse replaced flames. Maybe one day someone would come and douse them out, but until then I was stuck with her. Much as I wanted to run and flee—where would I go? I had no one to run *to*. Besides, she was all I knew. Better the devil you know and all that.

I managed to walk away from her, my mind filled with bad things—dragons, snakes, and giant lizards. Monsters like Scylla with six ugly heads, six sets of gnashing teeth, tongues lapping at me ready to feast on my young flesh. No different to Thursday nights when I think about it now, although at the time, I confused that shit with love and affection.

Any touch was better than none.

That afternoon, I played queens with Nelson for hours until daylight fled from my room and the blackness of night took its place. Hunger nudged my guts, and I ventured downstairs, hoping that Mam's afternoon of work had ended. I poked Nelson's face round the living room doorjamb and peeked into the room myself. Mam was on the centre seat of the sofa, chin against chest, eyes closed. I scooted past her into the kitchen and sat Nelson on the worktop so she could learn how to make supper. The fridge, bare except for half a pint of milk, dampened my spirits. How I longed for it to be full of yoghurts and jellies, processed cheese slices, and slabs of ham. Did Mam ever do a weekly shop? I don't recall that she did.

The larder held a tin of beans, half a loaf of hardened, uncut bread, and some tinned corned beef. And a mouse. It sat at the back on the middle shelf, black beady eyes glaring at me, whiskers moving. The tiny thing lifted its front paws and sniffed the air, nose twitching. Its mouth hung open, showing white teeth, and I conjured images of huge scary mice the size of houses, spittle slithering from their chops.

Abruptly, the mouse darted to the far corner of the larder and disappeared through a hole, its tail the last thing I saw—a pointed worm.

I wished that I were a mouse, able to get through small spaces and scurry away from the life I led. I'd be a princess mouse with a pink tutu for a dress and a golden crown, each of its points topped with a marble-sized emerald. I stared at the hole the mouse had escaped into for what seemed a long time, lost in thoughts of feasts fit for a king, a table laden with such palatable delights that my mouth watered.

"Carmel? You in the house?" Mam's harsh, grating tones jolted me from my daydream. "If you are, make us a cuppa and something to eat. Fucking starving, I am."

*Uh-oh. Your mam's awake.*

"I'm just making some supper now, Mam." Sighing just a little so Mam wouldn't hear, I cleansed my mind of childish yearnings and busied myself preparing the food. I burned the toast, having cut the bread too thickly, and warmed the beans for too long, the end result more like mushy peas.

"Good. Make sure mine's a large portion. Literally worked my arse off this afternoon, if you know what I mean, and I reckon I'll be doing the same tonight. You don't need anything to eat anyway. I'll give you some money to go up the shop."

*She had her medicine, Carmel?*

"I'm not sure," I whispered.

My bottom lip wobbled. I'd wanted to surprise Mam and make us a meal and just once eat it together like a proper family. I backhanded my tears and concentrated on using the little metal key to open the tin of corned beef. Vision impaired, my hand slipped, and I cut a slither of skin from my finger on the sharp tin edge. It bled, but not profusely, and didn't hurt nearly as much as the ache in my chest and the lump in my throat.

I served all the food onto one plate, corned beef sliced after a fashion next to beans on toast. I opened the cutlery drawer and reached inside.

"What's up with you, kid?" Mam said directly behind me.

I jumped. My hand slammed against the knives and forks; the sound of metal jangled too loudly. How did she sometimes creep up on me so stealthily? My ears were usually so well-tuned. Captive to her warped care, I'd grown accustomed to looking out for myself, knowing when she was coming. Perhaps I'd lowered my guard? I didn't know, but my heart beat fiercely, and that lump in my throat swelled enough that I struggled to breathe.

Voice strangled, I said, "Nothing's wrong, Mam."

*You sound like that mouse in the larder might. Squeak-squeak.*

She leaned over my shoulder and said, "Looks like shit but I'm sure it'll taste all right." Her bare feet slapped against the lino as she made her way to the small table and chairs behind me. The chair legs scraped on the floor, and the plastic seat cushion hissed when her backside met with it, sounding much like the cruel exhalations she made through the small gap in her front teeth.

Selecting a knife and fork, I picked up the plate full of food and turned, took Mam's supper that looked like shit, and placed it in front of her on the table. She snatched the cutlery from me and began to eat.

It may not have looked appetising, may not have been the best meal in the world, but my stomach voiced its hunger, the hollow growl protesting against what my eyes saw but would not nestle in my gut. Mam tucked in as if ravenous. Baked bean juice dripped down her chin and plopped onto the plate.

*She's dirty. I don't want to look at her anymore, Carmel.*

My brain ignored Nelson, and I continued to stand and ogle Mam.

Her mouth full of beef, she didn't turn to me when she said, "Stop staring at me, kid. Always bloody staring. You're weird, you know that?" She swallowed and shovelled more beans and toast into her spiteful trap.

"Yes, Mam."

"You know, that's kind of your cue to fuck off away from me. Bit slow, aren't you? Stupid and retarded. It's a wonder the school haven't written to tell me you need to go to one of them special places." Plate half-cleared, she ranted on. "Haven't got that kind of luck, though, have I? That school you need to go to—the kids sleep over all week. Only go home at weekends. That'd suit me fine."

*That'd suit you fine, too, Carmel. You'd get nice food and a clean bed, I bet. Reckon you should act silly in the head so you can go there.*

My feet leaden, unable to step away from the monster that had birthed me, I watched the food on her plate disappear.

"Still," she continued, "I'll admit I'd be lonely if I lived by myself. Wouldn't have anyone to be mean to, would I?" She laughed, a crazy-arsed sound that skittered round in my head long after it ceased flowing from her thin lips.

"Carmel?"

"Yes, Mam?"

"Why are you still standing near me?"

Mam turned to face me, her knife and fork poised midair.

Quickly, I said, "I was playing a game. I'm a waitress and I'm waiting to take your plate away."

Did tears fill her eyes? Was Mam about to *cry*?

She turned away, slapped the knife and fork onto the plate, set her jaw to its usual rigidity, and leant back in her chair. Arms crossed over her chest, she said, "Well?"

"Well what, Mam?"

"Take the plate! Jesus. Some fucking waitress you'd make."

I blinked to banish the tic flickering beside my right eye and reached forward to take Mam's plate. Her hand shot out quick sharp and grabbed me round my thin wrist. My tummy churned, and I gripped the plate edge with sweaty fingers.

"Hungry, kid?"

"Yes, Mam."

"Well, guess what?" She smiled, and although her black-stained teeth should have made me shudder, a small part of me lit up inside, for that smile also reached her eyes.

"What?" I said breathlessly, hope burgeoning within me like a forgotten plant receiving water, guzzling, grasping at the small display of affection.

"I'm not!" Her laugh cut the air, a loud guffaw that came from the depths of her belly. She let go of my wrist and roughly shoved me backwards, but I managed to keep hold of the plate. The knife and fork clattered to the floor, yet I righted myself and stood before her still. "Waitress? Go and wash the dishes before I telephone your boss and tell her you're crap at your job. You don't want me to do that, do you? I've heard your boss is a mean old witch. Reckon she'll shear off the hair on your head if she hears about your slacking." Mam's lips formed their trademark thin line, and she snatched a cigarette from a crumpled pack on the table and lit it.

I turned from her, walked to the sink, and washed the dishes from the past week. No other words passed between us. The sound of water in the sink sloshed along with the seemingly constant exhalations of the smoke from Mam's lungs.

# Chapter Nine

On tiptoes, I hung my cardigan on my peg in the deserted cloakroom at school that Monday morning. Mam's shouted reminder to steal a coat thudded around in my head, and I stored the request. I'd go to the lost property box later and see what I could find.

Lunchboxes stood on the shelves above pegs that held many coats—I was late for school, as usual. Slipping off my shoes, I sat on the floor in search of a pair of plimsolls. Grotty socks encased my feet, and my toes poked from holes. Shoes weren't allowed to be worn in class, so yet again, the other kids would snigger at me from behind palmed mouths. Just as I moved to get up, defeated, I spied Belinda's white plimsolls sitting on the low shelf under the bench seat. I reached over, picked them up, then put them on. Even with the laces tied they gaped at the sides of my feet, but it didn't matter. At least no one would see the holes in my socks.

I opened the door between the cloak and classroom and could've sworn the air was filled with ill will. Children seated on the story carpet in the 'home corner' turned towards me as I entered, and Mrs Draper's face looked pinched and drawn. She appeared so pale, as if her skin were the paper we would later paint on.

"Ah, Carmel. Come and sit down, dear. I was just about to explain something to everyone."

I walked to the home corner and sat behind the assembled children.

"Right, as I said before Carmel came in, I have some very sad news to tell you all."

Hands in my lap between crossed legs, I stared at the kids in front of me. Every face appeared solemn, as if by our teacher's very tone they knew to be good and still, not to fidget, or flick their fellow classmate. All eyes bar mine faced the front, riveted on the elderly woman before us.

Mrs Draper cleared her throat. "Well, children. Something very sad happened. What I'm going to tell you might be very upsetting for some of you. If, when I've finished speaking, you want to talk about it, I'll try to answer your questions. Now then…"

I moved my gaze to Mrs Draper's face. Crêpe skin sagged from her jaw line. Sometimes, when she shook her head, her jowls jiggled like living beings. Her mouth moved, yet I didn't hear a sound coming from her lips—lips that didn't match in size, the top one thin, the lower full. Decorated cerise pink, they opened and closed, stretched and twitched with her words. Mist shrouded my vision, a red mist that eddied and swirled before me, the dense fog of winter, where I spent freezing evenings outside, sometimes getting lost on the streets, my sense of direction deserting me like society had.

"…terrible accident. Belinda won't be coming back to school because…"

I squirmed, uncrossed my legs, and moved them beneath me so I sat on my heels. My bladder needed blessed release, but I had to stay still, had to wait until Mrs Draper's mouth stopped moving, until her fingers stopped wringing the hem of her cardigan.

"We'll maybe sing a song for Belinda at home time—perhaps her favourite—and she may hear it in Heaven…"

At last, Mrs Draper's lips closed. With watery eyes, she looked at us all, sighed raggedly, and placed her hands one upon each knee. Her fingers wiggled, reminding me of a spider's legs.

"Now. Does anyone have any questions?"

A hand raised to my left.

"Gary. What would you like to ask?"

"My dad knows Belinda's dad, right, and he said Belinda got killed at the park, and this spike thing went through her head, right, and she was all mashed up and stuff and she had blood all over her face and—"

"Gary!" said Mrs Draper. "I don't think that kind of talk is appropriate behaviour right at this moment. We don't know exactly what happened to Belinda. Let us just know she had an accident and she's now in Heaven watching us and looking after us, all right?"

"But my dad reckons some messed up motherfucker is going round killing kids, and I'm not allowed out no more just in case—"

"Gary! Your language is atrocious. That is quite enough from you. If you can't stop telling scary stories—for I'm quite sure that's what they are—you'll have to go and explain yourself to Mr

Kendry, and I'm *sure* you don't want to have to do that, do you?"

I kept my gaze on Mrs Draper, but out of the corner of my eye saw Gary hang his head.

"No, Miss," he said.

"Right. Does anyone else have anything to ask?" Mrs Draper looked at each one of us in turn. Her gaze met mine. "Carmel. You and Belinda were very good friends. Do you have something you want to ask, my dear?"

All heads turned towards me.

"No, Miss."

Mrs Draper frowned. "Anyone else?"

Children shifted and shook their heads — rustling leaves in the wind, they fidgeted under Mrs Draper's scrutiny.

"Well, then. If you feel the need to ask me any questions during the day, you must know you are free to do so. A special letter will go out to your parents this evening just in case you find yourself getting upset later on. Who wants to choose this morning's activity? I think we'll spend today doing arts and crafts."

Arms shot up in the air, many waving hands, kids wanting to be the one to choose exactly what we would do. I didn't raise mine. I wanted to learn — to read and soak up information that I could think about in the times I spent alone — not paint or do jigsaws or mess around in the sand pit. I shifted my position again and brought my legs in front of me.

Stared at Belinda's plimsolls.

"Painting it is, then. Everyone select an apron and put it on. I'll get the paints. First one with an apron on and tied properly can go to the paper drawer and hand out one sheet each. Second person can hand out the paintbrushes… No rushing!"

A flurry of movement, and the classroom became a hive of activity, children bustling from one place to another. I watched them all—ants obeying their queen—and noted how clean and tidy everyone looked, it being a Monday morning and all. I thought of Belinda and her cleanliness, of me and my dirty appearance. With each child that brushed past me the stench of my clothes swirled anew—as did my resentment towards everyone in that classroom whose passing odour resembled flowers on a beautiful summer's day.

Life hurt.

In a corner where two outer classroom walls met one another, I huddled away from the blasts of wind that jostled and shunted other children playing unshielded on the playground. A whoosh of wind sought me out and found my hiding place. It blew me spitefully, whipped at my scraggy hair, and I marvelled at how even the wind was a bully, just like Mam. I shoved my bare hands into the sleeves of my cardigan, but the sharpness of the breeze froze me to the core.

Furtive glances to my far right showed me the coast was clear enough to sort through the lost property box without anyone taking much notice. The big red plastic box, situated beneath an awning, displayed an overflowing jumble of material. I prayed a coat or at least another cardigan would be there for the taking. Everyone seemed busy running away from the gale, keeping themselves warm with exercise, just like Mrs Draper had advised prior to our departure from the classroom. I hunched my shoulders and jaywalked across the playground.

The box stood waist-high. Like a professional, I sorted through the clothing. Sweaters, skirts, T-shirts—all manner of things lost but not my size, either very small or much too big. Some too distinctive to steal; someone would undoubtedly recognise their things. But, wonder of wonders, I found a coat, one that most girls wore—a parka with a fluffy trim around the hood—just like I'd prayed would be there. Only it wasn't pink or purple, but baby blue. No nametag inside. My size. A quick glance behind me to check no one watched, and I slipped that coat on. The coldness of it soon dissipated with the heat of my body. I zipped it, yanked the hood over my head, and secured it with the Velcro tabs beneath my chin. I felt so posh. *So posh*, you know? I smiled and looked around at the other girls who wore something similar. I belonged.

Back in my corner space the wind didn't seem quite so vindictive, the grey cloudy sky not so threatening, and my inner peace not so aggrieved. Hands in fleece-lined pockets, I imagined myself an Eskimo. The playground became a vast landscape of snow, the children penguins. I'd brave the wintry storm knowing if the snowdrifts blasted me, I'd be warm enough. A huge polar bear walked towards me, its cream fur bristling in the strong breeze. It snorted a puff of white air.

"Why're you standing in the corner?" asked the bear.

Large, inquisitive marble eyes stared at me, and I reckoned they tried to pierce my soul.

"To keep out of the wind."

"Don't you like the wind?" Without waiting for an answer, the bear went on, "Wonder if it's cold and windy in Heaven?"

The bear stuck out the tip of its tongue to catch a dangle of mucous.

"Don't know," I said.

"D'you reckon it's true what Gary said? Imagine having a bleeding head." The bear's eyes widened, and its lips pursed, its muzzle elongated and strange.

"Don't know if it's true."

*I want a cuddle, Carmel.*

Nelson? Confusion stole over me, as did goose bumps. Nelson was wrapped up in my blanket at home on my bed. How could she speak to me when she wasn't *with* me?

The bear sniffed, cuffed another drip from its nose, and ambled off into the white wilderness to frolic with the penguins. I told myself everything would be okay. Told myself it was an *accident.* Told myself, told myself…

"I heard about your friend today, kid." Mam's lips retracted from her rotten teeth, showing pale pink gums. "What you going to do now? Where you going to hide out? Doubt anyone else will want to play with *you*."

I'd come in from school, thankful to shut the front door on the hateful wind that had relentlessly shunted me all the way home, only to be presented with another bully. I didn't answer, just stood in the living room doorway facing the dragon with smoke chundering from her nose. The wind had chapped my legs, my sock tops having lost their elastic, exposing my bare skin to the elements. Mam gazed at me with half-lidded eyes. I placed my legs together and shuddered at the utter chill of my skin.

"Reckon she got killed, so Bob said. Some nutter going round bumping off little kiddies. You'd better take more care of yourself when you go out at night. See you got yourself a coat, then?"

I nodded.

"Warm is it?"

"Yes."

A trail of smoke spiralled from Mam's cigarette. My mind transported me to a hilltop where Indians sat around a blaze. Tobacco pipes rested against bottom lips, and sounds of hummed tunes swirling in the darkness. A gust of wind blew acrid bonfire smoke into my face, and my eyes watered. I blinked, and the hilltop scene faded, replaced by Mam's face inches from mine.

She looked strange bent over like that, her head suspended on air, seemingly unattached to her neck and body.

"Run to the shop for me, will you?" Her breath whispered on my nose; I bit back a retch. "Need some fags. Hemmings will serve you — knows what'll happen if he doesn't. Besides, you gotta give him his usual."

Mam trudged to the kitchen, returning with a large brown envelope. She slapped it and a ten pound note in my hand, and I left the house. I would have loved to have taken Nelson but thought it best I go right away.

The shop enveloped me in its warmth once more. Mr Hemmings sat on the stool behind the counter, his beaming smile like a balm on my young soul. I walked to the counter and held out the money and the envelope.

"Mam would like some fags."

Mr Hemmings glanced round the shop before sliding the envelope under the counter. Turning to the shelf behind him, he selected a multipack of Mam's cigarette brand. He placed them in a carrier bag, handed them to me, and said, "Tell your mam she doesn't need to pay for these ones."

Mr Hemmings did that sometimes. Especially when I gave him the brown envelope.

I shoved the money in my coat pocket. "Okay."

"How are you feeling today, Carmel?"

"All right."

"Sad about your little friend?"

"Yes."

*Hurry up and come home, Carmel. I haven't seen you all day.*

"I gotta go." I dashed out of the shop, ran home, and pelted up the stairs, not caring that Mam shouted at me for her cigarettes. Nelson's cheek cold against mine, I squeezed my dolly to me tightly. *So tightly.* I wished that no one else would ask me how I was, or how I felt about Belinda.

# Chapter Ten

❦

She's been my only *true* friend, has Nelson. She saw everything: sitting on the chair in the posh back room, taking it all in with her glassy stare; perched on my bed when I cried until I thought my eyeballs would burst; placed her arm in my hand when we hid together in the smelly cupboard under the stairs. Hugged me on Thursdays after Bob left.

Bob seemed different the Thursday after the *accident*. He looked at me oddly, tilted his head like a garden bird, and said, "Pictures went down well, Carmel. Everyone thinks you're a star."

I smiled, uncertainty hurting my insides. Something wasn't right. The air bristled with static, and the roots of my hair stood up.

Mam giggled. "Same again tonight, Bob?"

Bob hawked phlegm, swallowed it. He reached inside his jacket and pulled out a brown paper bag. "Similar, though I've got a little something here that will make it different. Can't expect people to pay for the same kind of thing again and again, can I? Also, got to keep these ones under my hat, know what I mean? Dangerous territory. The pretty dress ones, well, they could be anyone's niece, see? This new venture—got to make sure I sell to who I can trust."

I think that was the first time I'd heard Bob say so much in one go. He usually spoke one or two sentences at a time, but mainly one-word commands.

"I'll have to reprint last week's pictures again—high demand. If they like those then I'll show a sample from this week. Charge a higher price, too." Bob handed the small bag to Mam, and she took it, opened it, and peeked inside.

She squealed. "Bob. You're so *crazy*!" She hugged the bag to her chest. Her face became animated, her lips opening as laughter spilled out, and she bent over double. Her hilarity stung my eardrums, my eyes, made my bottom lip wobble.

Bob tapped the top of her head, and Mam straightened again, wiping tears from her ruddy cheeks.

"Stop messing about," Bob said. "I've only got an hour."

We trooped into the back room.

That hour seemed like ten.

Belinda was the talk of the school for such a long time. Too long. Gary said she'd been buried in the Catholic cemetery a month after she'd died.

"My dad said she was cut open and all her guts fell out on the table at the hospital. He reckons her tummy had a big X on it, all sewed up like Frankenstein's monster's face. He said no one could go and look at her in the coffin because she had a massive scratch on her face that made her skin flap open. I think it must have really hurt to fall on that spike. D'you reckon she screamed and stuff?"

I didn't answer him, just dumbly stared at the mole on his right cheek. Big and round like a one pence piece—slightly fuzzy with hair. I wondered if it hurt or itched.

"I reckon the worms will eat her for their supper. The spiders and stuff will get in the coffin with her and scoff her up."

I thought about that. Wondered how long it would take and how many creatures it would need to eat a whole body for their tea. I imagined big worms, the size of snakes, spiders growing from ant-size to tarantula after feasting on Belinda's chubby arms and legs.

Gary's face lit up during our conversation. He'd always liked gore and scary things, confessing once that his dad let him stay up and watch horror movies. Belinda's death obviously brought his imagination to the fore, and he gorged on tales of her demise for months afterwards. I felt a little proud inside, that something I'd done had caused so much pleasure to Gary. That everyone spoke of the *accident* with such awe-tinged sorrow.

I had made that happen. Me.

But it was an accident.

Gary puffed out his cheeks. He pursed his lips, a chicken's arsehole as Mam would have put it, and bowed his arms out by his sides. He took large stompy steps up and down before me, his eyes wide.

He said, "I am a worm and I've eaten some Belinda for my dinner." He dramatically collapsed onto the home room carpet, on his back, laughing. He kicked his legs and waved his arms. "That Belinda, her meat was out of date. Given me a belly ache."

I giggled, really giggled for the first time in ages. My tummy muscles hurt from the unaccustomed exercise. I joined him on the carpet, adopting the same pose, and we both kicked our legs like bugs.

"Hello, Bug-girl," he hollered, and I laughed again.

"Hello, Bug-boy."

"You come down this way to eat some Belinda? Be careful now, she's out of date. My belly hurts so bad that I reckon if I fart I'm gonna poo my pants," he shouted, bringing us to the attention of Mrs Draper. She clapped—two sharp cracks—and strode in our direction.

"Oh, bloody hell," he said. "Bug killer's on the way. Her breath is made of Raid. One whiff of that and we're goners."

This may have been said to sober me, but it had the reverse effect. I laughed harder. Mrs Draper's breath *did* smell like Raid, faintly perfumed, like she constantly ate Parma Violets.

She loomed over us, a spider casting her gaze over two flies in her web. "What do you two think you're doing?"

She looked misty, like I viewed her through a mottled glass bathroom window. Fisting my eyes to clear them, I laughed, the sound resembling a pigeon I'd once heard in town. It pecked at cake crumbs on the ground, tossed down by generous shoppers, and cooed as it ate. With hands on her hips, Mrs Draper reminded me of that pigeon. Her arms created a triangular shape—pigeon's wings—and her nose became a beak.

Laughter bubbled inside me again, and Mrs Draper warbled on. I didn't hear what she said, just knew she spoke. I chanced a glimpse at Bug-boy. His face had contorted, morphed into something resembling him but not. His bunched-up eyes and rounded cheeks, his reddened skin and skewed lips, all told me he was about to burst.

"Gary. Ga-ry," I managed. "St-op laugh-ing."

He turned to me and opened his eyes wider. "I ca… I ca-n't help it."

He kicked his arms and legs faster—a bug sprayed with Raid—and that thought set me off even more. My tears, though of laughter, must have been from pain too; my ribs and stomach shouted their protest.

Mrs Draper's strident voice cut through our wailing. "That is *enough!* Whatever has got into you two?"

The thought of Belinda being what had 'got into us', her raw flesh gone bad inside our guts, had Gary and me so far down the road of hysterics it would take a huge fallen tree trunk across our path to stop us going farther.

Or the threat of being sent to sit outside Mr Kendry's office.

We silenced immediately, let our legs and arms flop to the carpet, dragging in ragged gulps of air to steady our breathing. My stomach muscles throbbed, and my arms were leaden—trying to lift them from the carpet to sit myself up left me defeated.

"Right," snapped Mrs. Draper. "Both of you, get up."

She looked a fierce pigeon while glaring down at us. Her beady black eyes glowed with malice. We'd ruffled her feathers, all right, although I did wonder why our laughter made her so angry. Shouldn't she have been happy to see her students carefree?

We stood before her, side by side. I looked at my feet—Belinda's plimsolls had become mine—

and concentrated on their gaping sides as if they were the most fascinating thing I'd seen. To look sideways at Gary would have been my undoing, and I'd have found my bottom firmly placed on the hard wooden bench outside Mr Kendry's office.

The pigeon stooped to our level—her arthritic knees clicked. Her wings became arms once more, and she placed her hands in her lap.

"Now, let me tell you both something. It isn't nice to pretend you're bugs that are eating Belinda."

Gary let out a strangled protest, cut short by the pigeon raising her hand, palm towards us. He sniffed, and his foot punted the carpet.

"I heard you both from right across the room. And if *I* heard you, the other children probably did too. This is *not* appropriate behaviour. I do *not* wish to see it repeated. Do you both understand?"

I nodded.

Gary said, "Yeah."

"Good."

Mrs Draper stood—more clicks, crickets on a summer's evening—and moved away from us. I lifted my head and turned to face Gary.

"My belly hurts from that meat," he whispered.

"Mine too!" I whispered back.

That must have been about the time our friendship was cemented.

⊚⊜⊹⊰⊚

Gary sought me out most break times. We zoomed across the playground pretending to be the flies that feasted on Belinda's hand that poked out of the earth, the only part of her that, in our fantasy, hadn't become encased in her coffin. We loped from one side of the playground to the other, worms that tunnelled through the earth and coffin wood to devour Belinda's head. Once, Gary said he was a rat. He mimicked gnawing at the coffin until he succeeded in making a hole wide enough to fit through (which reminded me of the mouse in our kitchen cupboard), and went in search of Belinda's elusive eye. I became his rat friend, who stood guard outside the coffin hole in case a dog or fox dug into the ground to claim us for its supper.

"Did you find the eye?" I said through the coffin hole.

"No. Not the real deal, Rat-girl. But I did find a glass one. We'll use it to play marbles with." Gary emerged from the hole and held up the eye.

The thought of rolling Belinda's wet glass eye on the playground where it would gather dirt had our imaginations running. We scurried, rodent-like, across the playground to our *lair* (the space behind the lost property box), and hunkered down next to one another to marvel at our find.

"I'd say we should snatch out her teeth next," Gary said. "Rip them out one by one. After that, I'll saw off her nose, cheek, and forehead bones. Once we've collected every bit of her skeleton, we'll put it back together, piece by piece. A jigsaw puzzle." Gary leaned to his left, closer to me, and lowered his voice. "My dad reckons her skin will be like leather in a few months, all dried and stuck to her skull. I'll have to peel the skin away before I can saw off the bones."

The image Gary presented didn't turn my stomach—if anything it piqued my interest.

"How did your dad get to know so much about dead people?" I asked.

"Aw, he knows lots of things. Like it takes a while before a body starts decomposing."

"Decom what? What's that mean?" I asked. Gary sometimes used big words.

"Decomposing. Rotting. Dad said something about this liquid stuff they put in the bodies before they get buried. That's what stops them from turning to mush."

I stared across the playground. Belinda stood right over the other side. She looked exactly the same as she had before the accident—podgy and well-fed, clean and wholesome. She smiled, and her teeth fell out one by one. The sound of them as they met the playground asphalt reminded me of the twang of Mrs Draper's guitar strings at music time.

One eye socket changed into a red cavernous void and widened, eventually obliterating her features until her whole face became that eye socket. It looked sore, like if I dashed a pinch of salt at her she'd release a wailing sound so awful that I'd never forget it as long as I lived. A little like the noise she'd made when she'd met with that metal spike.

"She's standing over there, Gary." I nudged him in the ribs and I pointed to where she stood. "Her teeth have all fallen out. Shall we go and collect them?"

Gary jumped up. "Race you!"

He dashed in the wrong direction. I chased after him, wanting to tell him Belinda wasn't over that way, but he continued to the far end of the playground, his tooth-finding mission obviously his main priority.

"Gary, wait!" The wind dashed into my open mouth, wrapped around my tonsils, and robbed my tongue of moisture. I snapped my lips closed and swallowed. The dryness of my throat—if I didn't know better I would say it audibly crackled—made me think of the deserts Mrs Draper had told us about the previous week, and the need for a cool drink of water overrode any desire I had to play out the fantasy of collecting my dead friend's teeth. I stopped running after Gary and turned to my right to see Belinda had gone. I switched direction once more. Making my way towards the waterspout under the awning above our lair, I noted the pipe that the spout was attached to had rusted since the last time I'd used it.

I frowned, and I know I did as I remember my forehead hurt from the concentration. Hadn't I used the waterspout just last week? The pipe hadn't been rusty then; I'd studied myself in the shiny silver, saw how my features changed. Last time I did this, Gary said I looked like a face in one of those mirrors at the funfair. I didn't know what he meant—I'd never been to a fair before— but took his word for it. It brought to mind me staring at myself in Belinda's gold bathroom taps, and a pang of sorrow wrenched my guts. I inhaled sharply and whimpered.

I stood in front of the rusted pipe, bent down slowly, and moved my head towards it, a tortoise bringing its head cautiously from its shell. I peered at the pipe. A burnt-orange, flaky substance covered the metal. A slight breeze danced against me; some of the flakes dislodged and flew into the air and filled with...blood?

I stepped back. It *was* blood, fresh and bright red, and it dripped down the pipe to the concrete slabs. Another breeze snapped past me, snatching the blood in its invisible hands. Droplets coasted through the air, only to land in splatters when the small gust of wind abated. Those splatters reminded me of fat raindrops, the pattern of them a circle with several streaks pointing from the arced edges.

A drop of wet landed on my hand, and I looked up. No rain clouds drifted above. The sky, a beautiful blue, obviously didn't harbour any bad weather. I stared at the back of my hand. A spot of blood, the size of a one pence piece, blared its redness; it had landed on the webbing between my thumb and index finger.

"Blood on your hands. Blood on your hands, you little bitch."

I whirled round to face the voice. Belinda, a red eye socket for a head.

"You're nothing but a scab-bag, Carmel. A killing scab-bag."

I clamped my teeth shut, catching my tongue between them. Blood seeped inside my mouth, the sensation similar to times when hunger gripped my guts and I saw and smelled food I wouldn't eat—cakes in the corner shop, pizza in a red satchel on the delivery guy's back—and saliva filled my mouth.

"They'll find out it was you, Scab-bag."

I stared at Belinda, aware that her voice came out of that red eye socket but from no discernable mouth. Translucent liquid coated the socket and drizzled down her neck. Tears?

"You're a cry baby, Belinda," I said. "A cry baby who probably screams for her mam every night, hammers against the coffin lid hoping someone will hear you, when no one will, because no one cares that you're dead."

The clear liquid dried as quickly as it had appeared, to be replaced with more blood—blood that dripped so quickly it drenched Belinda's dress. The dress she'd probably been buried in, for it was a pretty baby pink with ruffles round the neck. A human red shape, she lifted her arms before her, fingers twitching, maybe wanting to grab at my hair and hurt me, drag me to wherever the hell she came from.

"Little scabby bitch." The words came out garbled, a liquefied parody of her former voice. Her colour began to fade; the rich red of fresh blood changed to pink, changed to nothing as she disappeared.

I blinked and looked down at the paving slabs where she'd stood and caught a glimpse of swiftly drying, bloody footprints before they, too, vanished.

I swallowed the blood in my mouth. Gary called my name, breathless.

"Where did you get to?" He panted. "I went over and picked up all her teeth by myself. Got them in my pocket." He stuffed his hands into the opposing sleeve of each arm of his coat.

"I came over to get a drink, but the pipe…"

I turned back to the waterspout. The pipe no longer blood-rusty, it winked as it caught a reflection of the sun.

"The pipe what?" he asked.

"Nothing," I said and walked over to the spout. Turning the circular tap to make sure the water was indeed water, I leaned forward to take a sip. Belinda's face stared back at me from the metal water bowl—her real face, not the eye socket—where my face should have been reflected.

"Bitch," she said.

I told myself it was a hiss of air escaping through the spout and not her omnipotent voice.

"What did you say?" asked Gary.

I let go of the tap, swallowed the last of the water, and paused for a beat. I turned back to face Gary. "Nothing."

The bell signalling the end of playtime rang. I skipped towards our classroom, images of Belinda dancing in my mind's eye. I hoped she would appear again. I found her presence…fascinating.

# Chapter Eleven

*I*'ve told you before, it just isn't possible to waltz over there and do what you say. People might see me. I'm quite happy to wait for an opportune moment. All good things come to those who wait, so the saying goes. What? You've never heard of that one?

I came close to being caught last time. That isn't something I want happening again. Nor do I anticipate anyone even suspecting it's me. We've made the plans; we just have to wait before we execute them — sometimes longer than we have in the past. Patience. I wish Mam had called me that, for, as an adult, don't I have plenty of it?

*No. No, I'm not going to listen. I want this one to be done right, no mistakes. There is no way I'm going to put myself out there in a crowd and risk being spotted.*

*What? The crowd affords me a better chance of doing it undetected? Are you insane? No, don't answer that one.*

*Let me think about it. Give me some space, and I* mean *space. Don't speak to me for a few hours, preferably not until the morning. I'd like to weigh all the pros and cons without your voice twittering in my bloody ear.*

# Chapter Twelve

꧁❀꧂

Mam aged considerably over the next few months. Her teeth grew blacker, her veins more collapsed, and the wrinkles on her face were more ravine-like. Mid-twenties, and she could easily have passed for two decades older. Hard living does that to a body.

One time, as a teenager, I wondered about her, you know, properly wondered. Did her parents know she'd had a baby girl, know where she lived and what she did for a living? I suspect they did—probably why I never saw them during my childhood. I pondered on the fact that if she'd been outcast by her kin, she'd know how it felt to be unloved and lonely. This begged the question in my adult life: Why did she treat me as she did? Perhaps she really did think I was the blight on her existence, that my presence caused her pain. Yet, it can't have all been bad. I made her lots of money.

My friendship with Gary continued, as did our Belinda obsession. We progressed from being worms and rats to Ghost Catchers and, as Gary obviously didn't see Belinda like I did, I constantly veered him in her direction in an attempt to catch up with her. I wanted to touch her, see if she felt as real as she looked. But Belinda evaded the grasp of our small fingers every time, usually with a gleeful peal of laughter normally reserved for real children, children who played tag.

Despite her ghastly appearance, Belinda acted as though she were indeed still alive. On the odd occasion she turned malicious—spat blood, grew teeth as long as a rabbit's, leapt forward to sink those teeth into my neck—but for the most part she was one of us, the third person in our gang, albeit with an eye socket for a face. And the latter didn't disturb me one bit.

One particular day, the sun came out from its winter hibernation and shone down on the playground during morning break time. Blonde-haired kids looked blonder, brunettes' tresses shimmered myriad hues, and cheeks held the glow only kids' cheeks can. The shrubs and bushes that lined two edges of the playground seemed to have flourished overnight—I was sure yesterday their branches jutted out like blackened, arthritic fingers—and bright green leaves, the new growth of spring, still dew-laden, almost glimmered in the sunlight.

It was warm enough to shed our coats like snakes. Piles of them dotted the playground, and those heaps of material made me to think of a mountainous range.

"Gary, look! Belinda's standing on top of that mountain," I whispered.

We'd taken to whispering, convinced that if anyone else overheard our fantasies, or if Belinda herself got wind of what we were up to, our playtimes would be ruined. The spell would be broken if outsiders became aware. So adamant were we on this, that when we did whisper, our voices came out so low we had to strain to hear one another amid the shrieks and laughter of the other school kids. Gary's ears must have grown accustomed—mine were already sharp, what with having to listen out for Mam creeping up on me—and he turned to me and smiled.

"We must ride our horses up the mountain, then. Catch her and take her back to headquarters."

We playacted our ascent onto our horses' backs—mine was black with a white star between its eyes, the same as the mare in the TV programme *Black Beauty*—and kicked our steeds into a canter. The act of galloping across the playground gifted freedom to my mind and body. The warm wind flicked its tongue through my hair, caressed my face like Mam's hand didn't. My heartbeat quickened, throbbed, dashing blood through my veins that I felt arrive at every avenue of my body. I tingled all over; giddy excitement flared within, and I let out a squeal. A squeal of happiness? I'm sure it was.

Belinda stood on top of the mountain farthest from us, but Gary stopped at the first pile of coats.

"Whoa, you horsy beast," Gary shouted at his transport (a white one with a black star on its face).

A sense of belonging spread through me when he'd told me that, back along when we'd first introduced the horses to our game. Gary had chosen the opposite colours to my horse—an honour, surely? And, of course, that he called it

White Beauty was the small blob of icing on the mouldy cake that was my life.

Deciding not to stop and coax Gary to the far side of the playground, I cantered past him shouting, "She's legged it. See? She's over there now. That mountain far away. Quickly, before she disappears again."

Gary's trotting footsteps resumed behind me, the spaces between them meeting the asphalt growing shorter. I guessed he would catch up to me quickly, would want to overtake so that *he* was the first of the Ghost Catchers to reach our ghoul.

He'd said once, "Why don't you ever let me choose where Belinda is?" I'd answered that he was always allowed to reach Belinda first, and that the way we played it was fair. He'd shrugged, his pixie features sullen, and dashed his long mousy fringe away from his eyes with thin fingers topped with bitten, dirty nails. Still, he'd conceded defeat on that one, but never failed to be the first one to say where we could find Belinda. Give the boy a round of applause for persistence.

Gary overtook me, his hands poised in front of him as if he held the reins of White Beauty, and he glanced to his right at me, his smile as broad as an elephant's width.

"Race you!" he yelled, his voice falling behind him, carried by the wind as he surged ahead.

I picked up speed, gripped Black Beauty's reins more tightly, and laughed. "I'm catching up, Gary."

A harsher gust of wind slapped my face, bringing with it a bug of some kind. It splattered on my right eyeball. By instinct, my eyes closed, and I galloped valiantly onwards, despite my eye leaking and sting-itching.

I saw the layout of the playground in my mind, knew I had a way to go before I'd meet with the corner of bushes where the two rows met. I didn't anticipate the arrival of a new mountain in the scant seconds my eyes had been sightless, but upon opening my eyes, that mountain seemed as tall as a real one, blurred by my watery vision. Black Beauty didn't have a chance to change course, and she jumped to avoid the obstruction. Her hoof caught the mountaintop, and I launched out of the saddle and into the air. Three or four seconds—and those seconds seemed like minutes—saw me airborne. I windmilled my arms in an attempt to bring myself to an upright landing. A boy streaked past me to move out of my way, his startled shriek sounding like a girl's. His arm whumped into my stomach and turned the direction my body had been taking. I sailed downwards, past the soft landing the mountain would have given, and crashed to my side, hipbone first, onto the unyielding ground.

Laughter, gasps, and shouts applauded my fall. I kept my eyes bunched closed. A yell of, "Miss! Miss! Carmel's hurt!" gave a small nugget of comfort—someone cared—and it sustained me through the pain that throbbed in waves down my leg. I didn't cry, didn't let the building sobs leave my mouth. I'd endured worse in my time, and this pain would soon leave my body, a big purple bruise the only evidence it had ever been there in the first place.

Heavy footsteps bounded behind me. The sound of someone gasping for breath—and those breaths rasped and whistled—grew louder along with the footsteps. I opened my eyes to see numerous feet shod in different styles of shoes. T-bars, closed toes, trainers, even a pair of Wellington boots, green in shade with yellow eyes complete with black pupils—a frog? The largest pair of shoes, black sturdy lace-ups, belonged to Mrs Judd, the playtime supervisor.

Her legs, clad in black hosiery, bent at the knee. She lowered herself onto her haunches and peered at me. The sun shone behind her, her head creating an eclipse, and the urge to giggle, despite the pain, jiggled in my belly.

"Are you okay, Carmel?" she asked.

I nodded, my head grating against the ground. Small stones dug into my scalp—the kind of stones that usually found their way into my shoes and viciously bit the soles of my feet.

"Shall we try and get you to stand?" she said.

I nodded again and took the hand Mrs Judd offered. Her palm felt surprisingly rough. A cat's tongue, that's what it was like, damp and coarse. I'd expected it to be smooth to match the softness of what her cheeks promised. I looked at those cheeks, with their fine white blanket of tiny hairs, the sun enhancing their presence. She could almost be classed as having a beard.

Fear lurked in the back of my mind and whispered, its tone ethereal: *Wonder if you've broken your leg? I hope you have. It'd mean you couldn't come to school for a while, and you'd have to stay at home with your wretched mam…*

I blinked and batted the thoughts away, stood, and took one or two steps. Although I hobbled, I smiled with relief. I hadn't broken any bones.

*Damn, I was almost sure you'd…*

"Well done, Carmel," Mrs Judd almost yelled. "Let's get you to the nurse's room so she can take a look at you. Maybe you'll want a little rest on the bed there? You look too pale for my liking."

She stood by my side and placed her right arm across my back, clasped my elbow with her hand, and guided me towards the front of the school. The sea of children parted, and their hasty footsteps let me know the show was over; they were going back to whatever game I had interrupted.

"Carmel? You all right?"

Gary skipped along beside us, crab-like, his hands still out in front of him, holding on to White Beauty's reins.

"Yeah," I said.

"We'll play again later. After lunch."

"Okay," I said and allowed Mrs Judd to steer me into school.

The school nurse wasn't comely, buxom, and motherly like the TV hinted all nurses to be. With a body as thin as a hosepipe, her features sharp and pointy, nurse Helen reminded me of a ferret, her arms and legs short like the latter, too, her forearms fuzzed with brown hair. Surely she hadn't been made right. I stood in the medical room doorway. Mrs Judd ushered me inside then left. The faint tinkle of the big brass bell sounded; she must have collected it on her way back outside, ready to ring it to signal the end of playtime.

Nurse Helen gazed at me, her head cocked to one side, and sniffed. "So," she said. "Did you have a tumble, then?"

I nodded.

"Sit up on the bed. I'll take a look at you."

Her voice brought to mind the sound chalk made on the blackboard when Mrs Draper wrote out words. Wavy, it went up and down. She didn't come from around here; she had an accent, one I'd heard on the radio. A female version of Terry Wogan. He was on TV too; he hosted the game show *Blankety Blank*. The microphone he used looked like a giant matchstick.

"Ouch," she said. "You've grazed your knees quite badly." She turned to her medicine cabinet. Bottles clinked against one another, and the rustle of polythene sounded.

I looked down. Both of my knees sported angry scrapes, the redness dotted with grit. As if it wanted to be the chief source of upset, my hip protested. A sharp pain, followed by an angry, dull throb attacked my hipbone, and I imagined if my hip had a face it would be grimacing.

Nurse Helen returned to the bed with a small bottle of Dettol. Next to it, she plonked a large polythene-encased roll of cotton wool; it made a dull thunking sound, and a hiss of air escaped the hole in the top of the bag.

"Right, let's clean your knees first, shall we?" she said. The lilt in her voice calmed me but didn't match her appearance. I'd first heard her voice when she'd visited our class to discuss nits, and I'd expected her words to sound tinny, as if spoken through a megaphone, and sharp, sharp as broken china.

Nurse Helen bent to retrieve a metal bowl from a lower shelf. She placed it on the top next to the cotton wool. The resulting clang made me jump, and my ears buzzed. Her small arms moved in front of her, and I became entranced by the way her short, stubby fingers opened the bottle of Dettol and poured a little into the metal bowl. Quickly, she opened the cotton wool bag and snatched off a chunk; it squeaked.

I knew by the smell of the Dettol it would sting, even though I'd never been cleaned with it before. The odour, though, I savoured. It smelt of cleanliness, something I didn't encounter very often. As it bit into the grazes on my knees, I concentrated on its scent, striving to capture the smell of it in my mind forever, where I could retrieve it at leisure.

Finished, she said, "Did you hurt yourself anywhere else?"

I nodded. "I banged my side, and my head is sore."

Nurse Helen smiled, placed the dirty cotton wool into the metal bowl, and moved towards me, her arms extended, fingers splayed.

"I'll check your head, all right? And then we'll have a look at your side."

Her fingers gently parted my hair into sections.

"You only have…grit in your hair, so that's good, isn't it? I'll need to write a note to your mother and ask her to buy you some special shampoo."

I wondered what the shampoo could be for but dismissed taking the thought too far. What was the point in hoping for the luxury? Mam wouldn't buy the shampoo anyway.

"Right, Carmel. Swing round and put your legs up on the bed. That's it. Now, point to which side hurts and where."

I did, ensuring the end of my finger didn't jab my hip, that it hovered just above the pain site.

"May I lift your skirt so I can take a look at your hip?"

I nodded. Nurse Helen tucked the hem of my skirt into the elasticised waistband. The smell of Dettol wafted into my nose from her hand's movements.

"Oh. You must have taken quite a bang, young lady. You've got a bruise already, the size of a small apple, I'd say, except it isn't green or red but purple."

A big purple bruise. Mam and Bob wouldn't be happy. My face must have held a disbelieving expression. I know my eyes had widened.

"Don't you believe me? Take a look for yourself," she said.

I peeked. My stomach plummeted.

# Chapter Thirteen

The afternoon sun blazed upon the front door handle, its heat against my palm the only warm welcome I'd get at this house. I opened the door a little—it wouldn't fully open. I peeked around it. The contents of the cupboard under the stairs were piled high behind it, and I squeezed through the small gap. A muffled scratching sound, reminiscent of a scrubbing brush moving through soap suds met my ears, and the soles of Mam's dirty, bare feet poked out of the doorway to the cupboard.

I closed the front door quietly and tiptoed towards the living room in the hopes that Mam wouldn't know I'd arrived home. The scratching stopped and, never to be fooled, Mam blew out an impatient breath. Her voice echoed out of the cupboard.

"School nurse rang me today, kid. Said you fell over on the playground. That right?"

She scooted backwards on her hands and knees, looking ludicrous in a short black skirt and a cerise pink vest top. She lifted her torso and threw whatever had been in her hand into the cupboard. What sounded like the slap of water jerked my nerves.

"Yes, Mam."

Mam stood, not bothering to straighten her skirt, which had ridden up her thighs. She barged past me into the living room and through to the kitchen. I followed. The stench of dirty water lingering in her wake attacked my nostrils, and I suppressed a gag.

Her strident voice sailed towards me. "Reckons you've got nits."

*Nits.*

I reached the kitchen doorway. Mam sat with her back to me at the kitchen table, a cigarette packet in one hand, a bright yellow Bic lighter in the other. "She *also* reckons I should buy you some nit shampoo." Mam turned her head to face me. "Tea, kid, and make it snappy."

*Nits.*

I walked to the kettle and lifted it to check how much water it contained. A quiet slosh indicated near emptiness, so I filled it at the sink. The weight of it, once full, bunched my muscles, and I staggered back to the worktop and thumped it down.

"Break the kettle and I'll break your neck."

Mam's lighter clicked, and she inhaled and exhaled, inhaled again and held her breath as I held mine. I inserted the wire into the kettle base and flicked the ON switch. Mam exhaled.

"What *I* reckon," she said, "is that there isn't any point in buying nit shampoo when I've already got something that will get rid of them just as well. I'll wash your hair in it later."

I stayed with my back towards Mam and stared at the grimy tiles on the wall, listening to the sounds around me. The kettle creaked and popped while the water heated. Mam sucked at her cigarette and blew the smoke out. Birds twittered in the trees outside, and one of them shrieked so violently that many pairs of wings flapped as they flew up into the air in fright. The clock on the wall ticked, and I flashed my gaze at it, matched the ticks to the steady movement of the second hand. I must have zoned out, perhaps mesmerised by the clock hand. The slap to the side of my head stung.

"The kettle's boiled, you silly little cow. Tea. Make it."

I blinked and scrunched my eyes closed, opened them again, and prepared to make Mam's tea.

"Carmel? Get up here. I need to wash your hair, and then you can have a bath."

I flung my blanket from around me, grabbed Nelson, and scampered up the stairs. I sat Nelson against the wall and undressed on the landing. I remembered the bruise on my hip. Mam would see it. I took tentative steps into the bathroom, hid behind her, but she turned and gripped my shoulder.

"Hurry up and get your arse in front of the bath. I have to wash your hair."

I knelt beside the bath and hung my head over, mindful of shielding my hip from view.

I looked to my right at Mam. She smiled— black teeth in an equally black hole—turned, and picked up a glass milk bottle filled with yellow-tinged liquid. She swung back round and dashed the liquid over my head. The stench exploded and almost choked me. It reminded me of the times I'd walked past the petrol station. I didn't have the chance to close my eyes and turn my face to stare at the bottom of the bath, and some of the liquid dripped onto my eyeball—the one the bug had splatted against—and it stung. Burned so badly I could have sworn my eye was melting, that it would dissolve into goo and I'd forever have to walk round without an eye like Belinda did. I twisted my head straight, gasping.

Mam's harsh, phlegm-filled laugh filled the small room.

Another dash of cold liquid—I closed my eyes this time—and Mam slammed the bottle on the bath ledge and massaged my head with uncaring hands, her fingertips spiteful and harsh. I gulped in a lungful of cloying air, feeling as if my chest would disintegrate, and exhaled with a shudder.

"This'll get rid of the little fuckers," Mam all but shouted. She cackled and pummelled my head, aggravating my scalp.

I opened my mouth to breathe but kept my eyes closed. Liquid dribbled onto my bottom lip, and I blew it away, conscious not to inhale deeply in case the substance got sucked into my mouth. I clamped my teeth together and tried to bring the scent of Dettol to mind; prayed the memory of it would override the stink of the odious liquid that continued to travel in cold drips down my cheeks.

Mam piled my hair on top of my head, although some strands flopped down to touch my back, my forehead. I resisted the urge to cry, concentrating once again on breathing in short gasps, on keeping my eyes closed so tightly that no liquid could get in.

Mam stopped messing with my hair. I shivered—with shock, perhaps—and listened to the sounds of water splashing into the sink, the *schlup* of the soap as it came free of the old flower-patterned saucer it usually rested on, the squelch-slop-squelch of Mam washing her hands.

"Stay there for a minute while I fill the sink with clean water," she said.

The plop of the plug being inserted gave me something to focus on. I hoped that soon Mam would rinse off that infernal liquid and I could have a bath and get out of the room. A spurt of water sloshed into the sink for what seemed like very long minutes before it stopped. A rustle quite close to me indicated that Mam touched a towel—getting it ready for when I got out of the bath? Drying her hands?

A strange quiet descended around me then, and, young as I was, I recognised the sense of foreboding that stole over me, so acute that I shuddered. Unable to open my eyes, and with scant space between sensing danger and hearing the click of Mam's Bic lighter, it took milliseconds to realise what that foreboding had signalled. I opened my eyes and mouth simultaneously, gasped in air, tasted fuel. And screamed.

"Shall I burn the bastards, kid? Yes?"

I jerked my head up and flung my arms out, starfish hands, fingers splayed.

A terrible sound filled the bathroom, intertwined with Mam's insane laughter. I turned my head to look at her, my jaw aching from my mouth being open so wide. She smirked and zoomed the lighter towards me, the flame wavering.

*Your mam's wicked, Carmel. She's gonna burn your hair off.*

Mam continued to wave the lighter in my direction and then whip it away just as I thought she'd set me alight. Back and forth, back and forth, and each time she withdrew the flame she laughed.

Abruptly, she turned to the sink. I realised that terrible sound had been coming from my mouth.

"Lean back over the bath," Mam shouted.

I obeyed immediately, despite my fear, and the dash of more fluid slapped against the back of my head and dripped into the bath. Only water. A hiss like a collective sigh echoed inside my mind, and the slosh of water—rinsing, rinsing—registered before I blacked out into merciful oblivion.

# Chapter Fourteen

Something poked at my back. I'd felt that sensation before, but my sleep-addled brain struggled to recall what caused it. My eyes refused to open, their lids seemingly made of concrete, and the grit from them scratched my eyeballs. That poke, it jabbed relentlessly in the same spot near my right kidney, and with each contact, the achy pain grew. I attempted to raise my arm, to use my hand to bat the poking object away, but my limb was too heavy to lift. The effort too much.

"Wake up, you little cow."

A harder, more vicious poke. The concrete in my eyelids dispersed, leaving them light enough to open. I flung my arm out and caught the ends of my fingers on the edge of the bath. While they stung, I ignored the pain and asked myself: What am I doing down here?

I sat up, inhaled the horrific odour, and memories resurfaced.

"What was that little episode all about, eh?" Another poke, this one to my stomach—Mam's index finger. "You've scraped your knees and have one fuck-off big bruise on your side. And, to top it off, you banged your fucking nose when you blacked out. If you've broken it, tough shit, kid, I'm not taking you to the quack. *And*—Bob is gonna brain me for this. Stand up, you dopey little shit."

I scrambled to my feet, and her mentioning my nose acted as a catalyst for pain to stand up tall and say hello in a loud, searing voice. Cold air nipped at my bare skin; the window yawned open. I hugged myself, rubbed the tops of my arms. Mam gripped my chin, lifted it so that I had no choice but to look at her.

"Get in the bath—I've even filled it. Wash your hair then come downstairs. I've got something for you."

Mam never bought me things. What could she have for me but a slap or a pinch? Still, a glimmer of hope blossomed inside me that she may well have bought me something *nice*. I climbed into the bath under her watchful eye, my legs shaking. I slid into the water and dunked my hair. Mam still stood there, staring, staring. I reached for the cheap shampoo.

The click of Mam's lighter echoed around the room and entered my head, exploding as loud as a firecracker. I squealed and knocked the bottle of shampoo into the bath. The glug as it disappeared beneath the surface and the *schwoosh* as it bobbed back up joined the fireworks in my mind. Mam laughed, clutched at her stomach, and threw her head back. It didn't look like she owned a single tooth, so black were they in the gutter of her mouth. Busy...I'd keep busy washing my hair and ignore the terrible sound that came through her lips.

Thin liquid dribbled onto my palm—snotty green, supposedly apple fragrance so the label on the bottle stated—and I slapped it onto my head and massaged. This wasn't the kind of shampoo I'd seen on TV, where the user's hair frothed with a burst of thick white suds like an old granny's perm. No, this shampoo smelled of washing up detergent, the exact same liquid I used to wash the dishes downstairs, mixed with the other awful stuff Mam had splashed on my head.

Finished with washing, I eased back and lowered my head into the water, moved it from side to side to rinse out the bubbles and pretended to be a mermaid in the ocean. I closed my eyes, uncaring if Mam decided to inflict anything else on me. When I opened them again, she was gone.

Once dressed in dirty, ragged pyjamas, the days of their vibrant pink colour long gone (if, indeed, they had ever come to me brand new in the first place), I grabbed Nelson from her position on the landing and made my way downstairs. The smell of fuel still lingered in my hair, and I suspected it would always be there no matter how many times I washed it.

Mam sat on the sofa, legs curled beneath her, an elbow digging into the sofa arm, her hand cupping the side of her face.

"Go and brush your hair. Looks like a bird's nest," she said and trained her gaze on the TV.

I walked into the kitchen, the linoleum warm against the soles of my feet; the late afternoon sunshine still blazed through the window set in the back door. I placed Nelson on the table and rooted around on the worktops for a hairbrush. Debris, so much of it, littered the surfaces: dirty, blackened spoons, old newspapers and magazines, filthy crockery, hairpins, even a ball of mould sat proudly on top of a pile of used teabags. The dark green mould had hair, a fuzzy white outcrop, and I thought about sea anemones and fish under the ocean, swimming freely through a rainbow of coral.

"Get a fucking move on if you want what I have for you," Mam called.

I quickened my search, found a brush, complete with a wig of its own, so much hair that hardly any of the bristles were visible. Yanking it through my knotted hair, I tidied it as best I could, placed the brush back on the worktop, and returned to the living room.

Mam leant forward and picked up a bottle of medicine and a spoon from the scarred wooden coffee table in front of her. Not that I could see the state of the wood; the table was covered much the same as the kitchen worktops, minus the hairy mould. But the scars resided there all the same. A little like me, really. The main scars are all within, some of them visible on my skin, but the real scars, the ones that cause pain as if they're fresh wounds, hide inside my mind. No one would know; no one would particularly care.

"Come here, let me check and see if those little bastards are dead or not." Mam indicated impatiently with her hand, and I scooted to stand in front of her. "Well sit down, then. I can't fucking see from down here."

I sat. Mam fiddled around with my hair. I shivered.

"Yup. Looks like they're all dead. Their little bodies will all fall out eventually. Who knows, you might even wake up in the morning and find them on your pillow."

Mam laughed so much she coughed. The crackle of phlegm bubbled in her throat; it snapped as she inhaled ready for another burst of coughing. Damn, that phlegm was stubborn. Seemed it didn't want to be hawked up and spat out on the carpet today. I waited. Placed my hands in my lap and studied a picture on one of the magazines on the coffee table.

A beach with white sand. The sea frothed like the adverts for shampoo as it met with the shore, and the blueness of the water farther out was the best colour blue I'd seen in a long time. Well, since I'd first seen the blue coat in the lost property box, that was. The sky, a light shade of azure, held no clouds, none at all, and it wasn't for the want of me searching. A tree with a trunk like a pineapple bordered the left side of the picture. Its green leaves resembled those of some tulips I'd seen on a birthday card at our little shop. Would that sand be hot beneath my feet? And it wouldn't matter if the sand *was* hot—I could race down to the sea and plunge my feet in its coolness, swim in it if I wanted, and soothe my sun-baked skin.

Mam coughed on. And on.

A boat appeared in the picture, a great big cruise ship. It pulled up onto the beach much like a car parking. A door opened at the base of the ship's black bow, and a set of metal steps stretched out, the bottom one disappearing into the waves. Someone appeared on the top step and waved at me. Someone with an eye socket for a head.

"Carmel, get me…a…drink…of water… Sitting there… letting…me choke."

I blinked, and the magazine picture reverted to its original image. Scuttling into the kitchen, I filled a filthy glass with water and rushed back into the living room. Mam snatched the glass. Water sloshed from it, formed a perfect ball of liquid. It moved in slow motion towards the magazine picture, splatting onto it with a wet thwack.

The sound of Mam guzzling made me shake the fuzziness from my mind. I glanced at her red face, at her cheeks mottled with purple splotches, and wondered if I would look like her when I grew up. She plonked the glass on top of the mess on the table—it teetered, threatened to fall, but didn't—and drew in a deep breath. The air wheezed in her throat, whistled shrilly, then gusted out again. She cleared her throat, once, twice, and said, "Now, remind me when *you* next get a cough to ignore *you*."

Nothing out of the ordinary, then.

Mam reached for the medicine bottle and began to unscrew the cap. It clicked—safety lid—and frustration birthed on her face, twisted and ugly. Anger helped her to free the lid, and she placed it on the table and picked up the spoon. A dessert spoon.

"Come here. This medicine will help with your cuts and bruises," she said. A small "hmph!" escaped her lips—perhaps the start of a laugh and she'd thought better of it?

I took two steps, my arms hanging at my sides. Mam poured the medicine onto the spoon, and I leant forward to receive it. Spoon not quite in my mouth, I closed my lips. Medicine dribbled over Mam's fingers and down my chin. She cursed and yanked the spoon out, the metal edge paining my lips, the tip clanking against my top teeth.

"You're meant to wait until the *whole* spoon is in your mouth, kid. Jeez, what a dumb fuck. Here." She jerked the bottle at me. "Drink it from the bottle. About half should do it."

Of course, I obeyed, didn't question her instruction. Why would I? I had no concept of what a dose of medicine *was*. Hell, I don't think I'd ever had any medicine before that moment. A headache or sore tummy apparently didn't warrant any.

The medicine tasted…different to anything I'd had before. Bitter, but tasty at the same time. With each swig, I checked how much I'd swallowed. Mam watched and said, "More."

A burning sensation travelled from my throat down into my tummy. I knew exactly when the liquid ended its journey to my gut. Warmth spread there similar to what I imagined love would feel like—a pleasing glow—and I closed my eyes to savour it.

"That's enough for this time. Let's see how you get along with that."

I'm not sure how long I stood in front of Mam after taking that medicine. I just know that a swaying motion took over me, as if my ears had been affected by a virus, my balance off-kilter. The loving warmth spread from my guts to my limbs, right down to the ends of my toes and back up to the tips of my fingers. I imagined the medicine floating, its mission to reach every single part of me and make me better. Fix me.

My knees gave way, bent, and then snapped straight again. My torso jerked forward, and I nearly pitched into Mam. Had her eyes grown? Yes, they had. They bugged, big as tennis balls, the same yellow-green colour too. They looked as glassy as marbles, yet I had a feeling they wouldn't be as hard. That I could reach out and grasp one of them—and my fingers wouldn't stretch the whole way round it, of that I was sure—and squeeze it until it popped.

A low hum began in my head, growing in volume, the sound of a fly drawing closer. Light laughter tittered far off, as if travelling out from the bottom of a well. Its eerie echo flitted round the room, an unseen moth, seeming to bounce from the walls at me.

Mam wasn't laughing. Her stretched lips remained closed, reminiscent of two hotdogs glued together and attached to her face. Her features blurred, and her head moved from side to side—or was that me swaying?

The light laughter grew in strength, eventually reaching such a high octave that I placed my hands over my ears to deaden the sound. Piercing, so piercing—who *was* that?

I turned to look around the room, to check if anyone had come into the house without my knowledge. Someone had appeared all right, but it wasn't Bob or a male visitor that I'd expected. Belinda loomed in the living room doorway, her eye-socket head as large as Mam's. A snake's tongue protruded from it, licked the air, and tasted the scent of the fear that I felt growing inside me, multiplying at an alarming rate and coursing through my body, much like the medicine had done.

I backed away from Belinda. The base of the sofa met my calves, and I flumped onto the cushion next to Mam, who stared at me. I gawped from her to Belinda. The laughter from the well erupted again and repeated itself over and over. Belinda clapped, slowly at first, quickening her hands' movements until each clap merged into the next, creating a maddening accompaniment to the laughter.

I stood, teetered, and stepped forward, skirting round the coffee table on unsteady legs, away from Mam, closer to Belinda. In my fuddled brain, an apparition of a cadaver seemed safer than my own mother. Mam's breath zoomed from behind me, creating violent gusts of air that flung my wet hair in front of me and dried it. That air reached Belinda. Her eye-socket face lost its wetness, drying it into a big old prune. The snake tongue retracted and disappeared into one of the arid ravines on Belinda's face.

The well-laughter also dried up, an animalistic howl taking its place. My eardrums buzzed and hummed, vibrated to such an extent I momentarily wondered if they would pop.

"Go up to bed," yelled Mam.

I turned to her, saw her hotdog lips open and close in slow motion, her voice matching their lethargic movement.

"Go up to beeeed, yooou sillee coooooow."

I leapt towards the kitchen, the need to have Nelson with me uppermost in my mind. I could hug her in bed—hug her if the strangeness of this current situation followed me up the stairs and continued its assault. The carpet seemed covered in gunk, a sticky substance that clung on to the soles of my feet in an attempt to stop me walking. I willed myself forward, the muscles in my legs screaming in pain with the effort it took to take one step. Hours passed, it seemed, hours that left me drained and breathless by the time I reached the kitchen. I grabbed Nelson, now the same size as me, and she walked beside me through the living room, the gunky carpet back to its usual filthy, dry state.

"Got yourself a new pal?" asked Mam, her voice far off.

Perhaps she'd gone and fallen into that well?

Belinda, still standing in the doorway, appeared as if she had no intention of letting us pass. Her prune head wobbled, and she gripped her chubby hips with fingers made of over-ripe bananas, the yellow skin fading in vibrancy, black bruising indicating that the flesh beneath would be mushy and inedible.

"Get out of our way," said Nelson. "Move, or *I'll* kill you this time."

Belinda disappeared so quickly I had to blink to take in the information. In her place, a violet mist hovered and grew in density, filling the small hallway.

"What did Nelson meeean jussst thhhen, kkkkid?" asked Mam.

I didn't answer. Nelson stepped forward and pulled at my hand, urging me through the violet mist and up the stairs. My legs leaden, the effort to climb each step brought tears of fatigue to my eyes and a lump to my throat. We rounded the top banister, and Nelson pushed me from behind, nudging me along the landing and into my room. My bed had never seemed so inviting. It no longer had the ratty sheet and the stained pillow, but a puffy quilt, its cover a pretty pink with tiny red roses.

I fell forward onto it; its softness surrounded and embraced me in a cocoon, and the last thought I had before sleep claimed me was that I hoped, so dearly hoped, that the gunk from the carpet downstairs didn't ruin my beautiful new bedding.

# Chapter Fifteen

⸙

Sleep brought a strange dream.

"See this?" Belinda said and walked towards me. She held out the medicine bottle. "Know what it is?"

Bravado grew inside me, spread itself to my tongue, and I said, "Why? Don't you?"

"Oh, *I* know what it is, you freak. But you...don't."

Indignation overrode bravado. "Yes I do. It's medicine. I hurt myself at school today, and Mam gave it to me to make me feel better."

Belinda laughed, and her face morphed from the features I knew her to have in life to the ugly, singular eye socket. It oozed lime-green pus, which dripped from where her chin should be. Chunks of goo landed on the roll of queen-dress material at her waist. Mucous sprang to mind, and I stifled a heave.

"Except it didn't make you feel better. Did it?"

"No," I said and cursed myself for admitting that.

"Made you feel like a sack of shit, didn't it?"

"Yes."

"Wanna know what kind of medicine it is?" Yellow translucent liquid leaked from the eye socket's surface, creating a mini lake complete with waves, ripples. "It isn't the kind of medicine that cures sore knees or apple-sized bruises on your hip." Belinda's laugh issued from the round socket, and the mini lake jostled further. Excess liquid sloshed into her ears, travelling down her neck.

"What is it, then?" I asked.

"Phenergan. Meant to be for travel sickness, but *you* don't travel anywhere in a car. Meant to be for hay fever, but *you* haven't got that either, have you? *Meant* to be for many things but for nothing *you* suffer with. High doses, well, they make your knees and legs heavy, make your mind go all funny. Make you tired."

"Tired? Why would Mam want to make me tired?" I blinked and swallowed the lump forming in my throat.

The yellow liquid churned, and more laughter exploded from the socket. Droplets landed on my face as if Belinda had spat at me. "Why would Mam want to make you tired, indeed? So Bob... No. I've said too much. Think on, little bitch. You're a clever girl. You'll work it out."

Thick violet mist replaced Belinda's form, loitering in the air like a fog outfit upon a coat hanger. After several blinks, I turned towards the sofa.

"Want some more medicine, Carmel?" Mam said, Gary beside her.

Her lips pulled back, showing her stubby teeth. She laughed, and her breath puffed out as a visible thing. It shunted towards me, a heavy, black rain cloud. The stench of blocked drains and stagnant water hit me. I clamped my palm over my mouth and nose, swiped at the tears as the reek swirled around me. I gagged, and spittle pooled under my tongue.

"What's the matter, divvo?" said Mam, another cloud floating out of her mouth.

I turned to run into the kitchen, but my legs wouldn't move. My feet seemed stuck to the carpet. The second cloud enveloped me, and my lungs shuddered with lack of air. Heat blossomed on my cheeks, my pulse thudded in the vein on my neck, and I had no choice but to wrench my hand away from my face and breathe in the foul odour.

Gary jumped up. "Come on, Carmel, I've got to show you something."

He tottered towards me on his bare heels, syringe-toes tapping against one another, sounding like the empty plastic cotton reels we made necklaces with at school. As he drew closer, the syringe sound amplified, bringing empty Coke cans being shoved down the pavement by a vicious gust to mind. He reached for my hand, and I took it.

"That's it, you show her, Gary," Mam said. "Then bring her back here and she can have some more nice medicine."

Eager to get away from Mam's breath, I allowed Gary to pull me through to the hallway and out of the front door. The pitch black sky held a million or more stars; so many that they joined in places to form ridges of light. And those ridges appeared as a staircase. Amazed at the sight, I stared upwards to capture the scene, wanting to keep it in my memory forever.

"Look at the sky, Gary," I whispered.

Gary tugged at my wrist. "I know. That's where we're going."

Stumbling behind him, still staring at the sky and trusting my best friend to lead me, I said, "We're going up into the sky?"

"Yes, but we've got to get to the forest first. Gotta show you something. My dad said Belinda should be leather by now. Wanna go and see? If we go to the forest and tunnel down by the old brick wall, we'll come up the other side into the cemetery. Can't get into the cemetery any other way, see."

Puzzled, I yanked my gaze from the star-steps and took in our surroundings. How had we travelled so far, so fast? A road lay ahead and behind us. Either side, hay swayed in a chilly breeze, rustled, whispered.

*Carmel? You asleep? Oi...*

Something sharp poked my side—reminiscent of Mam's finger—and I glanced round to see if she'd followed us. No one there.

*She's asleep. I gave her the dose you told me to...*

*Can't be too careful. Just checking...*

"The hay's whispering, Gary." I quickened my pace, brought myself abreast of him; I'd been lagging behind despite him holding my wrist.

"Hay doesn't talk. Come on, we're nearly there."

Gary pressed on with more vigour. The road ahead led to a far-off tunnel on the other side of a forest. The hay had grown when I blinked and now stood higher than we did, their middles bending in a soft arc, their tops meeting over our heads. The swish and whoosh of their movement sounded like sheets snapping on a washing line, paper being scrunched into balls.

*Put that clean sheet on the floor…*

*Hang on, I'm trying to open this bloody package.*

A shudder ripped through me. "Did you hear that, Gary?"

"Hear what?"

"The hay…"

"Look ahead. Stay focused. We need to reach that clump of trees." Gary lunged forward, determination on his face.

I looked ahead. The forest was before us, seemed to be right there, yet we walked without getting any closer. Gary squeezed my hand and let out a frustrated sigh.

"Come *on*, Carmel."

I pressed on. Trees with eyes stared back at me. Not carved from wood, but real eyes. I felt as though we walked on a moving panel, that if we jumped to the side we could step forward and into the forest. I shook my wrist to free it from Gary's grasp. He tightened his fingers.

"Nearly there. A few more steps." Gary squeezed harder.

"Ow! Let go of me," I said through gritted teeth.

*All set?*

*Yup. You sure she won't wake up?*

*Nah, she's dead to the world…*

Sweat beaded my temples. My calves burned. An immense gust of wind rattled through the hay and shunted us forward onto the forest floor. Ground debris bit at my knees and palms. I stood, swiped at my knees, and rubbed my palms together. Gary did the same. He looked at me.

"Ready to go into the forest and find the wall?"

I glanced around and saw the wall and the cemetery beyond. "It's over there," I said. "There's a gap in the wall, look, where you walk through to get into the cemetery."

"We're not meant to use the entrance, Carmel. Aw, I don't know about doing that." Gary frowned, pursed his lips. "We've got to dig to reach her. We're rats, after all."

We stepped two paces forward, and the wall zoomed to greet us. Gary hunkered beside the opening and burrowed at the ground.

"Come on. Get down here and help."

"But the entrance is right here…" I stared at the stone wall, at the space we could walk through, the rows and rows of gravestones. "We don't need to dig if we can just—"

I found myself down on hands and knees inside a mud tunnel. I turned to see how far we'd dug. Nothing but blackness behind us.

"Upwards," Gary said and clawed at the earth above our heads. "I can smell her." He twitched his nose like he did when we played at being rats on the playground.

A muffled voice—was it coming from the depths of the mud? In my head?—said: *A couple more and we're done.*

"A couple more what, Gary?"

"What? Keep digging."

I obeyed and wondered: Why doesn't the mud cave in around us? How come it doesn't fill my mouth, clog my throat, and choke me to death?

We popped through the surface, surged into the air, dolphins at sea, and came to rest on top of a star-cloud that hovered near the ground.

"We did it!" Gary flung his arms around me. His wispy hair tickled my cheek. He pulled back, looked at me. "Come on. Let's climb the stairs."

Though his enthusiasm enticed me, I frowned.

*What is this all about, Carmel? What do you need to climb the stairs for?*

I didn't want to see Belinda as a piece of leather, didn't harbour the same urge to inspect her corpse like Gary did. After all, she appeared to me every day.

Gary bounded up the star-steps, stopped on step five, and turned to look down at me. "Come on. We have to go. Time's running out."

His urgency penetrated my confusion, and I followed him up the stairs. Infinite night sky surrounded us and, far from being scared when I stared down at Earth, exhilaration winged through me on angel's wings. A feeling of safety stole over me, and I glanced up the stairway to see how many we had yet to climb. The staircase stretched on for what looked like miles. My feet gained weightlessness, and I bounced upwards from step to step. My insides—had they been sucked out?—felt gone, a hollow in their place.

Sweet liquid filled my mouth—I think I tasted freedom, then—and I reached the last step.

"Gary?"

Where had he gone?

I turned to regard the stars, the sky, and Earth below. Such a vast place down there, a huge mass of land and sea. My sight zoomed down, latched onto Mam's house, enabling me to see through the roof, the ceilings, and into the 'posh' back room. A small person was on the bed, a leather mask on their face.

"What are you doing here? Mam give you too much medicine, did she?"

I wrenched my gaze from Mam's house, turned to look at the top step. Belinda stared at me—the Belinda with a face, though her skin resembled the person on the bed down there, leathery.

"Gary brought me here."

"Gary? So where is he, then?"

I shrugged. "Dunno." I climbed two more steps. Elation surged from my toes to my fingertips, making the hairs on the back of my neck stand up.

"Stay right there. No way are you coming any farther." Belinda held her hand out, palm towards me. Her skin changed from little girl hue to a beige-orange. Like the dried pigs' ears in those baskets outside the butcher's in town. "It's not your time yet. That's annoyed me, that has. I wanted to go back down these steps but my granny wouldn't let me. Yet you—you get to go back down there. So not fair."

My body floated off the step. The urge to climb higher, to *drift* higher, assailed me, and I ground my teeth together and ducked my head ready to ram Belinda aside. *I must get to that top step.*

"No!" she screeched and thrust her palm against my chest.

"Let me pass," I yelled. "I don't wanna go back home. I don't wanna be down there anymore."

The force of her palm zapped the air from my lungs and my feet from the steps. I sailed backwards, as if on a slide at the park—"Don't think of that park, you spiteful little bitch."—and the starry sky zipped past me with ferocious speed. My gut re-filled, slowly at first, but the closer I got to Earth the heavier it became. Phenergan replaced the taste of freedom on my tongue, and dread encompassed the liberty that had briefly allowed me airborne. I landed at the base of the steps on my back and looked at the stars. Tears pricked my eyes. I closed them.

# Chapter Sixteen

"Carmel! Wake up!"

Mam's strident tones pierced the fug of sleep—an ice pick on apple skin. I jumped, sat upright. Head heavy, I flopped back down again, my flat pillow no comfort to the ache at the base of my skull.

"Carmel? You fucking ignoring me, girl?"

I strove to respond, but my tongue felt too big for my mouth and brought to mind the time I'd bought sweets instead of a sandwich. Marshmallows. So hungry, I'd stuffed half the bag into my mouth, and that's what my tongue felt like: marshmallows.

I staggered out of bed on unsteady legs, legs that seemed too brittle to carry my weight. They wobbled, and I wondered: *If I fall and black out, will I see the star-steps again, make it to the top this time?* However, my legs betrayed me, and I managed to walk to the top of our stairs and grab hold of the newel post to stop myself from swaying.

Mam stood at the foot in her bottom-of-the-stairs pose and blew out a plume of smoke. "You look a bit peaky, kid. Feel rough, do you?"

I opened my mouth to answer. Couldn't.

Mam sucked on her cigarette, blew smoke out again. "What's up? Cat got your tongue?"

A shiver whipped up and down my spine, and gooseflesh sprung up on my arms. I glanced down at myself—naked.

*Why don't I have my pyjamas on?*

"Gotta make yourself scarce. Yeah, yeah, I know it's Saturday and you usually get to hang around, but I got a couple of specials on today. Also got some important people coming round with Bob. So, get a move on and get the fuck out."

Mam moved away from the bottom of the stairs. Her bare feet slapped against the floor, quieted when she trod on the living room carpet. I turned around. My knees buckled, and I stumbled into the bathroom.

Leaning over the sink, I dry-retched. Saliva dangled from my bottom lip, my innards jitterbugged, and my arms slapped against my sides. I groped for the cold water tap, twisted it on, and, with my elbows wedged inside the sink, cupped my palms beneath the water. Bringing my hands to my mouth, I guzzled the cold liquid, never so glad to have a drink to soothe my sore throat, my arid tongue. The water shot down into my belly, and I imagined the splash of it in my stomach as it hit the base and pooled there in an icy sea. It threatened to come back up—my jaw shook, my guts roiled, but I swallowed, inhaled deeply, and kept it down. Another sip, another, and I stood upright.

Shutting off the tap, I plunked onto the toilet and peed. I lowered my forehead to my knees, hugged my shins, and thought about what I would do that day, where I would go. With no destination in mind—did I ever have one?—I readied myself for the hours ahead.

Once I was downstairs, my equilibrium returned to near normalcy. Nelson hung from my hand, and I placed her on the kitchen work surface so she could watch me make Mam's tea. Mam sat at the kitchen table, a newspaper in front of her, as well as her near-finished cigarette perched in an ashtray. The kettle weighed heavy in my hand, wrenching at my elbow, pulling the muscles in the tops of my arms. I could quite happily have dropped it, but the ramifications ensured I stayed my grip. Kettle on top of its base, ON switch flicked down, I slouched over to the fridge to fetch the milk.

"My, my, we're tired today, aren't we? Had a good sleep, too. You were out from teatime until this morning. Lazy bitch."

I retrieved the milk and returned to the work surface, shifting various items to make enough space for Mam's cup. A mug tree, devoid of mugs, sat towards the back, a twig body with too many arms. A stick insect. I shuddered.

Dirty cups sat on two dinner plates in the sink. Sighing quietly, the sting of tears near, I squirted washing-up liquid into the bowl and turned on the tap. A gush of water had me longing for a bath, the smell of the washing detergent better than my current odour.

"You're only doing that because I called you lazy." Mam's lighter clicked. "Still, I'm not complaining."

A page of the newspaper turned over. Its crackle hurt my head.

I switched off the tap and washed the dishes, the cups. The kettle flipped off, the sound of bubbling water loud. Drying a cup, I turned and plopped a teabag and two sugars into it like an automaton.

"Haven't you fucking made that tea yet? Guts think my throat's been cut. Hurry up."

Another turn of a newspaper page. A gasp.

Tea made, I took it to Mam and placed it on the table on top of a stack of women's magazines. Why did Mam buy those? I never saw her reading them.

Mam didn't look up from reading. A bold, black headline stretched across the top of the page. It took me a minute to read it.

"What are you standing there for? Go on, fuck off. There's a fiver on the coffee table. You can have it all. You gotta stay out all day, evening, too. Don't come back until past nine."

I left her there, swirled the headline round in my head. MAN ARRESTED FOR KIDDIE PORN. I shrugged. It meant nothing to my young mind. The fiver, crisp and new, crackled against my palm. I'd go to the shop and buy something for breakfast. Maybe I'd feel more like myself then. I pulled Belinda's plimsolls out of my school bag and slipped them on, placing the five pound note inside beneath my right foot. The house harboured a chill; outside would be colder. After shrugging into my coat, I slipped past Mam again and grabbed Nelson from the worktop. Mam stared out of the glass in the back door, her finger pointing under a line of text on the newspaper, still open on the same page.

A breeze gusted through our street, bringing with it a biting chill. In breaks between wind bouts, the air felt quite pleasant. The sun shone— maybe this afternoon would be warmer?—and I dawdled to the shop.

*Bit nippy, isn't it, Carmel?*

"It is, Nelson, but Mam's busy today so we can't play queens and have a sleep this afternoon."

*Will you buy sweets at the shop?*

"Dunno. I might buy some later. Reckon I need to see how much I have left after I get my breakfast, lunch, and dinner."

*Oh.*

The heater above the shop door blasted a welcome that brought on a smile. I made straight for the bread aisle. It being early, I might find a cut-priced loaf left over from yesterday. I swooped down to the floor and rummaged towards the rear of the rack and found a treasure of sorts. A yellow reduced-price sticker attached itself to the back of my hand. Glancing up and down the aisle and seeing no one, I ripped the sticker off and placed it on the cellophane of a freshly baked, uncut loaf at the front of the rack.

The warmth of the bread seeped into my palms, and I worried whether Mr Hemmings would spot my duplicity. Deciding the risk was worth being caught for, I walked to the fridge and selected a pint carton of milk. The contrast of the cold milk in my hand and warm bread held against my chest brought on a shiver that flicked through my body. My tummy growled. I clutched Nelson tightly in my other hand.

At the counter, I waited behind two chatting women. No one worked the till—something I'd never seen before.

"You'd never have known, would you?" said one lady in a loud whisper. She fingered her chin.

I stared at her perfectly painted nails then looked at my own.

*When you're older, you can have nails like that, Carmel.*

I nodded.

"No. I'm absolutely stunned," whispered the other lady, her back to me. Her voice triggered a memory—of piss-sullied floors and hosiery-clad legs. Belinda's mam! What was her name…? Ma…Mar…Margo?

I wanted to shrink or run. My bladder pained, but with no fluid inside it, it didn't issue its usual stream. I clutched the bread, and the cellophane crackled. The woman with the fancy nails made an odd eye movement, jerked her head, and Margo spun round to face me.

"Why, Carmel! Hello, love. How are you?"

I looked into her beautiful eyes, smiled, and tension slipped away. "I'm all right."

"Good, good. What have you been up to?" she asked.

"Nothing much."

Painted Nails jabbed at the brass counter bell, dinged it several times, and huffed out a sigh. "If someone doesn't get behind this counter soon, I'm walking off without paying." She laughed, as did Margo.

"You could leave your payment on the counter," said Margo, turning back to her companion.

"What, and have some little scumbag steal it?" Painted Nails stared at me. "Not bloody likely."

Margo smiled at me. "Carmel wouldn't take the money, would you, love?"

I shook my head and stared at the floor—Painted Nails' glare proved too searching, too intrusive.

"Well, I'll take these things and pay for them next time I'm in, all the same," she said. "See you at the group on Friday?"

"Yes, yes. I'll be there. See you then," said Margo.

I looked back up. Painted Nails trotted out of the shop on impossibly high heels. I wished she'd trip over the threshold, but she didn't.

"So, Carmel. Up to anything interesting today?" asked Margo.

"No. Mam's busy so I'm to keep out of her hair."

"Oh, right. And what will you do to keep out of her hair?" Margo's smile warmed me just like the bread against my tummy.

"Dunno."

"Well," she said and hunkered beside me, "what do you think about coming to my house for the day? Would your mother mind?"

"No, but Arsey might," I said, the words out before I could stop them.

"Arsey?" Margo's smile grew wider before her lips formed a pout.

"Um, Belinda's dad might not like me going to your house."

Laughter barked out of Margo's mouth, a pleasant torrent of sound. "Oh, Carmel, you *are* funny. *Arsey* won't be there, my lovely. He's never there now. So, would you like to spend the day with me?"

I nodded, willing my bladder to let out even the smallest of squirts so that I could have a bath in her tub.

"Come along, then. I'll pay for what we've taken next time I'm here."

Margo stood and held out her hand. Shoving Nelson into the crook of my other arm with the bread, I clasped Belinda's mam's warm palm.

Life would be good today.

⁂

Belinda's house didn't smell the same as it had on my last visit. An odour I recognised but couldn't place permeated the air. The living room harboured dust on the TV cabinet and the windowsill, and Margo's usually clear-of-debris coffee table held glasses, an empty wine bottle, and dirty plates. Though untidy, it still wasn't as filthy as Mam's house.

Margo led me through to the kitchen. The same untidiness met me there.

"Sit yourself at the breakfast bar," she urged, her hand on my back, "and I'll make you a milkshake. Do you like milkshake?"

I nodded, still clutching my bread, milk, and Nelson.

"Put your things on the side, look. That's it. Would you like me to make you some toast with your bread?"

"Yes, please."

Margo made toast differently to the way Mam and me did. We used a decrepit toaster. Margo sliced my bread into thick hunks and placed them under a grill that hung over the hob of her cooker. She turned a knob and held a white implement under the grill that clicked when she pressed a red button. Blue flame created a sheet of fire as it lit; one curl of heat poked out like a tongue, licked the air, then settled back inside the grill. The toast cooked quickly.

Butter, my first taste of it. Mam used margarine—the cheap kind that left an aftertaste lingering at the back of my throat. And that butter, it was wonderful. With two slices of toast devoured, and a strawberry milkshake still to consume, I let warmth spread through me where I perched on that breakfast bar stool. Again, I thought about the many differences between here and home. And I realised how lucky Belinda had been. Previously, I'd thought her lucky because her lavish bedroom held everything a young girl could want, and her bathroom held things that had the ability to clean even the dirtiest of children. And although Arsey wasn't particularly nice by any means, she'd had two parents. Two that gave a shit.

Other differences made themselves apparent now. The kind Belinda would most certainly have taken for granted. Butter, milkshakes, that sense of being cared for, that how you felt *mattered*.

Margo stared at me for a long time. Tears dribbled down her face, and she stood in front of the cooker wringing her hands.

*She's thinking of Belinda, Carmel. She's seeing you sitting there and wishing things were back to how they used to be.*

I sipped my milkshake and shoved Nelson's words to the back of my mind.

"How come Belinda's dad isn't here anymore?" I asked and licked my milkshake moustache.

Margo blinked, snapped out her trance, and palmed her face. "Oh, after Belinda went, he went too. Things didn't work out."

"Oh. Don't you get lonely?" A burp rumbled in my throat, and I swallowed it. The bubble of trapped air hurt my windpipe. I winced.

A sad smile tweaked her lips. "Oh yes, but I don't miss *him*, not really. Besides, I've made some new friends at a group I go to. Kind of like going to school—lots of people there with the same alco...problem—and we learn to accept things." She dived towards the sink with such vigour it made me jump. Preparing to wash up, she said, "Anyway, enough of all that. How about clean the dishes, do a quick tidy round, and we go and play in Belinda's room? Would that be nice?"

I nodded. "I'll help you clean."

"Oh, what a good girl you are. Belinda would never have... Well, what a good girl you are, Carmel, that's all."

We played queens. One of the petticoats fitted Margo—she'd lost weight since I'd last seen her—and a brief thought of Mam prancing about in the same garb flitted through my mind.

*Mam would never play with you like this.*

"I know."

"Pardon, love?" Margo said, pausing in her walk up and down the bedroom.

"Nothing." Heat rushed to my cheeks, and I glanced at Nelson, who sat next to Belinda's dolls on the shelf.

Margo followed my gaze. "I wonder, would you like Belinda's dolls?"

I stared at them all, glassy-eyed, their poses somehow sinister. "No, thank you. I love Nelson; don't need any more dolls."

Margo smiled. "What about a new dress for Nelson, then?"

"All right."

She took Nelson from the shelf and handed her to me. "Which dress do you think Nelson would like? Pick any dress from any of these dolls." Margo seemed over-bright, manic.

*I'd like to wear the pink one with the ruffles.*

I pointed to the dress Nelson had selected. "That one."

"Righty-ho!" Margo reached up, grasped the doll, and undressed it quickly. "You know, I haven't been in here since… Well, you know, and I really must take my group leader's advice. Now then, is there anything in here you would like to take home with you? I should sort this room out really, start afresh, stop wallowing in the past. Oh," Margo placed her fingers to her mouth, "what am I thinking? Talking to you like you're an adult. I'm very sorry, Carmel, I shouldn't burden you with this kind of talk. Silly me."

I looked around the room. Though it was filled with most small girl's dreams, I didn't want anything in it except the woman who stood before me as my mother. And I couldn't have that. I shook my head.

"Nothing? Nothing at all? What about some clothes? Would clothes be okay?"

Margo bustled over to the chest of drawers and yanked one open, bringing out a pile of T-shirts. She placed them on the bed, sat, and put her hand on the top garment. Her fingertips rubbed the material, picked at the sequins that rounded the neckline. Her face crumpled, and she closed her eyes, that action urging two fat tears to plop down her cheeks. She sat like that for many seconds, and I mimicked her actions, fingering the sausage of material around my waist.

Trousers, jeans, skirts, sweaters, all came out of the drawers and the wardrobe. Some looked to be too big, Belinda being a plump child, but others would fit. I looked at the clothes longingly, wanted more than anything to wear the pinks, purples, yellows, and blues, but Mam would go mad if I took them home and said where I'd got them from.

Margo sat on the clothes-covered bed, a smile on her face. "Well? What do you think?"

I stared at Margo then shifted my gaze from her to the clothes. "Mam won't let me have them. She reckons being given stuff is bad."

"Hmm." Margo looked at the ceiling, bit her bottom lip. Returning her attention to me, she said, "What happens if you find things?"

"Oh, I can have anything I find. And I'm allowed to take stuff." I didn't have any qualms about admitting this; after all, Mam said it was okay.

Margo's eyes widened then narrowed. "Well, why don't you say you found them? If your mother thinks it's okay to find things and keep them, and you'd only be telling a tiny lie, do you think that would be all right? Though Lord knows I shouldn't encourage you to tell fibs."

"Yes. That would be okay. And telling lies is fine, because Mam tells me to do that sometimes, although I'm not allowed to lie to her, she said. If she finds out I've lied to her I'll be in trouble."

A sigh left Margo. "Well, I'll go downstairs and get a black bag for some of these clothes. We'll put the big ones in one bag, the smaller ones in another, and I'll put them out by the rubbish bin. Perhaps *someone* will *find* them and take them away before the dustbin man collects them, eh?"

# Chapter Seventeen

❧

After the clothes had been bagged and deposited next to the metal dustbin in the driveway, we settled in the kitchen for lunch. Using my bread, Margo made wedge-sliced sandwiches and filled them with grated cheese and cucumber. The butter thickly spread, its rich taste blending with the cheese was one of the best things I've tasted. A cup of tea, drank from a china cup, topped off the meal, and my eyelids grew heavy. I placed my hands, one above the other, on the breakfast bar, and rested my chin on them.

"Are you tired, love?" Margo asked.

I nodded.

"Do you want to go home? Won't your mother be worrying where you are by now?"

I shook my head.

"Are you sure?" Margo shook *her* head slightly at my response, her mouth a grim line. "Well, in that case, maybe you could have a little sleep on my sofa? Nelson might like that too. She's had an exciting day, getting a new dress."

Nelson sat on the breakfast bar against the wall. Margo had brushed her ratty hair, and a pink ribbon adorned the two pigtails either side of her head. She looked a different dolly altogether, if you discounted her cracked face and poorly eye.

*Yes, we can have a nice sleep on the sofa. We could, couldn't we, Carmel? Your mam doesn't want us home until tonight, and where else would we go if we left here?*

"Nelson would like a little sleep."

"Oh, good. Do you want a blanket?"

*No, it's warm enough in here, what with the fire being on.*

"No, thank you," I said and slipped from the high stool. Taking Nelson's hand, I walked into the living room and flopped onto the sofa. Maybe the medicine from yesterday still circulated my system, maybe the kindness bestowed on me proved too much. I closed my eyes and hot tears scalded my cheeks before blessed sleep claimed me.

*Isn't Belinda's mam nice, Carmel?*

"She is," I said and hefted the black bag beside me—a struggle, it was heavier than I thought it would be—mindful not to let it drag on the floor. My elbow and shoulder bore the strain.

*What are you going to tell your mam? About the clothes, I mean.*

"Dunno. I'll think of something."

*If you get to keep the clothes, what will you wear tomorrow?*

"Dunno. There's so much to choose from. Will you shh for a minute?"

Memories of hours gone by ran amok in my mind. I'd woken on the sofa to the sound of running water and Margo humming. I sat up, stretched, and followed the sounds. Margo leaned over the bath and swished water around, creating an eddy. Thick white bubbles grew up the sides of the tub like Mam's hair mousse on the rare times she expressed it into her palm. I reached out and touched Margo's shoulder.

"Oh!" She jumped, stood upright, and faced me. Water dripped from her hand. "Awake, I see. I've run you a bath, thought you might like one after that sleep."

Oh my.

Margo left the room, ensuring a huge pink towel hung on the back of the door, and urged me to use whatever shampoo and soap I liked. Before my bladder betrayed me, I snicked the lock across the door and made it to the toilet in time.

That bath, I'll never forget it.

I also never forgot to wind the plug chain round and round the tap afterwards.

While walking home, wind whipped my face, wafting the scent of the posh shampoo I'd used from my hair. I felt the cleanest I'd ever been, smelled like the poshest lady. You know, all perfumed and pampered.

The journey home went by too quickly. I didn't want to return to reality, smell the stink of Mam's house, see the filth of it. Belinda's mam had cleaned her home so it resembled the house of times past. I imagined I was her daughter, and we'd shared the chores, had fun. My palm against the door handle of our place infused my body with dread.

*Wonder what mood she'll be in, Carmel.*

"Dunno," I whispered.

The darkened hallway brought desolation to my soul—an ebony shroud of depression. I plunked the black bag by the door, clutched Nelson to my chest, and closed the front door. Dust, mould, those smells of home, how I hated them. I'd smelled Mr Sheen for the first time at Belinda's house, sprayed that furniture polish and inhaled deeply, marvelled at how it made the coffee table gleam with one swipe of the soft yellow cloth.

"That you, kid?" Mam's sleepy voice yanked me away from my thoughts.

"Yes, Mam."

"Where have you been?"

I walked into the living room and perched on the chair by the window. Mam was on the sofa, remnants of the day's make-up on her face along with a tired scowl.

"Around. Walked about mostly."

Mam's frown deepened. "What's that smell?"

My tummy rolled over. "Oh, I went swimming, used some shampoo that someone left."

"Swimming? With no costume?" Mam bolted upright, reached for her cigarettes, and levelled her frightening gaze at me. "You must think I was born yesterday, girl."

I squirmed in my seat. "No, honest. I found a bag of clothes outside the charity shop in town. There was a costume in there. That's what gave me the idea, see."

Mam narrowed her eyes, lit her cigarette, and seemed to consider what I'd said. "So, the costume will be wet when you show it to me then? And smell of chlorine."

A pain shot into my stomach; those nasty fists squeezed it tight. "Want me to show you?" I asked, my mind ticking over, frantic, scared.

"You bet I fucking do. Go and get the bag."

"I need a wee first," I said. Before she could protest, I lurched out into the hallway, opened the black bag, and retrieved the swimming costume. Stuffing it into my knickers, I raced upstairs. The cold tap on, I shoved the costume under the stream of water. The smell of bleach rose from the material—I'd smelled that for the first time at Margo's house, too—and I wrung out the costume as well as I could. Toilet flushed, I ran downstairs and thrust the costume into the black bag. Dragging it into the living room, I sat on the chair again and pulled the sack towards me.

Mam inspected every piece of clothing I gave her, some damp from the costume having rested against them. She brought the cozzie up to her nose, sniffed loudly.

"Let you off. Reckon you did go swimming, then. I tell you, you got quite a stash here. A lucky find, kid. Well done." She lay back on the sofa, reached out for an ashtray, and balanced it on her stomach. She closed her eyes. "Just makes me wonder what you dried yourself with. And where you stashed that big bag when you went swimming."

I busied myself placing the clothes back in the black bag. I sat for some time, waiting to see if Mam had anything else to say, whether she expected me to answer her musings. Seemed she didn't, so I sat Nelson on top of the clothes and carried my booty to my room.

I tried everything on, held Mam's old make-up mirror out in front of me to see what each outfit looked like. Although I couldn't see myself in full, the glimpses I did gain were enough. I needed a belt for some of the trousers and skirts—I'd snuck Belinda's silver one inside the bag when Margo had turned away—but other than that, the clothes fitted. I didn't recall seeing Belinda in any of them, except for a white towelling T-shirt with an embroidered butterfly on the left breast. I folded the dry clothes and placed them in a pile at the foot of my bed. The damp ones, I hung over the back of a rickety wooden chair that sat in the corner.

"Carmel?" Mam's shout invaded my pleasurable task.

Dressed in pink jeans, a matching jacket, and a white blouse, I skipped to the top of the stairs. "Yes, Mam?"

Mam's eyes widened. A small smile played out on her lips. "Well now, don't you look the business? People will think we've come up in the world. Anyhow, I wanted to ask you something. Get down here."

Sorrowful that she'd interrupted my game of dress-up, I descended the stairs, following her into the kitchen.

"Tea," she said.

I got on with the task. Mam sat in her usual chair at the small table.

"Did you go up the shop today, kid?"

"This morning."

"See Mr Hemmings, did you?"

"No. No one was behind the counter." I spooned sugar into Mam's cup then poured boiling water over the teabag.

"My, my. Bit lax, eh?"

I didn't know what she meant, what would be the correct answer, so I turned and smiled at her. Facing her cup once more, I squeezed her blood out of the teabag, turned the water almost black. Good job she liked her brew strong, else I'd get a smack on the side of the head for presenting her with dark tea.

"What did you buy?" she asked.

"Nothing." I poured in milk, stirred.

"Why, because no one was behind the counter?" The click of Mam's lighter jabbed at my nerves. I knew she was building up to something, and not knowing what it was had me fretting.

"No one could serve me, so I walked out with a loaf of bread and some milk." I handed Mam her tea. She took it then slapped me on the back, laughter spilling from her filthy maw.

"You clever little sod. We'll make a crim out of you yet. Fucking good day you've had, then. Free food and drink, and a bag of clothes."

I looked at the tabletop, worried whether Mam knew where I'd really been all day and was testing me to see what I'd say. Her free food and drink comment made my tummy squirm, and my bladder throbbed.

"How much did swimming cost?" she said and sucked on her cigarette as if it were a drink's straw.

*Here it comes…*

"Nothing."

"*Nothing*? So how the fuck did you go swimming?" Mam sipped her tea.

I continued to stare at the table, at four crumbs that had fallen there God knew when. If I drew a line between each crumb it'd make a square.

"I tagged along with a group of kids that went with their dad."

Mam laughed—and I mean *really* laughed. "Fuck me, kid. You've cheered me up no end today. Started out a bit shitty this morning, got some bad news about Mr Hemmings, but Jesus, you've given me some laughs this evening." Mam took a sip of tea then pulled on her cigarette. "So, you've still got that fiver left, then? Or did you need to buy some dinner?"

"I still have the fiver." *What had happened to Mr Hemmings?* "And I made friends with the kids at swimming, and their mam bought me a plate of chips in the cafeteria."

Mam choked on her smoke exhalation.

*Wish she'd choke for real.*

"Oh, my fucking God. You are priceless sometimes. There was me thinking you're useless baggage, when all along you're a proper little felon. Funny as fuck, you are."

For the first time in a long time, Mam yanked me forward and hugged me to her breast, pushed me down to sit on her knee. Confusion brought tears to my eyes, and I blinked them away. Aware that Mam could change tack at any second, I sat still, my body poised to leap away should the need arise. Conflict waged inside me. Mam was pleased I'd supposedly done all those naughty things. By doing them and telling her, she hugged me. Yet Mrs Draper spent a lot of time letting us know that honesty was the best policy. What was right?

"Carmel, I'm gonna let you keep the fiver as a reward. Besides, I made a packet today." Mam removed her hands from around my waist, shoved against my back. I stood up, faced her. "Wanna hear what happened to Mr Hemmings?"

I nodded.

"Well, the dirty old bastard had some pictures of little kids, see." My frown must have spurred her next explanation. "Not just normal pictures of kids. No, he had rude ones, like, kids with no clothes on. That's not allowed, you know. The police took him away because he's a pervert."

Sickness invaded my gut—not from what Mam told me, no, I didn't really grasp the importance of her statement—but because dear Mr Hemmings was in trouble with the police.

"Shocking, isn't it?" Mam asked and continued without waiting for my answer. "No one knows who the kids are in those pictures because they were taken with no faces in them. Or so I heard, anyway, but Mr Hemmings, he's in the shit, all right. Best thing is, it won't come back on me and Bob. What d'you reckon to that, eh? Someone's put the frighteners on the filthy old perv. Fucking classic, it is."

"It's great, Mam," I said, uncomprehending of frighteners, pervs, and classics. Would that mean I wouldn't see Mr Hemmings again? Did the police put people in prison for having pictures of children with no clothes on?

Mam must have read my mind—she was good at doing that—and said, "His wife'll probably sell the shop. The shame. We probably won't see the chubby old sod ever again. Shame for Bob, as well. Good customer, was Mr Hemmings. Still, there are more like him out there that are after what we can give them. We'll have a posh house in no time, girl."

Mam beamed, her filthy grin infectious, and, despite my confusion, I smiled too. Giggled. A *whole* posh house? That would be grand, that would.

"Anyway, kid. Bedtime for you. And you'll be wearing one of those new nighties, I reckon."

I nodded. Mam in this kind of mood was sometimes worse than her bad ones. With the bad, I knew what to expect. With the good, I walked on a tightrope. Before she could change from sunny day to tornado, I scooted out of the kitchen, up the stairs, and into my room.

With a soft nightshirt against my skin and the smell of posh shampoo in my hair—I'd pulled my hair across my face to better inhale its scent—I thought about Mr Hemmings all alone in a dirty prison cell, rats for company. I puzzled over having a mam that I loved and hated in equal measure. At how she could inspire fear one minute, and confusion with her nice side the next. Pulling my legs up against my body, I squeezed into a tight ball.

And let the tears fall.

# Chapter Eighteen

Monday arrived. What should I wear? Such indecision. Gone were the days where I had an either or option. I used to wear the same clothes for weeks on end. Funny how no one commented or took the piss out of me for that. Perhaps I was so insignificant to the other kids that my attire didn't warrant a mention.

Finally, I decided on the pink denim outfit and the towelling white T-shirt with the butterfly. Although obviously worn, Belinda's socks still appeared new to me, and I relished the thought of changing from my outdoor shoes to my plimsolls without fear of someone seeing my toes poking out. My own shoes were all that ruined my outfit that day. A size too small, the black patent leather scuffed across the front, I realised I'd have to look in the lost property box more regularly if I hoped to find a better pair.

Still, the walk to school seemed shorter, the sun brighter, the sky a sharper blue. I wanted people to look at me—what a change from previous days when I'd kept my head down and avoided eye contact—wanted them to notice the girl with the washed hair (that *still* smelled of posh shampoo) and the clean clothes. No one paid me any mind, though. On their way to work, lost in their own worlds, the people of our town bustled along as if I didn't exist. Which I barely did, really.

Gary sat on the wooden bench in the cloakroom, waiting for me.

"Carmel! I called round for you after school Friday, but no one answered the door. Someone was in, though. Heard noises through the letterbox. I peeked through and saw some bloke carrying you down the stairs."

He called round? For *me*? I knew we were friends at school, all right, but for him to actually seek me out afterwards, well… My eyes stung. I blinked.

"Oh, I went to bed early. Mam gave me medicine to make me better after I fell over, you know, on the playground. I don't remember a bloke carrying me."

Gary frowned and jumped up from the bench, stood while I proudly changed into my plimsolls. I wiggled my toes in the socks.

"Yeah, well, that's what I came round for. To see if you were all right. And you are, so that's okay. They new clothes?"

My tummy flipped, and butterflies danced within. "Yeah. Yeah, they are." Finished changing, I looked at Gary. Smiled.

"You look right good," he said and walked into class with his head down, the back of his neck red.

My mind tended to wander during boring school assemblies. Mr Kendry's voice droned, hummed like a bee. He looked like a bee, too, with his big round torso, short arms and legs. His tortoiseshell-rimmed glasses, their lenses thick, rested on his bulbous nose. Everest, we called him, you know, after the company that made double-glazing.

Today's lecture focused on being kind. Some children had apparently formed a gang. Mr Kendry knew who the gang members were, never fear, and he was watching them. We should mark his words...

My gaze roamed around the room at children's paintings on the walls. The theme: endangered animals. Tigers, elephants, monkeys, all depicted in various ways by many minds. Funny how one creature formed into a different creature on the page depending on whose mind conjured the image.

The tiger pictures fascinated me the most. Rounded faces, pointy faces, big teeth, little teeth. Thick stripes, thin stri—

"You should be paying attention, you little bitch."

Belinda sat next to me, though I didn't turn to look at her, just shifted my position. Uncrossed and re-crossed my legs.

"Mr Kendry has good advice on how to stop being bullied. On how to stop *being* a bully. Seems you're not listening."

A tiger with purple—purple?—eyes glared at me from the wall.

"I can't believe you have the cheek to wear *my* clothes, go to *my* house, be with *my* mam."

The assembly hall grew warmer. The air thicker.

"You're a horrible little girl, Carmel, d'you know that? Do you *know* what a nasty piece of shit you really are?"

I raised my hand, placed it beneath the right side of the pink denim jacket, and traced my fingers over the butterfly on *my* T-shirt. The embroidery tickled my index finger, numbed the skin.

"No one loves you. I wonder what that feels like? I mean, *I* wouldn't know. *Every*one loved me. What *does* it feel like, Carmel?"

Mr Kendry's buzz grew in volume, and the heat turned up a notch.

"I know all about you now. See everything that goes on. Stinky house, dirty mam, crappy doll. No wonder you didn't want me to come to *your* house for tea."

Belinda moved her head—I saw her in my peripheral vision. She craned her neck in an attempt to get me to look at her. A plop of eye socket juice splatted on the assembly hall floor. I looked at that instead of her, and it reminded me of Swarfega, that green goo Mrs Draper made us wash our hands in after we'd used oil paints in art once.

"Mr Hemmings is in big trouble. He looked at pictures of you with no clothes on. I know it was you. Know you were the one who took the pictures to him in the brown envelope. I'm dead because of you, and Mr Hemmings, well, he may as well be dead now too. People in prison can't stand people like him."

*Don't listen to her, Carmel.*

"Don't you ever think about how unfair it is? Like, I'm dead, and you're still alive. I had a great life, and yours is shit. I really don't see any justice there. Do you?"

I shook my head.

*No justice at all, Belinda. Because Carmel would give anything to climb the star-steps again and reach the top. Leave her alone.*

"Leave you alone? No, I don't think I will."

Belinda sat in front of me now, cross-legged, hands resting in the space between her legs. She wore the same as me. Wet mud streaked her clothes, her hands. The liquid on her eye-socket face bubbled. I stared at it, thought how it resembled the top of a volcano, and that any minute that pus could erupt, spew out over everyone in the hall. Fill the hall, trap everyone inside, burn us, drown us, cool down, dry out, and preserve us as fossils.

"My mam, she's been driven to drink, but you kind of knew that, didn't you? And my dad? He's off living the single life, acts a lot like your mam, except he doesn't get paid for it. Must have been a shock when you realised other people's mams don't behave the same as yours. That some kids are treated nice *all* the time, not just when their mams have had their medicine. *Medicine!*"

Belinda laughed. Her face goo gurgled. Mr Kendry hummed on. The tigers prowled on the walls, left their pictures, and congregated together. Safety in numbers. Monkeys jumped into the uppermost painting, settled on a tree, and looked down at those fearsome tigers. The elephants trumpeted, and the sound echoed off the hall floor. Children giggled. Mr Kendry shouted—*Releasing body odours in assembly isn't funny, now get out!*—and my throat tightened.

"I hope you have a terrible time for the rest of your life, bitch. I'm going to hang around and make sure I'm with you all the way. There when things go wrong, there when you suffer."

I jumped up, ran from the hall.

It wasn't until I reached my classroom that I realised people would think I'd passed gas. And it wasn't me. Wasn't me.

Mrs Draper followed me to class. "Carmel, is something troubling you?" she asked.

"No."

"Are you sure?"

"Yes."

"All right then. Off you go, out to play."

The lost property yielded a prize that playtime. A pair of girl's shoes—a size too big, but better than being too small—rested at the bottom of the box. Maybe a little worn, but they appeared in better condition than my current footwear. I squatted down behind the box and changed into them, reached up, and dropped my old shoes into the lost property.

The weather treated us well that day. Sunlight beamed, and I sat astride Black Beauty and chased Gary. We galloped over fields, jumped streams and fences. A road, much like the one in my dream, stretched before us, and we cantered towards the forest that sat on the horizon. The hay had been cut—an omen of things to come? (Mam hacked off my hair later that night in a drunken rage.) The hay shimmied in the breeze, whispered words I couldn't fathom. Forestry jumped from the distance and planted itself right before us. The trees had no eyes this day, the bark ridged like any other tree, the leaves a lush green. Birds cawed, and I caught a glimpse of two hares scampering through the foliage.

"So, where is she?" I said.

"Dunno." Gary lifted his hand, shielded his eyes from the unrelenting sun. "Reckon she's not playing with us today."

"Shall we ride through the forest to the graveyard then?"

"What graveyard?" Gary turned to me as we rode along, a frown on his forehead. "All I can see is the woods."

"There's a graveyard through here."

"Nah there isn't."

"There is. I've been there before. You can dig though the ground and come back up again by these steps that are made of stars. I climbed the steps and looked down at the whole world."

Gary laughed. "Your mind's whacko."

I laughed, though his words stung.

A bell jangled in the distance.

"Time to turn back. We've got weaving this afternoon." Gary turned White Beauty around, clicked his tongue, and dug his knees into the horse's flank.

I followed Gary back to the playground.

"Come along, children. Time to go in." A helper stood at the edge of the playground, hands clasped around a mug.

I often wondered why teachers got a drink at break time and we didn't. If they got thirsty, it stood to reason we would, too. Thinking of drinks ensured my tongue dried out. I skipped over to the water fountain, my new shoes rubbing a blister on my heel.

I leaned over the spout, watched for the rust to appear, for Belinda's face to morph onto the shiny silver bowl that caught the flow of water. Nothing happened. Partly relieved, for her visit to the assembly hall had unnerved me a little, I couldn't help but feel aggrieved. She usually played with us during break. Her visits gave my wandering mind something to focus on other than my home life.

I sucked at the bland water, let it take away the sting of thirst. Listened to the receding footsteps of the children going inside, the clatter of chairs being pulled out from under tables in the classroom situated beside the spout.

"Come along, Carmel. Stop dawdling." The playtime helper.

I wondered if she was someone's mam. Mams sometimes helped out. I couldn't imagine my mam offering her services in that way. And would I want Mam in my school? I turned from the spout, and on the way back into class I decided that no, I wouldn't want her invading the place that belonged to me. Yet at the same time, a small part of me yearned for Mam to be a proper one. Someone I could show off to the other children. I could tell my classmates she wanted to share in all aspects of my life. And the mam I wanted would be kind to the children, help them with their shoelaces, pick them up when they fell over. She wouldn't have a mug of tea; she'd drink from the spout just like we had to. Girls would forfeit playing just to walk around the playground holding her hand.

I changed into my plimsolls and faced the grim reality. Mam would have a mug of tea, and if a child annoyed her she'd think nothing of dashing that hot liquid into their faces. And she'd laugh, ridicule the scalded child, call them a baby, a pain, a worthless piece of shit…

"Carmel, we're waiting for you in the home corner." Mrs Draper stood in the cloakroom doorway, hands on hips.

"I need the toilet," I said.

A loud tsk issued from my teacher. "Well, hurry up."

She turned and stalked back into the classroom, leaving me feeling like I was a burden on everyone. That whatever I did, I would never be good enough.

# *Chapter Nineteen*

ou know, I've been thinking a lot about the
past. They say it catches up with you in the
end. I wonder how I haven't gone insane. What
do you mean, I have? You've grown bolder over the
years, d'you know that? So rude.

Sometimes, when I think about the things you
want me to do, sometimes I get to thinking it isn't
right. A small part of me knows right from wrong,
don't think I don't, yet the majority of me has been
conditioned to be the way I am.

Urges prod me all the time. I can usually fight
them off, but you, you insist on poking at me, shoving

*me to do what you want, listening to my thoughts. I could say I won't follow your orders, but if you want the whole truth, I enjoy doing what we do. Does that mean I'm a piece of shit? A bad person? Yes, it does. But if I'm bad, then I was made to be this way. I don't think I was born like it.*

*Who's next? We still have a few to go, don't we? I hope you're right when you say that ridding my life of everyone who ever hurt me will bring some form of peace. The risks we take…*

# Chapter Twenty

M uch of a muchness occurs, and time passes, lets us grow older. New experiences are added to our palettes, and we go forth and paint another scene. Our paintbrush may need new bristles, our canvas might crack, but still we paint on, don't we?

Twelve is a strange age. Neither child nor woman, I struggled with the new emotions surging inside. Of course, knowledge that my life was indeed wrong in so many ways became more apparent as the years rolled by, but what could I do? Bound to Mam, despite her obvious lack of care for me, I was stuck in her house, her life, until that wonderful age of sixteen sat on my overburdened shoulders.

Belinda continued to visit, though sometimes months passed in between. My friendship with Gary blossomed, spread to after-school meetings. We'd hang out at the park and sit on the swings, our gazes fixed to Belinda's death site, our tongues discussing her demise. Mr Moon smiled down on me, his star companions twinkled, and we'd swing up into the sky and play the game of who could kick Mr Moon in the head first. Gary always yelled that he'd done it, but I knew he hadn't, for didn't I swing higher than he did?

Other times, we'd visit the shop. During winter, especially, we'd take our time choosing what we'd buy, and I felt less alone knowing that act from my younger years was shared with someone else. The shop had been taken over by new owners, and it lost its friendly atmosphere, got revamped to look more like a convenience store. The penny sweet section no longer sat on the counter, the sale of them banished altogether, and ready-bagged sweets packaged in shiny colours replaced the huge jars of confectionery on the shelves. On the occasions I wanted to buy sweets, the joy wasn't the same. I missed the little white paper bags. I missed Mr Hemmings swooshing them round in the air as he sealed them shut.

Going to Gary's house always resulted in fun. His mam and dad, liberal parents, treated him almost the same as an adult. The banter between them, far removed from my strained relationship with Mam, served to make the differences more apparent. I didn't begrudge Gary his home life, although I was jealous of it. I spent many nights curled up in bed wishing I lived in a house with parents like Gary's, and it was amazing that I didn't want to hurt Gary for having something I didn't. The reason for that was simple. Gary saw me like no one else did, accepted me for who I was, and didn't let his peers or society dictate that hanging around with me wasn't good.

Gary was safe, then.

It was inevitable that I'd become an age where Thursday nights lost their appeal for Bob. Since that awful Friday night I'd first taken Phenergan, every Thursday evening saw me drinking a bottle of the stuff. I'd gain heavy legs, my eyes drooped, and Mam and Bob did with me what they would. I never visited the star-steps again during those times, maybe my body got used to the medicated abuse, but I slumbered, oblivious.

My feelings for Gary, aided by raging hormones and body changes, grew from friendship to…something else. I didn't know what love was, had never been shown it, nor did I know how to give it, feel it, so I put it down to a stronger like of my friend. He made me happy, caused my tummy to flip-flop in a pleasant way, and ensured my heart beat more quickly. I basked in his company, locked out the unhappiness in my life for the duration of our time together, and pretended. Pretended.

One particular Thursday drew round. Gary had long ago accepted that I couldn't go out Thursday nights, so his question threw me a little.

"Wanna come to the fair with me tonight? It's on until Sunday, but tonight's opening night, see. Free rides for the first hour, seven 'til eight."

Did I want to go to the fair? Hell, yes. I wanted to go more than anything, to feel the wind whip through my hair on The Waltzers, to squeal on The Ghost Train, clutching Gary's arm. That was what people did on TV, anyway. I'd never been to a fair before.

"I can't. Mam doesn't let me out on Thursdays, does she."

Gary kicked a stone on the road. It skittered and bumped over the tarmac before coming to rest beneath a red Ford Cortina parked on the kerb.

"What is it with Thursdays, anyway? Is it the night you do your chores or what? Surely your mam will let you off for one week?"

A smile played on my lips, and I said, "Yeah, it's chore night, all right. And nah, she won't let me off."

Gary thrust his hands in his trouser pockets, toed the ground some more. "But you haven't even asked her yet, so how d'you know she'll say no if you don't try?"

He had a point—one that would be valid with anyone else but me. I *knew* Mam would say no. She never had got her *whole* house posh, and over the years she'd made it clear that as long as there was breath in my body I'd work with Bob to ensure she did revamp her home. I thought about the ensuing argument if I brought up the question of me going to the fair. Her claw-like fingers came to mind, lunging at me, ready to scrape at my cheeks, pull out my hair. Her spiteful words swirled round in my head, her stinking breath touching my skin. No, I didn't dare to ask her.

"I dare you," Gary said.

*Oh no. He's dared you, Carmel. And you know you don't back down on a dare. You both made a pledge that neither of you would back down…*

Nelson, still my best friend.

"Shit," I said. "All right. But if you don't see me waiting at the park by seven tonight, you'll know Mam said no."

"Cool."

"You fucking *what*?" Mam switched her attention from the TV to me. "Who the hell do you think you are, coming in and telling, *telling* me you're going out tonight? Not bloody likely, kid. Thursday—it's *Thursday*, the one night a week I ask you to do something for *me*. Six days of the week you're allowed to do what you want, roaming around outside for hours on end getting up to God knows what, yet you want Thursday off *as well*? You ungrateful little bitch."

Mam stood, skirted the coffee table, and loomed in front of me, her face inches from mine.

"No *way* you're going to the fair. Not tomorrow or the weekend, either. Now go and drink your medicine. This discussion is *over*."

Hate for her surged through my body. Gooseflesh spread over my skin, my ears buzzed, and I clenched my jaw. "I *am* going," I said and stared at Mam, all fear of her gone as the unfairness of what she'd said swirled around my mind. "And I'm not taking any more of that medicine."

Mam's eyes widened. She glared at me, fists by her sides, her cheeks growing redder as the seconds ticked by. "What. Did. You. Just. Say?"

Where my gall came from, I don't know, but I said, "You heard me. And I'm not doing anything on Thursday nights again, either. Fucking perverts, the lot of you."

Mam swallowed, coughed, and almost choked on the spittle of her ire. "You little cow."

She lunged at me, grasped my hair in her fists, and shook my head from side to side, backwards and forwards. My brain hurt, almost like it rattled against the inside of my skull. She threw me back, and my hip met with the edge of the living room door. Unbalanced, I plunked down on my behind. Pain bloomed at the base of my spine, and I bit my lower lip in a bid to transfer the pain there. My scalp, if it had a mouth, would have screamed. My hair, ripped out by the roots, dangled from between Mam's fingers as she held her hands in front of her and stared at her palms.

"Get the fuck in that kitchen and take the medicine." Mam lifted her arm and pointed in that direction. Her hand shook.

I narrowed my eyes. Heart thumping, bile rising in my throat, I said, "No." I shifted my position, placed my palms on the floor to lever myself standing. Darting my torso forward, I said, "Fuck you!"

Mam had never had such open eyes before. I swear they would have popped out of her head if she hadn't closed them, which she did for what seemed a long time. She inhaled through her nose, nostrils flaring. Yes, she *was* a big old dragon, all right. And I wasn't scared of her. Not one bit. She'd beaten me, used me, and I'd had a tool I could have used against her all along. Yet I didn't possess enough of it. Courage. It had failed me in the past. It winged through my body now, screamed hello, waved its arms, and let me know it was there to help.

My breaths came in gasps. Mam's grew steadier the longer her eyes stayed closed. I stared at her, saw her for what she was: an addict who cared for nothing except her next hit. Holes punctured her body, some fresh, some with scabs, some so old they'd scarred. Her skinny frame didn't look strong enough to hold her head, and her hair... Well, men must have been desperate, depraved, or both to go with her out of choice.

Still with eyes closed, she said, "Go and take the medicine."

"Mam, I'm going out now," I said and left the living room. Walking through the hallway to the front door, I perked my ears for sounds of her stealthy approach. Expected her to jump me. The door handle cooled my palm, accelerated my beating heart. Cool air kissed my face, exacerbating the sting in my eyes. And I walked from that house on shaky legs, the sense of freedom and having won a small battle prevalent in my mind.

I say small, for I knew Mam. I wasn't stupid enough to think I'd won the war.

I sat on a swing and brushed my hair with my fingers. It took a while—Mam's grip had tangled it. With each movement, my scalp throbbed. The sky darkened, but I still had a couple of hours to kill before Gary showed up. Done with my hair, I pushed my legs out, pulled them back under me, and rocked my body to move the swing. The wind created from the swing's movement slashed at my hair. Every follicle on my head burned. Uncaring of the pain, I swung higher, closed my eyes.

Elation butterflies danced in my gut, coupled with fear of what would happen when I returned home later that night. I shoved those thoughts away, concentrating on the good feelings for once. I'd beaten Mam, and if this was the only time I'd ever do it, I wanted to revel in my victory.

Ever attuned to danger, and despite the breeze slapping at them, my ears picked up the sounds of rustling grass. Eyes still closed, I smiled, thinking Gary had come to meet me early, had maybe anticipated I'd be at the park by now. I stopped moving my legs, waited for the swing to slow, listened to the grass sounds moving closer. Stretching my foot, I let it drag along the floor, ceasing the swing's motion. Footsteps padded across the tarmac that surrounded the play area. I opened my eyes.

A screech, coupled with Mam's breath, hit my face. Her hands found my shoulders, yanked me from the swing, and pushed me downward by sheer rage-induced force. My torso flung over the swing's seat chest down, and the chains that held the swing to the brightly covered frame jangled. Wound across my neck. The metal chilled my throat, bit at the soft flesh. I opened my mouth to gulp in oxygen and was left wanting.

"You fucking little whore. I'll teach you to go against me. Who the fuck d'you think you are, eh?"

I didn't answer, couldn't.

"Eh? Answer me, you little bitch."

I brought my hands up to the chain, my fingers slipping against the metal, unable to find purchase. Gargled sounds came from my mouth, and I kicked my feet in an attempt to strike her, anywhere, give her pain so she released her grip. I stared at the sky, silently apologised to Mr Moon for kicking him in the head, pleaded with him to make the star-steps appear.

"She's one angry mother." Belinda.

She stood before me, chubby hands on chubby hips, her eye-socket face now purple. I conveyed my want through my eyes, hoped she'd understand what I needed.

"Oh, no. Not your time. Sorry, no star-steps for you."

The chain's pressure released, and I slumped forward, the swing's seat pushing on my chest. Mam's breaths gasped behind me, my own overtaking them in volume. I swallowed. Painful. Grit dug into my knees, and I toed the ground, stumbled upright.

With my hands at my throat, rubbing the skin to ease the immense soreness, I turned to face

Mam. She stood a metre away, hands by her sides, fingers clenching, unclenching to the rhythm of her exhalations. Her eyes held a wild glint, and her cheeks, I'd never seen them so red.

A sharp pain pricked my temples, and I swear my brain swelled, even for only a moment, before it shrivelled back to its usual size. Swallowing again — fragments of glass — I concentrated on steadying my breaths, reducing the speed of my heart.

"You," Mam said, raising a hand to point at me, "will be the death of me." She closed her eyes, lifted her face to Mr Moon, and laughed. "Fucking ironic, eh? I was nearly the death of you." She inhaled through her nostrils, a great snatch of air, then said, "You mark my words, kid. If you don't come back with me now, your life won't be worth living."

Though only twelve years old, I saw her. *Saw* her. A pitiful wreck. Someone who worked hand in hand with fear to keep me in line. Fear became *my* best friend now.

"And you mark *my* words, Mam. You touch me one more time, make me do one more thing, and I'm telling the police."

Her breath hitched. She opened her eyes, looked at Mr Moon again — had he witnessed some of her misdeeds too? — and then switched her attention to me. She stared with eyes that had frightened me witless throughout my life, and her irises dulled — a light went out.

"Your neck's swelling." She turned from me and trudged back across the park in the direction of home.

I walked to Gary's. No idea of the time, I banged on his front door with the side of my fist, rested my palm on the wall beside the door, and bent over. Pressure built in my throat from my position, and I straightened upright once more, swallowed the glass.

The door opened. Gary's dad, Pete, stood there, a smile across his face. His brown hair stood on end as if he'd been having a rest on the sofa. Stubble covered his chin, and specks of mechanic's grease dotted his cheeks. The smell of food — sausage and mash? — wafted from the house.

"Oh, it's you, Carmel. Come in. What the fu—?"

I stumbled on the doorstep, caught by his strong arms.

"What the fuck's up with your neck? What's happened?" asked Pete, steering me into their living room. I inhaled the scent of grease from his grey T-shirt. "Someone shut the front door, will you? Gary? Carmel's here. She's hurt."

I waved my arms, my hands flapping on the ends like rubber, and sat on the sofa. "No. It's…I'm okay."

Pete sat beside me, dangled his hands between his open legs. "'Ere, Sandra. Come and look at the state of this kid's neck. Fucking purple and swollen, it is." Spittle flew from Pete's mouth, and he flashed out his tongue to dismiss the globules that rested on his bottom lip. "Jesus. What you been up to, Carmel?"

I leant back, rested my head on the sofa. "Fell off a swing. The chain went round my neck." *Covering for Mam? No…*

"Reckon you need to see a doctor," said Pete as he turned in the direction of the kitchen. "Sandra? Where are you? Didn't you hear me?"

Sandra, Gary's mam, bustled into the room, her fleshy cheeks flushed. "What?" she said, a tea towel in her hands. "Oh, fuck me. What happened?" Her mouth dropped open, and her eyes devoured the state of me.

"Fell off a bloody swing, she said. Chain caught round her neck. Lucky she didn't top herself, eh?" Pete stood, placed one hand on his denim-clad hip; the other swiped his brow.

"Blimey," said Sandra. "Do you want us to take you home, Carmel? Get your mam to take you to the doctor?" She raked a hand through her short, curly blonde hair.

Pete's loud bark of laughter made me jump. "You taking the piss, love? That bitch wouldn't put a suffering dog down." He looked at me, adding, "Sorry. Uncalled for, that."

I smiled. Laughed. "No, it's okay. You're right."

"You sure you'll be okay?" asked Gary.

We walked across the field that housed the funfair in its centre.

"Yeah. It's fine, just a bit sore."

Gary frowned then smiled. "Knew she'd let you out."

I laughed quietly. "Yeah."

The ground throbbed with music. The beat travelled through my feet, up my legs. I kept my gaze forward—it hurt to turn my neck—determined to enjoy the evening's entertainment. Shrieks from riders flew into the air on wings of fun, and the low rumble of ride owners speaking into microphones sounded garbled, indecipherable. Despite the constant ache in my throat, excitement buzzed around me, enticed me to join in the revelry. As we drew closer, I spotted candyfloss stalls, Hook a Duck, the Rifle Range. Brightly coloured stalls lured crowds to gather round them.

The Waltzers' cars trundled around the platform, their inhabitants screaming, faces smiling. The Twister stood proudly in the centre of the field, spider-shaped, a riding carriage on the end of each leg. Those legs rose, the body spun, and the spider feet rotated and whizzed through the air, much to the delight of the people inside them.

Reduced to a child, a proper child, I broke away from Gary's side and ran towards the melee.

"Hey, wait up," Gary yelled.

I smiled.

# Chapter Twenty-One

❦

**M**emories. Those good ones are brilliant when regurgitated, spun back through the mind. I re-lived that evening on my walk home. It took my mind off what might happen when I arrived at Mam's decrepit shit hole. Yes, my neck was sore, very, and no, I couldn't scream on the rides, even when I wanted to, but the exhilaration that zipped through my body proved enough. I experienced freedom up there in the sky—that's what being on The Twister felt like. So much so, I went on that ride three times. My guts rolled, hair danced in the wind, face pulled in all directions, and the fun, sheer *fun* of being 'just a kid' was mine for a couple of hours.

The free ride sessions over, Gary treated me to some candyfloss, and I hooked a duck and won a crappy plastic ring, silver, with a huge fake diamond in the centre. Gary placed it on my finger and like a proposing sap, said, "We'll be friends forever, right?"

"Right," I said, hugging the knowledge to my heart that he *wanted* me as his lifelong friend. I placed it in a box in my mind, the one labelled SPECIAL. No lock on that box. Those recollections were free to swim through the murky waters, break through the surface into the sunlight.

I smiled again at the memory and ignored my thudding pulse as I clasped the handle of Mam's front door. It moved downwards, and the door unlatched with a soft click. I'd expected it to be locked. Surprise burst inside a small section of my mind like a flame, a stark contrast to the darkness that greeted me in the hallway. Instantly on guard, as Mam was usually still awake at ten o'clock at night, I quietly closed the front door and walked through to the unlit living room. Furniture shapes loomed, appearing bigger than they were with the light on—menacing, even.

I shivered and glanced through the doorway to the kitchen. A slither of light beneath the door of the posh back room lit a strip of lino, its continuity broken by grey shadows. I moved towards it, the beats of my heart growing faster and louder the closer I got. Muffled voices sounded—Mam's and Bob's.

*What are they doing in there without me?*

My toe stubbed one of the chair legs, and I cursed quietly, remained still with bated breath, hoping Mam and Bob hadn't heard the resultant scrape of wood against lino. Seconds passed. No door flung open, no questions regarding me being there blurted out of disgusting mouths. I took a couple more steps and, careful not to touch the door or the doorframe, I knelt. My knees sore from the grit at the park, I shuffled my position to one of more comfort. Leaning forward, I peered through the keyhole below the handle of the door.

My gaze landed on the bed directly opposite. A small form lay inert, its face leather-clad.

Bile surged into my throat. Confusion, fright—jealousy?—rumbled through me, and I blindly stood and ran through the house, choking back a sob. I sat on the bottom step in the hallway, caught my breath, and attempted to sort through the new set of muddles in my mind.

Tears flashed hotly down my cheeks. I pulled my thighs against my torso, resting my face on my knees. Pressure on my neck ensured I lifted my head again. All merriment of the fun evening fled as I crept up to bed and hid beneath my blanket.

Emotions raged. What was right? What was wrong? Why did I feel ousted? Wasn't that what I wanted—to be free of Thursday nights and all they entailed? Where had that person on the bed come from? Why hadn't Mam locked the front door if she'd been working? Scary thoughts taunted me, showed images of Mam abducting a kid on the way back from the park, her rage so prevalent that the child couldn't fight her off. Did they make that person drink my medicine?

*Of course they did, Carmel.*

And what was that mask?

*That mask, it jangles round the recesses of your mind. You can remember where you've seen it before…*

Up on the star-steps looking down upon the world.

*Yes.*

Who the hell had taken my place?

*Just some kid.*

I stayed in the same position for a long time. Tears abated, questions quieted. My mind loitered, just hanging there, thinking nothing.

Fuzzed voices from downstairs filtered through the fog. Noises from directly below told me Mam and Bob now stood in the hallway. My door, open a crack, allowed their voices admittance. They spoke in low tones.

"What time did your mate say he'd be here?" Mam.

"In a few minutes. He'll take her back home, put her in bed. Nobody'll be any the wiser," said Bob.

"Good."

"Been thinking about what you said, you know, about Carmel giving you grief. Ain't a problem. We knew this would happen sooner or later."

"Yeah. Growing tits now, she is. That's no fucking good to us."

"No."

The swish of tyres on the road outside and the arc of headlights flashing through the sheet at my window brought the 'mate'.

"He's here. Go and get the package," Mam said.

"Package?" Bob's laugh grew more distant— walking back to the posh room, then.

My face burned. They'd given a kid my medicine, brought the child here without it even knowing. What about the kid's parents? Did they know? Were there more parents out there like my mam?

*More kids live like you.*

The implications of this news weighed heavy on my small shoulders. What should I do?

*Rat on Mam and Bob.*

Where would I go then? There was no one to look after me…

Long after the shuffles in the hallway stopped, I waited in the darkness. Realisations thundered through my mind. Decision reached, I clutched Nelson to my chest and drifted into longed-for sleep.

"Carmel? Quick. Fucking wake up. Coppers are at the front door."

*Feign sleep. Ignore her. Let her deal with it by herself.*

My tummy muscles clenched.

Mam's spiteful fingers dug into my shoulder, shook me. "Wake up. Come on, you need to go down and do your thing. Get rid of them."

I sighed, smelt her sour breath, opened my eyes. Mam's face, inches from mine, appeared ghost-like. Her eyes glowed, reflecting the streetlight from outside, which peeked through the holes in the window sheet. Shrugging off her hand, I stared at her.

"Get out of the way, then," I said.

Mam moved back and stepped to the window. She pulled the sheet across a few inches, staring outside. "Two cars out there. Did *you* fucking call them out?"

"No." I slipped out of bed and wrapped my teddy bear blanket around my shoulders.

Another set of raps smacked the front door.

"What the fuck do they want, then? Unless… Aw, shit. Carmel, you tell them we went to the fair together tonight." She turned from the window and gawped at me. "And cover your damn neck. Looks black in this light."

I clasped the sides of my blanket together beneath my chin and padded downstairs. Two dark figures stood behind the patterned glass in the front door, their outlines fuzzy. I opened the front door a crack. Smiled sleepily.

"Hello, miss. Your mam in?" one officer said, his brown hair kinked, just visible beneath his peaked cap. Kindly blue eyes.

I nodded and gazed up and down the street. The two police cars had parked haphazardly at the end of the road. "She's asleep in bed."

"Can you wake her up? We need to have a word," said the other officer, a portly man, grey sideburns, brown eyes.

"Hang on," I said and closed the door.

"Tell them you can't wake me up!" Mam hissed.

I jumped. Mam stood beside the cupboard under the stairs, a shape in the darkness.

"Don't think they're here for you. Cars are up the other end," I whispered and moved away from the door, standing with my back to the wall beside it.

"Then why do they want a fucking word?"

I shrugged, realised she wouldn't see it in the gloom. "Dunno, but there are two at snotty's next door as well."

"Shit!"

Mam's fright pleased me, although a hint of fear kissed my limbs, and my knees buckled, my hands shook. "Just let them in, Mam. They'll get to you eventually, anyway."

"Fucking enjoying this, aren't you?" she said and stalked past me to open the front door. "Hello, Officers. What can I do to you tonight? Massage? Toe rub?"

One of the officers laughed. "Very funny, Annette. Just let us in, will you? Got some questions you might know the answers to."

I retreated into the corner, pressing myself against it.

Mam's working smile — she should have kept her mouth shut with those teeth — filled her face, and she patted her hair. "Good job you don't want nothin', really. I'm not presentable."

A choked laugh came from the other side of the door.

"Come in, then," Mam said on a sigh.

The three adults trooped past me in the gloom, my existence apparently forgotten. Again.

The living room light flicked on. Mam's breath huffed as she thwumped down on the sofa, her lighter clicked, and she said, "Questions?" She inhaled, exhaled.

The vein in my throat throbbed, freaked with adrenaline.

"The old chap at the end of the road. Mr Lawton. He a customer of yours?" I recognised the voice of the older policeman.

Mam laughed — a short, harsh burst of sound. "Mr Lawton? Not fucking likely."

"Know anything about him?" asked Old Cop.

"Nah. What with him being up the other end, I don't see the bloke. Why?" Mam sounded bored.

"Do you know of any other prostitutes that he might have visited?" said Blue Eyes.

"*Other prostitutes*?" Mam sniggered. "I'm a fucking masseuse, told you lot that before."

Old Cop laughed. "Fucking being the operative word, off the record, like."

"No off the record about it," Mam said. "I massage people for a living. Ain't no crime in that." Her inhalation sounded like a gasp of fright.

Body movements—the flick of a notebook, maybe?—sounded. Black leather shoes squeaked. "Let me rephrase that. Do you know of any *woman* Mr Lawton might have visited, been in contact with on a regular basis?"

"Let me answer that again for you. No, because I don't have anything to do with the pervy old fucker."

The air seemed to still. I held my breath, sure that Mam had said something of significance. My heart thudded, and I had the urge to run upstairs, but I stood my ground, fear like lead in my feet.

"You don't have anything to do with him, know nothing about him, yet say he's a pervert?" Old Cop said.

Mam's embarrassed titter danced on my nerves. "Well, when I've seen him walk past the house, he reminds me of a perv, that's all. You get to spot them in my line of work, know what I mean?"

"*Masseuses* get a lot of perverts, then?" asked Blue Eyes.

"Yeah," said Mam. "They think *something else* is on offer, don't they? Try it on all the time, they do."

"Right," said Old Cop. "If you think of anything or anyone who might bear relevance to Mr Lawton, let us know. No, stay there, we'll show ourselves out. Been here enough times to know the way."

"Ain't you just," said Mam, her voice low.

I pressed even farther against the wall, willed myself to become small. The two policemen walked past me, Blue Eyes leaving the house first. Authority bled from them, infected the air. Security too. If I just stepped forward, dropped my blanket, Old Cop might see my neck. Ask what happened. If I just…

"You'll get a chill stood there, miss," said Old Cop before he walked out of the house and closed the door.

I blinked, squeezed my blanket together more fiercely. Swallowed—still sore. The hallway seemed grey, so bleak.

"Carmel, get your arse in here, quick."

Mam's urgent call pierced my despondency. I pushed away from the wall and tiptoed, though I don't know why, into the living room. Mam stood at the window, peering through the nets.

"Look. Shit a fucking brick." Mam blew fag smoke out, the grey cloud shifting the nets.

I walked to the window. A policeman, his hand placed on top of Mr Lawton's head, pushed the old man into the back of a police car. The door slamming made me jolt away from the window. Tears pricked my eyes. Poor Mr Lawton. What had he done? I sat on the chair by the window, pulled my legs up, crouched into a ball. I flapped my blanket into the air, let it fall and encompass me. I tucked it around myself—I'd soon be too big to hide beneath it in this way—and stared at the pattern of holes.

Mam stalked from the window over to the coffee table. The telephone rested there, its wiggly wires knotted, and she snatched up the receiver, dialling six digits.

"It's me," she said. "Lawton's been busted. Yeah, they just left… Yeah… Reckon he needs the same as Hemmings? Me too… Yeah, squeal like a pig…" Mam laughed hoarsely, and shivers raced down my spine. She sat on the sofa. "It was *that* copper who came here. Yeah. Sure he'll sort it, but it won't hurt to give him another nudge. Right… Yeah. Bye for now."

Mam dropped the receiver into the cradle and leaned back. My breaths heated the air beneath the blanket; my cheeks grew warm, and I longed for fresh air to cool them.

"That conversation we had this afternoon, Carmel. Discussed it with Bob. We don't need you anymore. Do what you like on Thursdays, just stay out of this fucking house, right?"

I closed my eyes. Relief relaxed my shoulders. "Yes, Mam."

"And when you're sixteen you can fuck off out of it for good."

# Chapter Twenty-Two

***

"Fourteen years old, eh?" said Bob. "Who woulda thought it? Like, I've known you since you were a baby." He shifted his position on the sofa and turned to Mam. "Where's the fucking time gone, Annette?"

"Dunno," Mam said, "but I wish the next two years would hurry themselves along. Won't have her round my fucking ankles, then." Mam stared at me from beside Bob. I hid the revulsion that surged through me, sitting in the chair by the window as if nothing were amiss. "Eat your chips up then, kid. It's not like we have them often."

Chips from the chippy—birthday treat. Me and Gary often bought a cone of chips, warming our hands from their heat on winter nights, burning our windpipes because we'd eaten them too quickly, forgetting to blow. If our pockets stretched to it, we'd share a portion of battered cod, ripping it down the middle, or a saveloy. No, chips on their own definitely weren't something I classed as a birthday treat anymore.

Still, I ate them. Knew better than to waste food. Never knew when more would be forthcoming. I swallowed a gag—Bob stuffed half a fishcake in his mouth, eating noisily.

"Carmel?" he said, his mouth still full. "Been thinking. D'you wanna start working with me ag—"

"No, she doesn't," snapped Mam. She looked at me, narrowed her eyes. "I'm telling you, this kid'd call the fucking coppers on us. Leave her alone." She rammed a few chips in her mouth, black teeth chomping them.

Bob swallowed, ran a nicotine-stained finger beneath his nose. Sniffed. "Was just asking, like. I mean, she's getting older. Might have wanted to make a bit of money."

I continued to eat. Watched them.

"She gets enough money off me. Doesn't need to make her own." Mam nudged Bob in the side, scrunched her chip paper into a jagged ball, and threw it across the room. It bounced off the wall and landed on top of junk that had begun to accumulate beside the doorway leading to the kitchen. "Besides, she could go and get her own job now if she felt the need. Papergirl, shop assistant or something."

Bob belched, sniffed again, filled his mouth with the other half of his fishcake. "Yeah. I can see her doing a bloody paper round. 'Ere, Carmel," Bob turned from Mam to look at me, "reckon if you got a paper round you could dump the whole lot down by the warehouses. Save you postin' them. And it'd give the workers down there a free read." He grinned, showing food stuck between his teeth.

Mam laughed, reached forward, and picked up her cigarettes and lighter from the coffee table. "Yeah. Get paid for doing fuck all. Sounds good to me."

Bob whipped his head back round to glare at Mam. "So, you complainin' about your job now, eh?"

"Nope, was just sayin' —"

"Well, don't. Plenty more women out there gaggin' for your job. *Younger* women, know what I mean?"

Mam visibly bristled. Red spots snuck onto her cheeks, much like the heavier wrinkles beside her eyes had done of late. Her nostrils flared, and she drew her lips back in a sneer. "But these younger women, they don't know what I know, do they?"

Tension filled the air. Bob dispelled it with a hearty bellow, laughing until tears spilled down his cheeks. "But they also wouldn't use their daughter, sell her from a youngster, would they? And the coppers don't know what I know. Jeez, Annette. You're thick as pig's shit sometimes."

Mam's mouth gaped, and she glanced at me—with a look of worry on her face? No, couldn't have been.

"If I remember right, you made me think I had no fucking choice over what went on with Carmel."

Bob snorted. "Oh, give over, you silly cow. It was you who suggested it. Remember?"

Mam's eyes widened.

As did mine.

I stood, walked over to the sofa, and held my hand out for Bob's chip packet.

"Got her trained, eh, Annette?"

Mam didn't answer, just sucked on her cigarette and stared at the living room door. Her hands shook.

On my way to the kitchen, I picked up Mam's paper ball, threw all our rubbish on top of the overflowing bin. Shook my head at the state of the place.

"Couple of tins of peaches out there for afters, kid. Dish them up, will you?" called Mam.

I opened the tins, poured the syrup into a glass, and drank it. One of the good things in my life, that. Drinking fruit syrup. Tears stung. How could I once again have expected a birthday cake? Would I ever learn? Ever stop hoping for normality, for Mam to change?

Peaches in dishes, I swilled three spoons under the running tap, flicked them dry. Taking a deep breath, I picked my way through floor debris and handed Mam and Bob their bowls.

No thanks. And I didn't expect any.

On my way back to the kitchen, Mam said, "Your present. It's in the bin outside."

Butterflies fluttered in my tummy, swiftly ousted by a ball of depression that sat heavily, paining my guts. What the hell I'd find in that bin was anyone's guess. Tempted not to bother going out there to check, I said, "Thanks," and stood eating my peaches while leaning against the kitchen worktop.

"Not eating your pud with us, then?" asked Bob.

The slurp of him sucking peach syrup off his spoon made me shiver.

"Thought you two might want time on your own," I said and balanced my empty bowl on a pile of unwashed crockery. Sighed, squirted washing-up liquid into the sink, filled it with hot water.

"Nah, you come in here, kid. We don't mind," said Bob.

I closed my eyes in irritation, grinding my teeth. "It's okay. I've finished. Doing the washing up now."

"You sure you want that kid out of here in two years, Annette? You got a built-in skivvy there." Bob laughed.

"Shame she don't clean the whole bloody house, then," said Mam. "Earn her fucking keep."

I tuned them out, thought about how crap my birthday had been. Gary hadn't known, was only interested in rehashing Belinda's death, what with it being her anniversary. Also, I thought about the fact that Gary was off out with his dad; they'd gone to watch the footy. With nothing better to do, and to stop myself going out to that dirty metal bin to see what rubbish Mam had given me for a present, I made up my mind to clean Mam's shit-tip of a house from top to bottom.

I filled four black refuse sacks with crap picked up from the floor, tables, and worktops that evening, the fifth plump from the rubbish in the kitchen bin. Memories of tidying up with Belinda's mam came to mind, and I pretended it was her house I cleaned, that she stood beside me as I toiled. I conversed with her in my head while Mam filled her veins and Bob smoked weed. What he was doing there that night, I had no idea, because it wasn't Thursday. No customers knocked on the front door, either. Maybe the sole purpose of his visit had been to ask me to go back to work. Whatever, I tidied around them.

A lack of cleaning detergents hampered the urge within me to morph Mam's house into something resembling a habitable abode. I ran to the shop and used some of my saved stash to purchase bleach, polish (Mr Sheen), yellow cloths, and scouring pads. Armed with my weapons of germ destruction, I returned home to find Mam and Bob in the same place I had left them—slumped on the sofa. Beer cans littered the coffee table, the coffee table I'd cleared of debris. Sighing inwardly, I disposed of them, and knelt on the floor in front of the table, sprayed a liberal amount of Mr Sheen.

"Watch it," slurred Mam. "If I wanted to use that for perfume, I would."

I ignored her and wiped the table. The yellow cloth snagged on months—years—of grime, fluff attaching itself to the dirt. With a scouring pad soaked in soapy water, I concentrated on the task of lifting the filth from that table. Many minutes passed, minutes where I remembered where some of the stains originated. The times when Mam had knocked over her drink and left it to dry in a sticky puddle. Or when she'd flicked her cigarette ash and missed the ashtray. All of it came off, and underneath revealed a surprisingly nice wooden surface.

Finished, I stood and surveyed my work.

Mam lifted her feet and dumped her legs on the table. "Ah, got something to rest my pins on now," she said. Particles of dirt from her feet dropped onto the table.

Bob chuckled.

I swallowed the lump in my throat and turned away from them, walking to the cupboard under the stairs to try to find the vacuum cleaner. I was sure we owned one.

We did, one with poor suction. Mam watched me struggle to vacuum for quite some time before she said, "The bag'll need changing, though where the fuck the empty ones are is something you'll have to work out." Her eyelids drooped, and a smack-head's smile touched her lips.

I managed to dismantle a vacuum. How to improvise and cut the bottom off of the full bag, empty it, and tape the damn thing back up again for re-use. It sucked then, all right.

Lugging two black bags at a time, I placed them all beside the dustbin outside. The bin lid balanced precariously on top of other rubbish, and I reached out to remove it, to see what lay beneath. A large envelope, previously white and bearing the red postal frank of an electricity provider, sat beneath an empty packet of Walkers crisps and two moist, squashed teabags. The envelope had been folded over and resealed with Sellotape, and my name scrawled in black biro replaced our scribbled-out address.

I took it out of the bin, peeled back the Sellotape. My fingers slipped against a greasy substance—tuna fish oil?—but I managed to re-open the envelope. I peered into it.

Inside nestled a thick wad of money.

With the shaking fingers of one hand, I held the envelope much like I had those bags of sweeties from Mr Hemmings' shop. The other hand I swiped down my trousers to remove some of the grease. Heart beating wildly, for it wasn't every day I found an envelope stuffed with cash, I wondered what to do. Was this money really for me? If so, what had possessed Mam to give me so much?

I walked back into the house via the front door and stood before Mam and Bob. Mam, almost nodding out, stared at me, her glazed eyes reflecting the light from the bulb overhead. Her dirty hair rested against her forehead, and the pores in her cheeks had widened over the past few months.

Bob leaned forward and prepared his umpteenth joint.

"Um, Mam?"

"What?"

"My present…"

"In the bin, like I said," she slurred. "Unless some fucker's nicked it." She closed her eyes.

"The envelope—"

"Yeah, yeah, that's yours." Her lower jaw sagged.

*Gone. Out for the count.*

I transferred my attention to Bob. "It's filled with—"

"Ah," said Bob. He licked the gum strip on his Rizla, sticking it down to form a perfectly shaped joint. "She kept to her word, then. Fucking hell. Didn't think she would."

I frowned. "What do you mean?" I clutched the envelope tighter. The paper crackled, sounded foghorn loud in the quiet of the room.

"Lawton sent it."

"Mr Lawton?" Incomprehension wended up and down my spine. "He's been in the nick for ages. Is he out?"

Bob sniggered, dashing his thumb against the flint of his lighter, and lit his joint. "Oh, yeah. He's out. Out and praising the fucking Lord. Found God while inside. Wanted to repay you."

"Repay me for what?" Snippets of conversations, images from covert glances when no one thought I was looking, filtered into my consciousness. Dredged up along with memories from pre-Phenergan, my mind filled with the sludge of my early childhood. The reason for the thick wad of money highly apparent, a small smile twitched my lips.

Bob opened his mouth to explain.

"It's okay," I said. "I understand."

I turned from him, took an appreciative glance at how the downstairs of the house looked, sniffed, the smell of bleach and Mr Sheen a pleasing aroma. The walk up to my room took half the usual time. Closing my bedroom door, I dived onto my bed and brought the envelope up to my face, breathing in the scent of money. Heart ticking in anticipation—for those notes could be all fivers and wouldn't amount to that much—I reached in and pulled out the wad, fanning it on my bed.

Twenty fifty-pound notes.

*Shame every one of them dirty fuckers doesn't find God, eh, Carmel?*

I laughed and looked at Nelson.

"Fancy a new dress?" I asked.

I spent one hundred pounds—a vast amount—and hid the remainder in the hole in the back of the kitchen cupboard, you know, where the mouse went, checking every day that it was still there. Every day for the next two years.

The pastime of cleaning house afforded me a new outlet for my frustrations. I visited the world of me and Margo, cleaners supreme. With her in my mind showing me the way, I was able to keep thoughts of hurting Mam out of my head for a while.

Only a while, mind.

# *Chapter Twenty-Three*

❦

A man—he watched me weekday mornings on my way to school. Stood there every day, hands in brown jacket pockets, legs at ease. His boots, cumbersome-looking, poked from his denims like a strangulation victim's tongue. No idea what colour his hair was, his hood obscured my view. I stared at him, and he leered back at me as if he had the right to gawp. I couldn't stop him, really, free country and all that. If I told Mam or Bob about him, they'd have told me to change my route, or not walk alone. Or worse, laugh.

Rain spattered on my umbrella—one I'd bought with Mr Lawton's money—and I held it so low some of my hair got caught in the spokes. I liked hiding beneath that umbrella. Keeping my head down, gaze fixed on a pavement slick with nature's tears. I remember thinking that if I didn't look at the man again, maybe he'd lose interest, abstain from being there the next day. And anyway, who was to say he was even waiting for me? I must have been so steeped in my own self-importance that I assumed it was me he watched. I'd heard that line on *Dr Phil* while waiting for *Sally* to start. He had a programme on dysfunctional families and problem kids. I didn't watch it all. Hurt too much.

Jeez. I hated myself between the ages of fourteen and sixteen, you know? Like how I sometimes thought everything was about me when it wasn't. Or when something happened to someone else, I wished it *was* me—the meetings at the pizza parlour, Saturdays in town buying new clothes with a gaggle of girlfriends.

I continued walking to school. Shrugged, blinked. It wasn't me he waited for. I'd have to learn to deal with it like everything else.

I didn't socialise at secondary school, just hung around with Gary at break and lunchtimes. Once, a girl gave me a filthy look. You know the type of stare—narrowed eyes, lips pursed as if she were about to whistle for her supper. A whole crowd of people surrounded me, yet I'd assumed she'd looked at me. Our gazes didn't meet, and if I'm totally honest, she looked right over my head, but I'd like to think she looked at me, *saw me*. I told myself to talk to my counsellor—I'd opted to chat to one who visited the school each week. I told myself to tell her about the man and the girl.

Did those counsellor sessions do me any good? I still don't know.

*Remember when your mam got the letter about you seeing The Lighthouse? Remember what she said, Carmel.*

Oh, I remember, all right.

"So you *opted*—that's the word used in this letter here—to speak to one of those nut doctors, then?" Mam said and blew a cloud of smoke in my direction. "What d'you need to speak to one of them for?" She glared at me; her eyes glittered. Waving her hand in the air, she continued without waiting for my reply. "Best you don't be telling them anything, kid. Last thing I need is the Social Services knocking on the fucking door. Especially when I'm so close to you buggering off out of here." She cackled. "Well? You gonna answer me or what?"

I swallowed, said, "I just go for someone to talk to, that's all."

"Aw, hasn't Carmel got any friends, then? Is Carmel a Billy-No-Mates? What's happened to that Gary kid you were hanging around with?" Mam chugged on her cigarette, a steam train.

"Nothing's happened to him. I just wanted to speak to someone different." I sat in the chair by the living room window, staring at Mam through the haze of smoke that loitered around her.

"I'd talk to you, but guess what? I don't want to." She threw her head back, rested it on the sofa, giggled.

Boldness straightened my spine, lent me a little courage. "Mam, you're just as childish as those bitches at school." I waited for her to sock me one. Surprise raised my eyebrows when she continued to laugh. Laugh and smoke.

"Ah, fuck off out of it, Carmel. Can't be arsed with you."

I went to my room.

*If you opened a dictionary at the words selfish, conscienceless, spiteful, hypocritical, nasty, cruel — your mam's name would be beside every one.*

Memories, they hurt my eyes, made them sting.

I trudged towards the school, lifted my head. The man stood beneath the tree, his image distorted by the rain that fell like mist. As I got closer, I squinted. He appeared faceless. A black void inside a fur-rimmed hood. I sniffed—the end of my nose would be numb by the time I got into class.

*You sniffed. Are you sure you're not crying?*

"My nose is cold, that's all."

Tears, hot on my face. I wouldn't have been surprised if they froze. The man looked away so that the back of his hood faced me.

Like I said, my nose was *numb*. I shuffled into school. The girls' toilets smelled like a dirty hamster's cage, the mirror above the sink spotted with what looked like rust. Made me appear to have ginger freckles. If they were real, those freckles, I'd have had character. Instead, I'd been blessed with pale skin—so transparent, the miniature vein rivers beneath stood out, easily seen. A grey circle surrounded each of my sunken eyes. I tilted my head to the left, the right—a bird, an ugly bird. I *was* a bird, otherwise, why that urge to fly, to be free? I stared at myself, tried to see what *they* saw. Would I stare at me if I wasn't me? Would I think me weird?

The restroom door jerked open with a creak. Previous toilet visits invaded my mind: head pushed from behind, nose cracked on porcelain. The pain had spread like volcanic eruptions, with blood as the lava, splashing, dirtying the sink. Laughter, curse words—my ears rang with those sounds in anticipation of a recurrence. Eyes squeezed tight. If I didn't look, it wouldn't happen. If I didn't breathe, they'd leave me alone.

*Bullies. Bitches.*

I scooted into a toilet stall, let the door close behind me, and snapped the lock loudly. The sound echoed off the tiles and the mottled windows (people can still see through those, you know). Breath left my lungs, ragged. Hitch-gasp-hitch.

"What are you crying for?" asked Belinda, her voice kind and smooth. Alien.

"Not crying."

"Sounds like you are. Sorry, my mistake."

I sniffed quietly, fearing if I didn't, I'd be made out to be a liar. And I couldn't be one of those. Mam said lying to her was bad. That lying deserved punishment—*How come your mam hasn't been punished?*—yet I could lie about other things, to other people. I didn't understand. Just didn't get the hypocrisy.

The ominous creak sounded again—who was in the restroom with me? The man? The girl?—and I stumbled out of the toilets, shuffling down the corridor, arm brushing the wall, foot against wainscoting.

*Lean on the wall, keep out of the way. Don't bump into anybody.*

I turned the corner. Searing light stung my eyes. A huge skylight in the ceiling appeared like a cathedral painting. You know, the ones with cherubic angels, their legs podgy, hair in ringlets. I'd half-listened in the lesson where we'd learned about the paintings, one ear tuned to Mr Hicks' voice, the other on the titters from behind.

"Carmel's got nits. See them crawling?"

"I see 'em. My mam said she's filthy dirty, lives in a house that'd need fumigating if they ever moved out."

*"The Sistine Chapel has paintings depicting…"*

"Wonder if she knows she smells?"

"What, like, can she smell herself? Doubt it. She's probably so used to her own stench…"

*"Settle down, class. Yes, yes, I'm well aware the paintings are of naked people. Stop being silly now…"*

"Don't reckon she's ever heard of deodorant."

The classroom, warmed by our body heat, grew uncomfortable. I couldn't sit by the heater—home invaded school, then: the smell of Mam and her cigarettes. I needed to separate the two places. One mustn't overlap the other. I longed to be unseen at school, but those people, they stared at me, taunted me. Yet on the other hand, I *wanted* to be seen. Really seen.

It worked at home. I'd only be visible when Mam wanted a cup of tea, or for me to run to the shop. Or when a bad dose of medicine ensured anger flowed alongside the heroin in her veins, urging her hands into fists. She'd taken to packing quite a punch, her strikes like a bowling ball, me the pin. I'd topple over, hear Mam shouting, "Lucky strike!", her laughter a gargle, her needing a dentist springing to mind. I'd be prone on my back, skull-sore. Prostrate on the gritty carpet, eyes sore, eyes salty sore.

"What would you like to talk about today, Carmel?" The counsellor entwined her fingers and rested her palms on her stomach. A round stomach, probably comforting to rest my head on.

I shrugged the images out of my mind, blinked them away, and lifted my shoulders. I didn't know what I wanted to talk about, wasn't sure… Oh yes, I wanted to ask about the man by the tree, about the girl who'd looked at me but over my head. And Mam. I wanted to talk about

Mam, but I didn't know what to say or how to say it.

I toed the carpet. Blue carpet, my sea of hope. The first time I visited the counsellor, I'd stared at that carpet and told it some of my secrets. Not the dark ones. No, I didn't talk about those. Counsellor was The Lighthouse, steering me clear of the rocks, yet she urged me towards them, light beckoning. Crash time imminent, she bellowed her foghorn, catastrophe averted. The blue carpet knew many things about me, but not enough. No. Not enough.

Counsellor cleared her throat.

I looked up, inclined my head, and stared at The Lighthouse, at her enlarged eyes behind her spectacles, nose like a jackdaw. Her smile—thin, so thin it seemed as though she didn't own any lips. A skeleton at Halloween—except The Lighthouse had hair, scraped back in a bun. Her follicles must have been screaming.

"What about telling me what you've done since last week, hmm?"

My gaze returned to the blue sea—choppy waters, storm brewing, white crests upon the waves. Salt tasted sharp on my lips; that morning's tears lingered.

"Kept out of Mam's way all week. It's been okay."

"Anything happen that you'd like to get off your chest? The blue sea is listening, Carmel. It doesn't tell a soul, you know that."

"I know. Except the sea's choppy now. The water's jumping up and spitting on me, stinging my eyes."

"I understand. What about moving your thoughts away from your mother. Anything else you'd like to discuss?"

I nodded. Like my head rested on a spring. "The people. I'd like to talk about them."

"Go ahead."

"This man. Well, I think it's a man. He stands behind the big tree just outside school, you know the one?" I looked up.

The Lighthouse nodded.

"Well, he's there every morning. Like he's waiting for me. Stares at me when I'm walking towards the school gates."

"What does he look like?"

"Dunno. His hood stops me from seeing his face."

"Do you feel scared of this man, Carmel?"

The sea calmed a little.

"No. Not like the way Mam scares me. I only get butterflies in my tummy with the man. I can see him from right up the other end of the street. I get to the tree, walk past it, turn around, and he's gone. Like he ran away or something."

"Where do you think he goes, Carmel?"

"Dunno." I shrugged, stared at the blue sea.

The Lighthouse's beam shone on the top of my head. Her stare burned.

*Nothing is ever silent. It's quiet, but not silent. It never will be, so long as the sound of blood frantically pumps through my veins.*

I thought that then, in the quiet that descended upon us. Poked the toe of my shoe into the blue sea, splashed a little. The Lighthouse sighed. A gust of wind—an anticipatory or impatient breeze? I didn't want to look up, to see her features and find out.

"I'm gonna go."

"Your session isn't over yet, Carmel."

My chair toppled backwards, its steel leg scraping mine.

"Burning calf, sea salt eyes. What a little baby you are!" Belinda said.

"Gotta get home, because Mam…"

"Carmel…sit." Lighthouse brooked no argument.

Eyelids at half-mast, I turned and righted my raft, perched upon it, knees beneath my chin, hands clasped over shins. A ball.

*They get kicked around.*

"Mam ignores me most of the time."

"Go on…"

"And the people, the man behind the tree, and that girl, they stare at me then look away. But at least they stared in the first place. Tried to see me. I don't want to be looked at, just seen."

The droplets from my eyes morphed the blue sea from choppy waves to circular ripples. The circumference of each ring reached the walls, rebounding off them, creating small eddies.

"There are times when your mother notices you, Carmel. It's just unfortunate she notices you in the wrong way, hmm?"

"Yes."

"I can help you with that. You know, find somewhere to go when you're sixteen. We've discussed this before."

"I know. But if I leave her, she'll have no one."

"Sometimes, people don't deserve to have anyone."

"But—"

"I'll help you with it when you're ready, Carmel."

I nodded. Felt safe.

"Do you want to talk about why you need to leave home yet a part of you wants to stay? I can help you understand those feelings, if you'd like."

I shook my head. "What about the man. What do I do about him?"

"I'll watch for him out of my office window in the morning. If he's there, I'll go out and ask what he's doing. Sound good?"

"Yes. Thank you."

It rained all that week. Even when it didn't fall from the sky, it was still there. Dreary, wet, residing in my eyes. I wondered, when I grew older, just a little older, and I turned sixteen, would it all stop? I mean, if I moved out of Mam's, doing that wouldn't mean everything would get better, would it? I'd still have memories. Things swirling around in my head.

I thought of The Lighthouse, so right, so clever. She had an answer for everything. She told me once that even she got scared sometimes, but I didn't believe her. She appeared too comfortable with herself to be scared of anything. Besides, she didn't have a mam who liked bowling. At least, I didn't think she did.

*Must be nice not to be frightened, tormented, used, worried…*

I forgot my umbrella the next day. The rain dashed into my eyes, made me think I couldn't see the man.

*He must be there. He's there every day.*

I quickened my pace, drawing closer to the tree. He wasn't there looking at me, and the realisation hurt my chest—painful not to be seen. Even though I didn't want him there.

I didn't!

I sighed. What did it matter? Who wanted to be seen, anyway? I hurried past the tree, turned back to catch him out. Maybe he'd hidden while I'd made my way towards the oak? No. He hadn't. The Lighthouse must have ushered him on. I rushed into school, out of the wet, and bumped into the counsellor in the corridor.

"He wasn't there today," I said.

"I know, Carmel. I watched for him."

"Maybe he wasn't looking at me after all."

"That's entirely possible. Maybe he'd been waiting for a lift to work each morning."

The corridor filled up. People jostled The Lighthouse. She shouted, "Have some manners. And walk, don't run."

Foghorn.

School shoes squeaked on the tiled floor. Giant mice.

The Lighthouse wore a lamb's-wool jumper. Expensive, chic. I saw one in the window of Debenhams once, the mannequin slender and headless.

*Would you like to be a mannequin? Sightless?*

"I have a free slot available right after school of you want it, Carmel."

"No, thank you. I'll be all right now."

Mam's house smelt of sick gone sour. Of greasy chips, dried baked beans, and stale air. I closed the front door and swallowed the rising bile. Inhaling deeply, I then emptied my lungs through shaky lips, counted to five, and walked into the living room. I would do it today. Kill her. I would.

Mam was on the couch, dead to the world.

*Dead to the world. Don't you just wish that were so, Carmel?*

Heroin had been her friend again that day.

I left the room and trudged upstairs. It was like climbing a mountain, with nothing at the apex except dirt, dirt, and more dirt, despite my cleaning frenzies. I settled on my bed, flicking through catalogues, and imagined myself on the pages, curled up on one of those beds, quilt so puffy it hugged me whole. Through misted eyes, I gazed at my own blanket—thin, unhuggable.

I sighed and dragged myself off the bed and into the bathroom. Seated on the toilet, the sting down below burned, and I gritted my teeth. That sting: a tribute to the thrush that always seemed to be there during those two years.

*Nerves, stress, nerves, stress…*

I returned to the living room, walked through on soft toes to the kitchen. Ferreted around in the drawers for a while.

*Quiet, must be quiet.*

Back in the living room, I stood beside the ratty sofa and stared at Mam's inert form. Time passed. I blinked again.

Mam on the sofa, dead to the world, dead to the world. But she'd wake up. My courage had failed me once again.

# Chapter Twenty-Four

❦

The counsellor found a small bedsit that adequately suited my needs. The room, situated in an old Victorian house, measured the same size as Mam's living room. What, eighteen feet by twelve? Yes, that was about right. I bought a second-hand, metal-sprung bed settee and pulled it out nightly. Mornings saw me proudly folding it back up into a sofa, quilt and pillows hidden from view.

I finally got my eiderdown, one with a removable cover decorated with red roses—the bedclothes of my childhood dreams. It took some time to find one that closely resembled it, and although it didn't have ribbons on each corner, I loved it all the same. The bed settee, a brown velvet affair, held four scatter cushions by day, one of each in red, blue, yellow, and green. Sounded ghastly, but when you'd been brought up in a life devoid of colour, where everything was grey…

A kitchenette graced the left-hand side of the room. Four floor cupboards with drawers, a fake marble worktop resting on them, housed my pots and pans, drinking glasses, plates. I owned two forks, two knives, and two dessert spoons, all of them in a drawer with three tea towels. Gary, my only visitor, stayed for dinner some nights. Only beans on toast, egg and chips, that kind of thing, but I felt grown up, you know? And free. So fucking free. Cooking with that mini oven—I'd had some mishaps using that. Unused to a cooker that heated up to the proper temperature saw me burning pies, fish fingers and the like, but I got used to it in the end.

A small side table with a lamp and a coaster served as the place I rested my teacup and my current reading book. I'd purchased a flat-packed single wardrobe that Gary and I lugged home from the shop and put together one evening after dinner. I bought a few items of clothing from the local market, the kind I could mix and match, and hung them on silk-covered hangers. Often, I'd open the wardrobe and stroke the fabrics, smiling at the fact that I owned clothes that hadn't previously belonged to someone else, that had no holes and were clean.

The Victorian house, one of eight in a row, stood opposite a parade of small shops. A newsagent, convenience store, and laundrette serviced all my needs. I remember wondering what on earth a tool shop would be doing there, squashed between the paper shop and the laundrette, and who would frequent such a place that was so far out of town. But, if I looked out of my window when bored, or passed the shop on my way to work, I realised Tool City had a brisk trade.

Of course, I left school as soon as I could and secured a job as the predicted sales assistant in a women's clothes shop. Hardly something I'd planned—I'd had such high hopes for myself—but I could go to college later on. My exam results, certainly not shabby, would afford me entrance. My wages wouldn't stretch to the clothing in the store where I worked, even with my ten percent off. I examined the skirts, dresses, and tops when the new stocks came in, placed them on the rails with an idea of what the current trends were, and mimicked them with items bought at cheaper outlets. I paid six months' rent up front for the bedsit out of Mr Lawton's payment, and my wages would cover the small outlay after that.

My sixteenth birthday—that had been some day. I woke, emotions roiling inside me, so damn happy to be getting out of Mam's house. I placed Nelson inside a holdall I'd bought in readiness. The few clothes I wanted to keep joined her, as did a pair of boots, my toothbrush, hairbrush, and a book I'd recently bought. I left the bag on my bed and made my way downstairs.

Mam sat at the kitchen table. I stood in the doorway and surveyed the back of her greasy-haired head. Ribbons of smoke curled towards the ceiling—grey fog in a grey house—and her cup, no steam rose from it. No, she'd waited until I got up to make her second cup of morning tea.

What had she been thinking while looking out of the dirty, bird-shit-stained window in that back door? Would she have allowed herself to look back over the years, ponder on what could have been? Was she ever the kind of person to re-evaluate what had gone before, to sift through the disgusting life she'd led and decide to better herself, make amends for the way she'd treated me?

"First day of my new life starts today, kid."

Obviously not. The only thing she evaluated? Whether she had enough money to buy her medicine. Part of me faced that fact that day. You know, accepted that some people are as they are, and no amount of silent pleading on my part would make her change the way she was. Some people were born guiltless, had no conscience. Mam was one of them.

"Mine too," I said and walked into the kitchen. I filled that kettle for what I hoped would be the last time. Collected her used cup from the table, swilled it out, and placed a teabag and two sugars inside it. Tapped my fingers against the worktop as I waited for the kettle to come to a laborious boil, surprised the damn thing hadn't given up working years ago.

Brew before her, she continued to stare out of the back door while fumbling on the table for her cigarettes. I leaned against the worktop, my own tea in hand, and took in her profile. Her nose had grown hooked over the years. A ball of pointed gristle sat at the end of it—a witch, all right—and the skin appeared to have thinned. Red veins—yes, I saw them from where I stood—littered the bridge and spread across the cheek facing me. She'd always been slim, but I imagined she'd run to fat given a few more years, as her jowls had gained some baggage and hung from her lower jaw.

A scraggle of baggy skin congregated around her neck, and the bone in her throat bounced once, twice, as she swallowed her tea. She winced—the drink must have been too hot—and I smiled at that before blowing my own tea and taking a sip. I remember thinking then: *I'll buy myself a lovely set of mugs with no chips on the rims, no tea stains inside. Lovely, clean cups, all matching.*

"When are you leaving?" she asked.

"In about half an hour," I said and shifted my weight from one hip to the other. "Won't be coming back."

"Won't be letting you in if you did." She stubbed out her cigarette, reaching for another. Sighed. "You know, it wasn't *all* bad."

My eyes widened, and a snort of derision left me like I'd been punched in the gut. "Wasn't it? You tell me of a time when it was *good*, then. I'd like to hear that." I sipped my tea.

Mam studied the trees in the back garden. "Well, I…"

Silence lingered, a silence so palpable it swirled around me, rising in the air to join the cigarette fog that hovered between us. I stared at the tattered but clean lino, knowing filth would converge on it the moment I left that hell hole.

Mam cleared her throat. Sniffed. "Umm, well, there must be *some*thing…it can't have *all* been bad."

I pushed myself away from the worktop, emptied the remainder of my tea down the plughole, and placed the cup in the empty sink—a sink that would be filled by dinner time and would stay that way for fuck knew how long. Did I care? A part of me did, for hadn't I kept house the past two years, made it more presentable? Ensured more punters knocked on the door? Word at not having to walk through piles of crap to reach the back room must have spread, as business had picked up after my fourteenth birthday. Yes, I did care…a little. But—always a but, so they say—I'd be getting out of there and making a new life for myself. Painting my own picture.

"You fucked up, Mam, simple as that. And you're a fuck-up yourself. The only thing you've instilled in me is not to waste my money by shooting it into my veins. Oh, and treating any kids I have to a good life. Something you'd know nothing about."

A tear trickled down Mam's cheek. She was *crying*? "I had high hopes once, just like you have. But life isn't like that, kid. You'll see. The shit hits the fan, and you're fucked. Life is a bunch of crap,

Carmel. Not worth living. Robots, the lot of us, milling round trying to do the best we can with what we've got—"

I laughed. "The best we can? That's fucking rich, coming from you, Mam. You reckon you did the best you could, do you? Hey, even if you'd still been a prostitute—"

"A masseuse—"

"A prostitute, and hid it from me, stayed off heroin and loved me like you should have, it could've worked out." Anger bubbled in my guts, growing up my windpipe then spilling out of my mouth before I could stop it. "But you're too fucking selfish to give a shit about anyone but yourself, your needs, your wants. A dried up old hag who will see out the rest of her days—what you've got left of them—shagging old duffers that are too desperate to find someone more appealing. Shit, I reckon your *medicine*, especially the amount you've been taking lately, will kill you off before you know it. What does that prospect say to you? Can you tell me *that* before I go?"

Mam's wet cheek glistened from the morning sunlight streaming in through the window. Her breath hitched, and she hiccoughed in a lungful of cigarette smoke. Coughed, patted her chest, blinked. "Reckon it'd be a blessing," she said. "Got fuck all in my life worth staying around for."

That said, I left her there and walked upstairs to collect my bag and its meagre contents, not much from sixteen years of living. Pitiful. Another person may have been upset by her words, choked out a sob or two, and blundered blindly up the stairs and back down again, out of the house. Not me. I'd expected that answer, or something similar, and only anger at the injustices served to me flickered around my mind like angry wasps trapped between a net curtain and a windowpane.

I walked along our street, my holdall slung over my shoulder. No remorse at leaving the road I'd lived in all my life filled me, no what-ifs questioned me as I left the path and turned down a side alley that led to the park. Once there, I dumped my bag on the tarmac and sat on a swing to fly through the air and cast the clutter from my mind into the wind. Not all of it, though. The locked boxes of my mind remained, and would do so until I found the need, or courage, to open them. For now, the time to move on and start again had arrived.

*Reckon we're gonna have a good life now, Carmel. You and me against the world.*

"And Gary. Mustn't forget Gary," I said, my words thrown back at me by the breeze. I closed my eyes and let the early morning sun caress my face.

"And me," said Belinda. "I'll always be here."

My stomach contracted. Belinda hadn't visited for months. Her last appearance had been short—just a glimpse of her standing behind me as I'd looked in the bathroom mirror—and the time before that she'd laughed when Gary had told me he fancied me rotten, but she hadn't shown herself.

I opened my eyes and glanced to my right. Belinda's eye-socket face turned in my direction, yellow pus oozing.

"Yeah, and you," I said, my freedom tainted by her presence.

"Told you before, I'm with you all the way. Through the bad times—and let there be many of those." She laughed and threw her head back. It separated from her neck and hit the ground with a dull thud. It rolled, the moist flesh picking up grit and dirt, and stopped beside one of the poles that held the swing set upright. Her hair spilled out, fan-like, against the black tarmac, and her face from life morphed over the socket, eyes wide with shock, lips opening and closing. Grit grains embedded in her skin, over her nose and cheeks. They resembled black freckles. "Now that would have hurt at one time," she said.

I slowed the swing but remained seated. Belinda's headless body sat up, her hands reaching out to pat the ground in search of her head. I watched in fascination, willing her fingers not to come into contact with her hair that danced in the breeze just inches away from their tips. A gust blew a tress into the air, and it landed in the middle of one of her palms.

"That's it, my pretty," she said and dragged her head towards her body. She picked it up and plopped it onto her neck. The skin merged, ensuring her head wouldn't fall off any time soon, and a shudder rippled her limbs. "That's better. Now, as I was saying—"

"I don't care what you were saying," I said and got off the swing. Holdall in hand, I left the fenced-off play area, walking across the dewy grass, my shoes gaining a slick layer of moisture.

*Does that freak assume we want her tagging along?*

"No idea, Nelson, but I'm sure she'll persist in following us."

"I will," said Belinda, now striding alongside me.

*Three's a crowd.*

"It is, Nelson," I said, turning left out of the park and taking the path that led to my new home.

"Best your doll fucks off, then," said Belinda.

I sighed, lowered my head, and surged on. On towards a new life, one that would unfortunately contain two voices I could well do without.

# Chapter Twenty-Five

It was amazing that even after living a life of hell, a person could yearn for what they'd once known, longing for the acceptance of a parent who couldn't have cared less. The first year of living alone, I didn't have those wants, but the year and a half after that first heady rush of being self-sufficient plagued me with the need for answers. To visit Mam once more, to see if my absence had changed her—something I doubted. Nevertheless, I clung on to the slim hope that she may have seen the error of her ways.

Would that make everything better, though?

Was I bitter? Yes, I still harboured the desire to make her pay for her crimes against me, yet another part of me shouted that I should protect her from the sins she'd committed, that I was the stronger person and could deal with the atrocities better than a broken woman addicted to heroin. I despised myself at times. Small snippets of information I'd gleaned as a small child escaped from my locked mind boxes, rampaging through my head, and my emotions took a seat on a roller coaster that travelled through my musings, wreaking havoc.

Nelson and Belinda fought between themselves, their attempts mirroring the two sides of my mind. Nelson wanted retribution. She whispered that we could get rid of Mam, and only when that was done could we live a peaceful existence. Belinda, on the other hand, chose the opposite argument. Mam should be forgiven, for wasn't she a product of a society that had moulded her into what she had become? That as a young girl with fresh dreams, unsullied by reality, she'd set out one day on a walk to find herself flat on her back in a field, an older man above her, grunting his enjoyment. I was the result of that union and, hated as I was from my conception, my future had further been mapped out by Mam's parents disowning her.

*How does Belinda know all this?*

"Because I'm on the *other side*, you stupid doll. I know everything, I told Carmel that before. Her mam should be pitied, I tell you."

*Pitied? She should be hung for what she's done to Carmel. Annette endured desecration, knew what it felt like, yet she allowed her own child to go through the same thing time and time again. Sick in the head, Annette is. I'll never understand that woman, you hear me?*

"Exactly," I yelled. "What about me? I've had an unfortunate life. Don't I deserve any bloody pity?"

Belinda's lips turned down, and she cocked her socket head to the side. Had her eyes been present, she would have regarded me with her piercing gaze, I reckoned. "Um, prior to my death, yes. After that? No."

*But can't you understand why you had that accident? If you weren't such a spoilt little bitch, if you'd been a true friend to Carmel, none of that would have happened.*

I sighed, sick of hearing their voices, and clutched at the hair on the sides of my head. "Shut up. Just shut up, all right?"

I leaned on the windowsill in my bedsit, staring at the opposite row of shops. Nelson and Belinda's argument twittered on in the background, their voices swallowed by the low hum that started inside my head and grew in volume the longer they bickered.

"Enough," I shouted and whipped round to face them. Nelson sat on top of my wardrobe. Belinda stood beside it, looking up at the doll. "I'm going out, and if either of you follow me, I swear to

God—"

Socket Head turned to face me and laughed. "You swear to God *what*? That you'll kill me?" She bent double with laughter and, standing upright once more, wiped tears from her life-face, the socket gone. "Seeing as you've already done that, maybe you'll kill the doll here." She jerked her thumb upwards. "Fucking thing's ugly as sin, anyway. And at eighteen years of age, I rather thought you'd have outgrown the tatty bitch."

*Who the hell are you calling tatty? You, with your manky-arsed socket face, and when that isn't present, your features aren't exactly pleasant to look at. Seen better looking dogs than you. Dogs in the process of having their arseholes stung by nettles, I might add.*

I clenched my jaw. "Oh, please. *Please* shut up. I'm going out. Do *not* follow me."

I walked with no destination in mind. Let my feet lead the way, take me wherever they chose. Nelson's and Belinda's words ferreted through my mind, a beagle at a foxhole, relentless in their quest of torment. Images, memories, and long ago words jostled for precedence, fighting my rational side.

"Let it go," I said. "Just let it all go."

Their stubborn refusal to leave me be remained, cloistered in my brain, digging deep beneath the grey matter. Fugginess spread throughout my body. Lethargy made each step awkward, risking the hazard of me falling over the graves—the graves?—I wended between.

I blinked.

I stood on a flat-topped hill in the middle of nowhere, though nowhere, once my fuddled mind refocused, became the site of an old church to the west of town. Its ancient grey brick façade brought damsels in flouncy skirts to mind, knights astride black steeds.

Black Beauty.

Hundreds of women, their open parasols resting on one shoulder, walked across the graves of folk long dead. Men appeared, holding out crooked arms for the women to take, their stockinged calves poking out of knee-length trousers. So many of them, so many…

"Just think, a hundred years from now, you'll be like them," said Belinda. "No one can remember these people, and no one gives a shit about them. So, before you carry on feeling sorry for yourself, think about that for a moment. A few decades from now, not one person will remember you. No one will care what life you led, what you're about to lead. It'll all be gone."

I tried to ignore her.

"*Maybe* you'll wander round aimlessly like they are, like *I* do," she said. "*Maybe* you'll have unfinished business you'll need to attend to. Or maybe, just *maybe*, you'll be swallowed by the flames of Hell and won't need to go through the palaver of trying to get yourself through those blasted gates at the top of the star-steps." Belinda ran forward, walked and twirled amid the men and women. "But you've got to be pure to do that. Harbour no regrets and animosity towards anyone." She laughed. "So I guess you *will* be like us. In limbo, nowhere to go."

Annoyance addled my guts. "I told you not to follow me."

"Isn't that prospect fun, Carmel?" she said. "That not only will I be with you during your life, but I'll follow you through eternity, too."

I shuddered, turning from her and those…those people. Running, I reached the church and twisted the black, iron ring handle on the door. The heavy square of aged wood creaked open, its echo loud, masking Belinda's insane laughter that floated behind me. Two grey stone steps led down into the main body of the church. I took them, placed my feet on a harlequin-tiled aisle, and listened to the sound of my footsteps as I walked towards the altar.

What was that feeling? As if the air held a charge, as if a presence loitered, the inside of the church felt very different from outside. A nuance of being totally alone in the world stole around me. The thought that this very building housed my salvation rose within me. Was that what those people in town had meant—those that preached the word of the Lord from a homemade wooden podium in the marketplace, a microphone touching their lips? That if you only stepped foot inside a church, the good Lord would refresh you, take away the sins that bound guilt to your soul, and make you brand new.

Spooked—that's how I felt. Spooked and cherished at the same time. Peace settled on my shoulders, hugging away the fear that someone watched me from the far shadows of the church's innards. Eyes…I sensed them everywhere.

People…were those people from outside in here, sitting unseen in the pews, open Bibles on their laps, psalms waiting to be read?

Three stone steps raised the altar, ensuring it could be seen by all who rejoiced there. A white, sheet-like cloth, embroidered with a golden cross, was draped over the dark wood. I stood at the base of the steps and longed to touch the cloth, but dared not. Tainted, I didn't feel worthy enough to feel that material. I'd sully its goodness. Instead, I did what those on TV did: knelt, closed my eyes, and let the purity of that place seep into my bones.

I was sure I could have been saved that day.

A shuffle sounded behind me. The jangle of keys screeched like an eagle. I gasped, scrambled standing, and twisted round. A large old man, his back to me, stood poised by the door, keys held aloft, obviously ready to lock up.

"Wait," I said. "Don't lock me in."

Startled, he swung round. His white, fuzzy hair resembled cotton wool and stood out from his head in clumps, as if windblown and matted. With a hand against his chest he said, "Oh! You scared me then, my dear."

He chuckled, and as I walked towards him down the aisle, a nudge of recognition prodded my memory. Dark glasses framed his eyes now, and the lenses in those frames reflected light filtering in from the huge stained-glass windows to my right. Being unable to see his eyes unnerved me, made me feel beneath him in so many ways. A white beard covered the lower half of his face, the moustache full, as cotton-woolly as his hair.

"I was just…" Just what? Running from ghosts that probably still loitered on the other side of that door? Or not—perhaps they only existed in my imagination, as did he, for surely *this* man wasn't real.

"No problem, my duck," he said and smiled.

I stood before him now, looking up at him two steps above me, and it made him seem as tall as he'd appeared to me as a child.

"Mr Lawton?"

The man's eyes widened, and he shuffled back a step, his heels coming into contact with the door. His breath left him in stuttered gasps, and the keys fell from twitchy fingers to the floor. "No, no, my name isn't Lawton," he said.

I narrowed my eyes, peering at him. Blinked to clear my vision, to make sure I hadn't made a silly mistake. Mr Lawton still stood there, pink splotches on his cheeks, his chin trembling beneath that big old bushy beard. It was him, all right.

"It *is* you," I said and walked up the steps, my gaze on his face, that beard, those unseen eyes, still sequestered behind reflected light.

"It is him, yes," said Belinda from somewhere behind me. "Isn't fate a hoot? Just like his disguise."

"Shh!"

Mr Lawton blinked.

I stood nearly as tall as he did, and he looked nothing like the old man of my youth. Shoulders hunched, he reminded me of a scarecrow, its stuffing pecked out by a thousand starlings. Lines that had marked him as old back then rendered him ancient now. His once neatly combed hair, well, it stood in all directions.

His watery eyes came into view at last—maybe the sun slipped behind a cloud—and he regarded me, said, "Carmel? Carmel Wickens?"

I nodded. Smiled. Remembered the fifty p for the electricity meter.

"Well, I'll be! How are you diddling, my duck?"

I smiled again. Remembered the photos. "I'm diddling fine, Mr Lawton. You?"

"Oh, couldn't be better, the good Lord's seen to that. What brings you here? Salvation? A bit of prayer?"

Belinda snorted. "Fate brought her here. Here to break your fucking neck."

"Shh!"

Mr Lawton jerked his head back at the sound I'd made. "I'm sorry, dear. Didn't mean to offend you."

I laughed, a light giggle. "Oh, no. You didn't offend me. I was just—"

"Just what? About to tell him you tried to shut up your dead childhood friend?" Belinda's laugh rang through the church. Amplified. Too loud.

"Just here for a look around. I came out walking, found this church," I said and threw out my arm as if to encompass the building. "A shock finding you here. I didn't expect that."

Mr Lawton laughed. "Me neither, my duck. Still, things happen for a reason. Maybe God brought you across my path today. Perhaps he feels my prayers for you, my confessions of past sins concerning you, aren't good enough. Happen that today is the day I apologise to you directly and ask for your forgiveness."

"Forgiveness for what?" I smiled, heart thwumping. "Looking at pictures of my young, naked body? Fiddling with your cock while doing so? Oh, don't be silly. There's nothing to forgive.

It's not like you knew those pictures were of me. Is it?"

"Good Lord, no. No. I didn't know who they were. And truth be told, I should never have bought them. Your mam—not that I'm foisting the blame onto her, mind—was persistent when selling her wares. Another of my past sins."

Mr Lawton. *And Mam*? I shuddered.

He bent down to pick up the keys, stood upright, and twirled them in his hands.

"The dirty old fucker's wanting to lock up, get rid of you," whispered Belinda. "Make him wait, sweat a little."

"The past is just that, Mr Lawton. In the past. So, what do you do here? Caretaker?"

Mr Lawton visibly relaxed. "That and bell-ringer. My time…my time in prison," he crossed himself, glancing above, "gave me a new beginning. I left that place and came here. A fellow inmate—another soul who found the great and good God—saw the opening for this job in the newspaper. I applied via post, prior to my leaving prison, and confessed my sins, explaining that I needed the job, *wanted* the job. To be as close to the Lord as I could."

I swallowed. "And they *accepted* you? Even after your confession?" I frowned.

Mr Lawton smiled. "Oh, yes. Christians are good people. True Christians, I mean. And now I'm one of them."

He was a real Christian, despite his past faults?

"The mind boggles, doesn't it, Carmel?" Belinda's whisper further fired my already growing ire.

"Shh!"

"What's the matter? What did you hear?" asked Mr Lawton, a look of puzzlement on his face.

"Oh, nothing. I wonder…would you mind showing me the bell tower? I'd like to see that. Do you have time? I wouldn't want to mess up the rest of your afternoon." I glanced at my watch. "Well, early evening."

Relief relaxed his features. "Of *course* I have the time. Come this way," he said and placed the set of keys in his trouser pocket.

# Chapter Twenty-Six

I followed him down the aisle and veered right. Walking past the front pew, I noticed a wooden door set in a stone wall opposite. Brick ends formed an arch over the door, and again, the images of people from a bygone age danced in my mind's eye. Medieval men and women congregated beside the doorway and shifted out of Mr Lawton's path as he approached.

"I should tell them to spook the old bastard," said Belinda. "Put the frighteners on him, you know, scare the life out of him. Give him a heart attack. Mind you, that would defeat the object, wouldn't it?"

Mr Lawton fished in his pocket and brought out the ring of keys, holding them up, and squinted before selecting the one he needed. Slipping the key in the lock produced a click, and the door swung open with an insipid groan.

"This way," he said and stepped forward into a small foyer.

Flagstones covered the floor, and an image of it from the past entered my mind. Straw littered the flagstones. Sconces, placed at regular intervals on the walls, held lighted candles, and the aroma of burnt wicks lingered. I blinked. Electric lights replaced the sconces, albeit ones fashioned to resemble olden day lamps. The glass around the unlit bulbs reminded me of disused lighthouses.

"What made you think of that?" asked Belinda, shuffling her feet on the floor behind me.

I frowned, didn't answer.

A flight of wooden steps stood opposite us, and I cast my gaze upwards. Bells hung from a beamed ceiling. High, so high up.

Mr Lawton climbed the steps. I followed.

"Long way up, I'm afraid," he said. "My old bones are given a hard job doing this every day." He chuckled.

*Oh, my heart bleeds for you...*

"If it's a problem…?"

"No, no problem at all," he said. "I should be used to it by now. I did wonder why the bells needed to be rung each day." He wheezed. "What with this old church being so far out. Made me question who would hear them ringing. No houses around for miles, see. The vicar—he lives in town—he said it didn't matter if no one heard, that the fact they were rung would please God. So, I climb the stairs twice a day and pull the ropes. Good exercise if nothing else."

I smiled at his rambling. The air thickened as we stepped higher. The staircase twisted, winding like a spiral. I looked down. Dust motes tangoed in the air, easily seen via the lowering sun peeking through the lead-paned windows set in the walls of the tower.

Halfway up the staircase, Mr Lawton paused by one such window and leaned on the stony ledge to catch his breath. I stood beside him, my own breaths slightly laboured, and gazed out at the landscape. From this side of the building, the town wasn't visible. Hills dominated the horizon, some dotted with what appeared to be sheep or cows. A patchwork of greenery, interspersed with brown and beige, spread far into the distance. Trees and hedgerows bordered many fields, and I wondered if some of those boundaries had existed years ago, put down by those who originally owned the land.

How long had those trees been there? How many seasons had they seen? Idle thoughts, yet ones that inspired the want of understanding inside me. My childhood thirst for knowledge had stayed with me. Not the knowledge gained from secondary school, but that of infants and juniors. Tales told by Mrs Draper, those stories and fascinating myths remained, lingering in the recesses, and I reminded myself that day to join the library, to borrow books to feed the rekindled desire to learn.

"Amazing view, isn't it?" asked Mr Lawton.

"More amazing than a kid with no clothes on," Belinda said.

"Shh!"

"Yes, I quite agree," he said. "Needs to be gazed upon in silence. A little longer here, then?"

I frowned, catching on to his meaning. "Oh. Sorry, I keep shhing you. I don't mean it to sound rude."

"Not a problem," he said and seated himself on a step. "You continue looking. Take in as much as you can before the light fades completely."

The sky *had* darkened. The stairwell appeared gloomy, and I thought it would look either creepy or quaint when lit by the many wall lights.

"Shall we carry on upwards?" I said. "A quick peek at the bells—I've heard they're *really* big—and then I'll leave you in peace."

Belinda laughed.

At the top of the tower, vertigo hit me. I stared down at how far we'd climbed. Inhaling deeply, I clutched the top of a wooden partition that reached waist height. I steadied my breathing and looked at the four bells. They surely must have been taller than us.

"How did they get these up here?" I mused.

"I should imagine they were hoisted up on ropes. You know, many people pulling, enough people to bear the weight. These bells have apparently been hanging here well over two hundred years."

"Isn't that amazing?" I gazed at the intricate carvings on the bell sides. That someone could create such beauty without a machine stirred admiration inside me. "And those carvings. Wow."

"Are you being serious, Carmel, or taking the piss out of the old duffer?" Belinda asked. She sat atop a bell, hands clutching the metal mechanism that held it to the rafters. She wriggled, and the bell moved a little. It donged.

I clamped my hands over my ears. "That is so loud," I shouted.

"The reverberation fair tickles your fanny, too," screeched Belinda.

Mr Lawton laughed. "That's why I wear these while bell ringing," he said loudly and held up a pair of industrial ear protectors before placing them on his head. "Don't know why it rang, though. I hadn't pulled the rope." He frowned.

I glared at Belinda. She crawled from the top of the bell, down its side, and hugged it. The bell swung farther, donging louder.

"What the devil's going on?" said Mr Lawton. With wide eyes, he fingered his bushy beard then leaned out over the wooden partition and made to catch the edge of the bell, or at least let it bump against his arm until it came to rest. I thought the weight of the swing might push him sideways. Luckily, we stood away from the stairs if he should tumble.

Belinda's feet rested on the bell's rim. She bent her knees and pushed her weight downwards. Ringing as if Mr Lawton himself pulled the rope, the bell emitted an ear-buzzing toll. Again, I covered my ears. Mr Lawton flapped his arm over the wooden partition, leaning out a little farther. I moved behind him to pick up a second pair of ear protectors that were on the floor. Before I could, another ear-splitting toll shuddered through me, hurting my ears, and I jumped. Nudged Mr Lawton's backside with my elbow. His moving weight displaced the air, and wispy breezes caressed my face. I gasped, stood upright, and dumbly wondered where he had gone.

His scream mingled with the sound of the bell, growing quieter and hoarser the longer he yelled. I glanced at Belinda, who stood beside me, then stared at the bell that had stopped swinging, stopped ringing. And looked over the partition and down, just in time to watch Mr Lawton's head disintegrate as it slapped against the flagstones below.

"Another accident?" asked Belinda. "He's closer to the Lord now, all right. Or not, as the case may be."

I slapped my palm against my mouth to stop vomit escaping. Swallowed it. I heaved, but nothing burst out of my mouth and through my fingers. I shook from head to foot, inhaling a dust-laden breath, and removed my hand from my mouth. Pulling down the sleeves of my sweater over my hands, I rubbed them along the top of the partition. I turned, glaring once again at a smirking Belinda, and raced down the staircase, my sweater-covered hands wiping the handrails as I went.

Giddy, so giddy, my breath escaping in strangled gasps, I reached the bottom of the stairwell. I leaned over, palms on knees, and struggled to breathe, to regain my equilibrium.

*Calm down, calm down, calm down. It was an accident. Not your fault…*

"Oh, behave your fucking self. Delusional, you are. I mean, look at him. Tell me you didn't mean to do that," said Belinda.

I stood upright. My head spun, eyes watered, heart thundered. I steeled myself to turn and look at Mr Lawton, but instead, fled from the foyer, back through the church, and out into the fresh, early evening air. Swiping the arm of my sweater over the door handle ring and the door itself where I'd pushed it upon entrance and exit, I fled through the churchyard on leaden feet, stumbling for miles without seeing my surroundings or anyone that may have witnessed my presence.

"That really was very naughty," said Belinda.

She sat on the arm of my bed settee, leaning back to get more comfortable. Her socket face bled, though the blood didn't drip anywhere. As if shrink wrap covered her face and prevented the blood escaping, the red liquid churned and reminded me of water behind the glass of an automatic washing machine door.

*She's staying for the duration by the looks of it, Carmel.*

"Yes, I am," said Belinda, her tone brisk. "I want to discuss what Carmel's been doing, Doll. As you weren't there, you can piss off out of this conversation."

I sat with my back pressed into one corner of the settee, my legs tucked beneath me. I glanced at the wardrobe behind the sofa. Nelson still sat on the wardrobe, her one-eyed, glassy stare fixed on the back of Belinda's head. Her cracked face appeared to twitch—did she blink?—and her pale lips, once so pink, pursed. I was sure of it.

*I don't have to be there to know what happened. I'm everywhere, just like you seem to be, Belinda. The only difference is that I'm wanted.*

Belinda bounded from the chair arm, twisted round, and faced Nelson. "Look, I was her friend way before you came along. If it wasn't for you, none of this would have happened. Fucking weird little doll, you are. Telling her what to think and what to do." Blood bulged against the wrap-like skin, stretching it—water in a balloon.

*I'm weird? Check out your face.*

I closed my eyes and willed them to stop bickering.

A knock on my door startled me.

"Who the fuck is that at this time of night?" Belinda asked.

"I don't know, I haven't got the ability to see through doors," I said.

"Oooh! Get you," she said.

*Oh, be quiet, moron.*

"You be quiet," snapped Belinda.

"Both of you be quiet," I whispered, walking to the door. "Who is it?" I asked, my mouth close to the doorframe.

"It's me, Gary."

# Chapter Twenty-Seven

I opened the door. Gary stood, hands in trouser pockets, hair tousled and damp with sweat. His breath came in short spurts, and he appeared distressed.

"Bloody hell," I said. "Who rattled your cage?"

He brushed past me into the room and walked over to the sink. His hands gripping the sides, he leaned over it and took deep breaths. After turning on the cold tap, he filled a glass. With two swallows, he emptied the glass then placed it upside down on the drainer.

"Needed that," he said and swiped the sleeve of his jacket over his lips. "Ran all the way from the pub on our estate, you know, The Cross Keys. I was minding my own business, drinking my pint, and that Bob bloke walked in."

My stomach lurched. "Bob? And?"

"Well, we got talking, which surprised me because I hardly know him. He asked me if—"

Panic wrenched my solar plexus. "You didn't tell him where I live, did you?"

Gary sighed and shot me a contemptuous look. "Do you think I'm stupid?" He laughed. "Actually, don't answer that one. Anyway, he asked me if I knew where you were. Your mam's been asking for you, apparently."

Gary sat down. Belinda stood from the sofa arm, opened the wardrobe, and shut herself inside. I leaned against the kitchenette worktop and folded my arms across my stomach.

"Why the hell has Mam been asking for me? Did Bob say?"

Gary shrugged. "He said something about her nearly overdosing last night. That he visited her as usual, and she was out of it on the sofa, semi-conscious. Reckons her H was cut with quinine, whatever the fuck that is. I didn't even know your old dear took heroin. I thought she was just a piss head. How come you never told me?"

Thoughts of Mam dying from an overdose entertained me for a few seconds. Unable to explore my feelings on the subject fully, I said, "Didn't think it was anything to shout about, you know? I mean, who wants to admit their mam is an addict?"

I pushed away from the worktop and plonked down beside Gary. He placed his arm around my shoulders and gave me a little squeeze.

"D'you want to talk about it?" he asked.

"No thanks. Living with it was bad enough without going over it again with you." I rested my cheek against his chest.

"Pardon me for breathing," he said. "I was only asking."

"Yeah, well don't." Changing my surly tone, I said, "So, what else did Bob have to say?"

*What do you want to know for?*

"Yeah, what do you want to know for?" yelled Belinda from inside the wardrobe, her voice muffled.

I imagined the wet ooze from her socket face dirtying all my clothes and resisted the urge to jump up and snatch the wardrobe door open.

"Asked if I could let you know next time I saw you that your mam asked about you. Bob said she's gone downhill since you left."

I snorted, lifted my head, and looked at Gary's face to make sure he wasn't messing me around. "Downhill since I left? I'll never believe that. She's probably just missed the bloody housework being done."

Gary shrugged. "Bob sounded pretty genuine to me. Mind you, I don't really know the bloke, so I wouldn't know if he meant what he said or not." Sniffing, he glanced around my room. "Got a TV guide? I wanna see if that film is on tonight. You know, the one about that man who murdered those prostitutes. Jack the Ripper, that's it."

I smiled. Some things never changed, and Gary's quench for blood and gore was one of them.

"I haven't got a TV guide, but I think it's on tomorrow night at nine," I said and stood. "D'you want another drink? I've got some Coke in the fridge."

Gary tutted. "Now she tells me. Bloody filled myself up with water, didn't I."

Smiling, I walked over to the kitchenette and poured two glasses of Coke. Seated beside him again, I said, "Is Bob still at the pub?"

"He was when I left, why?"

"Fancy a drink?"

*What the hell are you doing, Carmel?*

Belinda's squeal sailed out of the wardrobe. "She's going to check on her mam. I told you, Doll, Annette needs forgiving, not ignoring."

*Forgiving my arse.*

"My sentiments exactly," I said.

"What?" said Gary.

"Nothing," I said, guzzling my Coke.

The Cross Keys was filled to the brim with patrons. Grey cigarette smoke lingered above the heads of those seated at the bar, eerily lit by lights hanging from gold chains. Raucous laughter mixed with mumbled conversations ebbed and flowed. The door swooshed closed behind us, shutting out the cold air. The stench of beer and pub food prevalent, I breathed through my mouth and followed Gary past the crowd.

Bob sat in a far corner, resting his feet on the edge of a table. His greasy hair looked more unkempt than it had the last time I'd seen him, and he now sported a beard and moustache. I still would have recognised him, though—his piercing eyes gave him away.

"Well, fuck me, if it isn't Carmel, my favourite girl."

The hairs on my arms stood on end, and a shudder raced up my spine. Memories of the past flounced through my mind as if the events had only occurred yesterday. I blinked and shut them away, forcing myself to think of the here and now.

Bob stood and dug his hand into his pocket, bringing out a handful of change and crumpled notes. "What're you drinking?" he asked.

"Coke," I said.

Bob held out a ten pound note to Gary. "Coke for Carmel, pint of Guinness for me, and whatever you're having. Good lad." He sat and patted the chair beside him.

Suddenly awkward, I didn't know whether I wanted to sit beside him or continue to stand. The urge to follow Gary to the bar grew strong, but I resisted, sighed, and sat opposite Bob.

Bob leaned his elbows on the table, and his face moved perilously close to mine. His beer breath tickled the hairs on my jaw. I stifled a heave. Blackheads, prominent on his nose, reminded me of when I used to stab my biro against the paper in my school books.

"So the lad there told you about your mam, then?" He nodded towards the bar.

*Well, obviously…*

"Yes." I turned to see if Gary had managed to get served yet. Two rows of men lined the bar, and Gary was in the process of elbowing his way closer.

"She was nearly a goner last night, kid."

I faced Bob again. "Really? Shame she wasn't. How much did she take?" I studied the tabletop rather than look at Bob's new facial adornment.

"Dunno. As dependent as a dog on its owner, is Annette. Old H got its grip on her bad lately. Been using more than her usual dose. I'll brain the fucker that sold me the dodgy batch." Bob belched.

I shuddered and imagined Mam's syringe and how full it used to be.

"So what does she want me for?" I asked.

"Scared herself shitless, didn't she. Reckon she thought she was gonna meet her maker, know what I mean?"

Gary placed a pint of Guinness on the table, and Bob sat upright, picked up the glass, and swallowed deeply. His Adam's apple bobbed up and down, and I envisaged a knife slashing his throat open and Guinness pouring out along with blood.

Taking the glass bottle of Coke from Gary, I indicated with my eyes that he sit beside me. "We'll drink these quick and be off," I said quietly.

Gary glanced at his pint and sat down. "Give me a chance."

"Lovers' tiff?" said Bob.

I glared at Bob and saw him for the insipid creep he was. Everything was sexually orientated with him. Memories barged into my mind, bringing unwanted images of the little girl I used to be. The flash of the camera, the click of the shutter, the tinkle of the chains on my 'new' outfit, the 'toys'…

I blinked and stood.

"I'll be back in about an hour," I said and registered the shock on Gary's face. "You stay and finish your pint with Bob."

Gary's mouth hung open, and I snapped it closed with my finger under his chin.

"Where you going?" he asked.

"I may as well nip and see Mam, save you rushing your beer."

I turned and elbowed through the crowd without waiting for Gary to protest. Some things were better done alone.

Her house looked exactly the same as it always had from the outside.

"Why shouldn't it?" said Belinda.

"Dunno. I just expected it to be…different for some reason."

I stared at the dirty net curtains hanging behind the equally filthy windows. Streaks of dried earth decorated the front door as if someone with muddy boots had attempted to kick it in.

*Angry punter?*

I stood on the paving slab in front of the door. The handle appeared to be broken. It dangled downwards.

*Someone's wrenched that bugger.*

"Bob did it last night. Your Mam didn't answer his knock, and he saw her through the window on the sofa. Thought she was asleep at first, but after rapping his knuckles on the window, he kind of guessed she wasn't quite right," said Belinda. "Despite his pitfalls, Bob realises Annette needs help."

"Despite his pitfalls?" I almost laughed. "He's the fucker who's been supplying the silly bitch all these years."

The sound of a door opening made me jump. I moved back from Mam's door, but it wasn't hers that had opened. The snotty cow from next door stepped out onto her path to my left with the fronts of her dressing gown clutched tightly in her fists.

"Oh, it's you. Back again, are you?" Snotty's hair rollers bobbed along with her head. "Thought we'd got rid of at least one of you. And you can tell your mother," she snarled, her top lip curling, "that we *normal* folk don't appreciate hearing *her* screaming at the top of her lungs late into the night." She flared her nostrils. "It's bad enough that I have to live next door to a prostitute, but to hear her carrying on last night you'd—"

I flew across the grass in front of the two houses and stood directly in front of her. "What she does is nothing to do with me. Never has been. And you can stop sneering at me like that, because I happen to agree with you. Why do you think I got away so young, why I haven't been back since I left? And her profession obviously doesn't bother you *that* much, otherwise you'd have reported her and got me taken away to a foster home. To someone who gave a shit about me, you pious old cow."

Snotty's eyes widened, and she gripped her gown tighter. Her cheeks gained a pink hue, the light spilling from her open door affording me a clear view of her face. Her eyebrows shot up and down. They needed plucking. I took another step towards her, anger at her reluctance to help me as a child seeping dangerously into my bloodstream.

"Oh, well… Right…" She stood for a few seconds, obviously unsure what to say or do next. Her bottom lip quivered, and a teardrop of spittle oozed from one corner of her mouth and turned into a glistening, liquid slug. With a quick shake of her head, she turned abruptly and stumbled into her hallway and closed her door.

*Fucking old bitch.*

I stood on the grass for a moment and contemplated knocking on Snotty's door and spilling out my vengeance. Snatching out her hair rollers and shoving them down her throat. She'd lived in silence all those years and must have known what my life had been like.

"Ignorance is bliss. If you pretend something isn't happening, you can almost convince yourself it doesn't exist," whispered Belinda from behind me. She walked to stand at Snotty's front door, a barrier against me ringing the doorbell.

*Oh, shut the hell up, girl. What do you know, eh? Leave us alone, you one-eyed freak.*

"Huh, look who's talking, Doll." Belinda's shoulders stiffened, and she straightened her posture in affront. Her eye-socket head morphed into her life-face. Crocodile skin sagged at her jaw line and looked as though it would slip off if I reached out and —

"Don't you dare!" she said and backed up against Snotty's door. "Leave me alone."

"Well shut up, then," I said and, turning away from her, took three paces over the frost-kissed grass to Mam's door. "I'm going in alone before you even think about coming with me."

A vast sigh from Belinda sailed to me and covered my face. I raised my hands and clawed at my cheeks to remove the breath-cowl. It stuck to my skin, and for a second I recalled the white glue we used at school and how, when it dried, it looked like peeling skin. The film tightened across my cheeks, my mouth, nostrils, and I fought for breath. A moan sounded inside my head followed by a primal growl. I twisted round to stare at Belinda. Her fuzzy form stood in front of me, her face a socket once more, the blood-inside-sandwich-wrap version.

"Now you know how I feel," she said.

*Get that fucking thing off her face.*

My lungs strained, and my knees threatened to buckle. Panicked, I ripped at my face and succeeded in pulling off strips of film. Belinda continued to breathe at me, resealing the places where my fingers had torn strips. I snatched a large hole over my mouth and sucked in air before Belinda breathed again, but she turned away from me and disintegrated. As if the cowl had never been, it disappeared with her.

*She's losing it, Carmel.*

I bent over, placed my palms on my knees, and sucked in gulps of air. My heart thundered, and the backs of my eyeballs throbbed. "I…know," I said. "But…it doesn't…help…when you…"

*I know. I should keep my mouth shut, but she annoys me.*

"Shhh…she might be…listening." Breaths steadier, I stood upright. My vision blurred, and I sensed a faint coming. "Need to…" I staggered to Mam's door and slapped at the handle. The door sprang open, and I lurched inside the house.

Childhood odours assaulted me. As if I'd never left, the house engulfed me in its familiarity, welcoming me in. Whispers seeped from the walls.

*Welcome home, Carmel. Come in…come in…*

Although the hallway light wasn't on, I recognised the same shapes in the gloom. The door to the cupboard under the stairs stood open, and a shadow mound of shoes was piled in the entrance.

*Your mam must have scrabbled about in there to put the electric on.*

I closed the door. "Mam?" My voice echoed back at me.

A shaft of light seeped from beneath the living room door. Hands out before me, I walked towards it.

# Chapter Twenty-Eight

﷯

The light from the bare bulb in the living room rendered me momentarily sightless. I blinked. Silver spots danced, and my vision gradually returned. I rubbed my eyes then glanced towards the sofa where I expected Mam to be. But the sofa, devoid of her drug-addled body, looked as worn out and abused as I once was. Mam's dream of making her house as posh as the back room had obviously not been realised, and a hint of sadness nudged my conscience.

*Make sure it is only a hint of sadness, Carmel. There's no room for pity when it comes to your mam. She had no pity for you...*

I crossed the living room, dodging pizza boxes, old magazines, and empty beer cans. The door to the kitchen stood closed, and I placed my ear against it. A tap dripped loudly, which meant the bowl in the sink was empty of dirty dishes.

*Or the drips are plopping into a cup.*

I nodded, whispered, "Most probably," and opened the door. The fluorescent strip light flickered on and off; the starter obviously needed changing. It gave the kitchen an ominous feel, made the appliances on the worktops sinister in the darkness. Nelson had been right; the tap water *was* dripping into a cup perched on top of a stack of dirty crockery. What looked like a splash of tomato sauce streaked the side of the yellow-white kettle, resembling a splatter of old blood.

A quick survey of the kitchen worktops yielded sights of toast crumbs, tea splashes, and empty food packages. A ketchup bottle stood lidless, the sauce congealed and crusty around the rim. The cutlery drawer hung open and leaned listlessly to one side, the runner broken. Dirt nestled in a line along the edge of the lino where it met the cupboard bases, the once white flooring now grey and brown.

A squeak sounded to my left, and I jumped. An altogether different squeak came from behind the door to the back room, and I knew that Mam was working. Doing her thing, massaging her client's—

*Back and shoulders. Yeah, right.*

I turned to the larder and opened the door. The mouse of my youth—could it be the same one?—sat on its haunches on the shelf. It eyed me warily, its front paws poised in front of it, clasped together as if in prayer.

"Praying for food, mister?" I whispered and moved to the worktop to swipe a smattering of breadcrumbs into my palm. Nearing the mouse, I expected it to flee into the hole in the back of the cupboard, but it remained in place, rigid. "Do you think if you stay still for long enough I won't see you, is that it? Ah, I've played that game many times, and it doesn't quite work like that. For one," I emptied the crumbs onto the shelf, "you don't have a blanket with holes to peer from, and two," I rubbed my palms together and hunkered down, "people have a habit of knowing that you're trying to hide. Then they give you their attention. Yet if you'd scurried off to your hole, their interest in you would wane immediately. Unless, of course, they wanted you for some reason—and then they'd come and find you."

I closed the cupboard door and walked back into the living room. Mam's mirror that she used for plucking her eyebrows perched perilously on top of a stack of *Good Housekeeping* magazines. The urge to laugh gripped me—insane, ironic laughter—but sadness snatched the mirth away, wrenching it in its fists along with squeezing tears from my eyes.

Angrily, I dashed them away, growling in frustration at the emotions Mam made me feel, even when she wasn't in the room. She would forever be the octopus in my sea, many arms reaching into every aspect of my psyche.

"What are you still doing here? Your mam is too busy to see you." Belinda stood in the doorway to the hall, hands on hips. "I did try and stop you coming in here, didn't I? But you knew best. Just had to come in. Overdose or not, that woman will work until she's dead, and it wouldn't surprise me if one of her punters came in and did her even then."

"You say that, yet defend her. You make no sense, Belinda."

She laughed. "It's all part of my plan to confuse your already fucked-up mind. Payback is a bitch, isn't it?"

I stumbled past her and out of Mam's house. The cold air whacked my sore face, seeping into the scratch marks I'd made. As I walked briskly along the street, the sound of Mam's door closing reached me, as did footsteps on the tarmac.

"Why don't you go back?" Belinda said, hurrying alongside me. "He's gone. She's in there hauling her sad and abused body off of her bed right now. She could use a hug."

"She could use a shot of H, Belinda. She could use a cigarette, a cup of hot tea, a snort of cocaine. But a hug? No, she couldn't use one of those, especially not from me." I thundered towards the pub, my cheeks stinging as much as my eyes.

*Go away, Belinda. You cause havoc every time you're near.*

"That's the idea, Doll."

Belinda's laugh grated on my last nerve, and I stopped walking and turned to face her. "If you're trying to make me go to Insane Land, forget it, because I'm already there. If you're trying to make me forgive Mam, hit the fucking road, Jack—that'll never happen."

I stared at the blood swirling beneath the film of her socket face. My fingers twitched with the need to rip it open and watch the blood spill onto the tarmac, splash onto my shins, on my face, in my hair. An image of her prone on the path entered my mind, and I saw myself jumping on her over and over again until she became nothing but sodden mulch.

"That's quite an imagination you have there, Carmel. Shame I'm already dead." She giggled and flicked her head back.

*You're a crazy bitch, d'you know that?*

"Oh yeah, Doll. I know. Aren't we all?"

My throat constricted, and I turned from her and continued walking to The Cross Keys. Eyes downcast, I concentrated on my footsteps and counted how many it took me to reach the pub. My shoes clip-clopped, the sound reverberating in the still night. Tears spilled, burned my cheeks, and upon reaching the pub entrance, I patted them away, wincing at the salty sting.

"Bet you ask Gary to stay the night at your place," Belinda said.

I sighed and turned to face her. "And if I do?"

Her life-face appeared, and her good eye looked heavenward while she contemplated her response. "Um, I think I'll come back tomorrow." She disappeared, though the stench of her rotting flesh lingered.

*Thank fuck for that.*

"Indeed."

I pushed the pub door open and shoved my way through the drinkers to the corner. Two empty pint glasses sat on the table. Bob and Gary held fresh drinks. I glanced at Bob before sitting beside Gary.

"What happened to your face?" Gary asked.

"What's up with it?" said Bob. "Turn this way, kid."

Ignoring Bob, I said, "I fell in a bush on the way back from Mam's, didn't I? Scratched it on the branches."

Bob guffawed. "Daft mare. Did you see your mam, then?"

I looked at him. Froth from his Guinness gave him a two-tone moustache. I squinted, and it looked like one of those fancy Belgian chocolates. You know, half white, half brown.

"No. I went in, but she was busy."

"Ah." Bob sipped his drink. "Still, there's always tomorrow, eh?"

I nodded. "Well, there's always another time."

*Another time, yes.*

Gary placed his half-full glass on the table. "I've had enough for one night. Come on, I'll walk you home."

We stood, and awkwardness gripped me.

"Um, I'll see you around, Bob."

He belched and wiped his palm over his moustache, the Belgian chocolate obsolete. "Most probably." He winked.

The insides of my ears tingled in disgust, and I quickly turned from him and snaked my hand through Gary's crooked arm. Once outside, I said, "Would you mind sleeping at mine tonight?"

Surprise lifted his eyebrows. "I hope you're not suggesting anything improper, young lady," he said with the voice of an affluent gentleman. "One couldn't condone such behaviour."

I giggled. "Don't worry, I won't accost you. But a cuddle would be nice."

He smiled and squeezed my arm against his side. "Ah, one can do cuddles. Cuddles aren't dangerous."

Gary's gentle snores lulled me into restfulness. The sound of an occasional passing car punctuated his breaths, and his steady heartbeat throbbed against my cheek. I was nestled in his arms, and contentment stole over me. A thought struck: I'd never shared a bed with anyone like this before—had never been hugged for such an extended period of time.

I opened my eyes. A streetlamp's muted light struggled to permeate the curtains, and a square glow around the drapes fizzled into the darkness of the room. My arm, draped over his stomach, rose and fell with his breaths, and the hairs on his legs tickled the skin on mine. Flickering images from the TV played on Gary's face, the change of lighting making him sinister one moment and sexy the next.

Sexy?

*That's what I was about to say. Sexy? Do you fancy Gary, Carmel?*

I don't know, Nelson. Do I?

*Probably. How do you feel about that?*

I'm not sure. Part of me thinks it's filthy. You know, wanting to have sex, to try it, see what it's all about.

*You've got your mother to thank for that. Besides, it's natural, isn't it? For your age. Most girls would have done it by now, anyway.*

I know.

*Are you going to do it?*

Nelson!

*Well, I'm just asking, because if you are, I'd appreciate you turning me the other way, facing the wall.*

*Did* I want to do it? Emotions raged through me, ones I'd experienced before but to a lesser degree. Everything inside me seemed to heat up, especially between my legs. Did Mam feel like that with those men?

*I doubt it, Carmel. She probably switches off and thinks of England. After all, she only does it for the money and for Bob.*

My cheeks grew hot—somehow feeling like this and having a conversation with Nelson didn't feel right.

*Shall I be quiet? Do you want me to switch off and think of England?*

Ummm, yes. Let me just—

*Sort through your feelings on your own?*

Yes. Thank you.

Shame brought further fire to my cheeks, and my stomach clenched. Had I offended Nelson? And what would I do if I did want to do it? Just turning Nelson to face the wall wouldn't be right. She would still be able to hear…

*No, you haven't offended me. And you could put me in the wardrobe.*

"I was going to say: Don't ask me to put her in the wardrobe."

*Belinda? What are you doing here? Get out. This is a private moment for Carmel.*

"Look, Doll, I'm here to fuck up Carmel's life, as you know. Like I'm going to let her do it with someone who I had a soft spot for. Not likely."

*Like Gary would have done it with you if you were still alive, anyway. Got ideas above your station, you have.*

"You'd know all about that, wouldn't you? Parading around in one of *my* doll's dresses. I mean, come on. We all know *clothes don't maketh the man. Don't* we, Carmel?"

Desire, if that's what it was, fled my body. I rolled away from Gary and huddled beneath the quilt on the other side of the sofa bed. The coldness struck a deal with my skin, goose bumps the payment. Belinda stood by the door, hands on hips, wearing her eye-socket head. My heart rate slowed, each painful thud loud, and I ousted thoughts of spite and revenge against Belinda from my mind. I'd never be able to get rid of her and lead a normal life. Not with Gary as my partner, anyway.

"Damn right you won't. Like I said before, I'm here for the long haul."

*So how come there are times when you stay away then, Ugly Face?*

Belinda's shrill laugh rent the air, and I jumped, pulling the quilt over my head. Why couldn't they just go away, leave me alone? Why…?

"You're calling *me* Ugly Face? Have you looked in the mirror lately? Oh, silly me. I forgot. You can't, can you? You need Carmel to do things for you. The only thing you can do for yourself is speak, and it's debateable whether you can even do that properly. Got a voice like a slowing gramophone, you have."

*Oh, get lost, will you? You're boring me.*

"Shh!" I whispered, my breaths hot beneath the quilt. "Be quiet."

"Aw, worried that Gary will hear us, are you?"

I nodded.

Belinda's scream ricocheted off the walls and through my mind, its ear-splitting pitch painful. I quickly shoved the quilt from my head and leaned up on one elbow, turned around, and looked at Gary. He slept on, oblivious. The scream continued—surely she'd have to take a breath soon?—and I bunched my eyes closed. Rage boiled in my belly, and the urge to jump up and throttle Belinda, to choke the scream out of her, tingled in my hands.

"Shh! Just shh," I said.

Silence arrested the room, the resonance of the scream drowning out any other sound. Slowly, as if filtering through, the thud of my heart, another passing car, and my uneasy breaths all grew in audibility, shunting the scream's echo away.

"Shh?" asked Belinda. "Why? It didn't bother him, did it?"

I opened my eyes, turning to face her. "No, but it could have. Maybe he's a deep sleeper?"

Belinda laughed and moved towards me. She knelt and whispered, "You just don't get it, do you?"

Frowning, I said, "Get what?"

"Forget it," she said and stood. "Thick as pig's shit, that's what you are."

Her words speared me—she'd used Mam's voice—and I rolled onto my back to stare at the ceiling. Tears stung the backs of my eyes, and I willed them not to increase in size and spill. Concentrating on Gary's low snores, I matched his breaths with my own, hoping to hypnotise myself into sleep. Belinda's presence drifted away, and I made pictures out of the Artex on the ceiling. A scene appeared in the white plaster, one of Mam on the sofa, a needle sticking out of her…

My mind settled once more, I closed my eyes and smiled.

# Chapter Twenty-Nine

*I*'ve got to be able to get a clear shot. I've told you this time and again. Your idea about doing it in a crowd was good, I'll give you that much, all right? I know I don't need any practice, that I've done it before, but what if that other shot was just a lucky one?

I'm going to pick them off, one by one. All of them—gone.

And there was me thinking I'd got the last one, that at last I'd have inner peace. Seeing...seeing inside that...fucking thing blasted my newfound equilibrium to Hell and back. And you know I've resided there my whole life. What about my little bit of Heaven, eh? Why *couldn't it have been finished back then—after I did* him? *Why did I have to go snooping inside and find…*

*Now look at me. I'm all flustered and out of sorts. Sweating—and you know how I hate being smelly. I'm going to have a shower now. Wash the memories of them off me.*

*DON'T follow me.*

# Chapter Thirty

Tired of hanging clothes on the sales racks, I entertained thoughts of bettering myself. Aged nineteen and working in a clothes shop…hardly my idea of a good career. Still, I had things I needed to do before I could even think about going to college. My mind had to be clear of the debris of my past. Three left, that's all, then I could shove everything behind me and start again. Maybe I'd move to a new town. No one would know me, and the stigma of my youth could stay in this stinking, shit hole of a place.

"It'll follow you wherever you go, Carmel."

Belinda slouched beside the clothes rack, yellow pus plopping from her eye-socket face onto the white-tiled floor. Funny that she'd stayed the same height as when she'd died—that she hadn't grown with me over the years. Strange that such a small being could inspire terror inside me when I stood so much taller. I'd always thought that once grown, I wouldn't be scared anymore, that the heebie-jeebies vanished upon adulthood's arrival. What a load of crap that thought had been.

"What the hell do you want?" I whispered and placed another black top on the rack.

As usual, she ignored my question. "No matter where you run to, it will follow. Wanna know why?"

I sighed, nodded.

"Because it's all inside you, thicko. You think that once they all cease to exist you'll feel better? Think again, dipshit."

I glanced around the store, relieved to see it mainly empty. "You don't know me and what I feel inside—"

"Yes I do, I know every thought, every—"

"No, you *don't*. And it *will* work, I know it."

Belinda snorted. "And if it doesn't? What will you do then? Kill yourself?"

I frowned. I hadn't thought of that scenario lately. The urges to wreak revenge had surpassed any urges to relieve life's burdens. Even though thoughts of the star-steps invaded my mind—and the longing to be there once again and experience that feeling of peace proved too much—I'd long ago realised why it hadn't been my time to stand on the last step and move forward into bliss. I had things to do before I could walk through the portal between this world and the next.

"No, I won't have to do that, because it *will* work. Anyway, don't bother me while I'm here. You don't show up for months, and when you do it's here. Piss off before my boss sees me and thinks I'm talking to myself."

"Who says she can't see me?" Belinda twirled, her burial dress billowing around her. "Maybe she has the ability to—"

"Belinda."

She pouted. "Don't you want to know why I'm here?"

"No." I shoved a hanger into the neck of the last black top and hung it up. "Sod off."

"Think about it. I usually turn up when there's something important to do, don't I?" She sniffed. The sound of yellow goo slapping on the floor turned my stomach.

"Do you? So, slinging shit at me is important? Arguing with Nelson and driving me mad is important?" I clamped my teeth, stomped over to the cardboard box of tops, and pulled them over to the empty rack near the window.

"Of course that's important, but I'm here for something else today. Something you'll be pleased about, though why I want to please you is anyone's guess."

I lifted a cerise top and placed it on a hanger. "I was about to say the same thing. Had a personality transplant, have we?"

Belinda gusted towards me. The displaced air held a tinge of menace, and I hung the top on the rack and stared at her, my heart thudding, hands trembling. Her life-face glared back, nostrils flared, cheeks reddened.

"You'd better fucking stop being rude to me or I'll—"

"You'll what?" Bravado had finally arrived. "Stalk me? Scare me? What?"

"Well…" Belinda rested a forefinger on her chin and looked at the ceiling. "Remember the breath cowl? Hmm? How you couldn't breathe? You know what I'm capable of doing, don't you?" Her gaze met mine.

My stomach churned. Determined not to let her see my fright, I laughed. "Yes, I know, but I suspect you're not actually allowed to kill me. Ironic, that, don't you think? That I was able to kill you, but you're not able to—"

"Shut the hell up and look out of the window. Quickly."

*Do as she says, Carmel.*

I stared in the direction Belinda's sausage finger pointed. Shoppers in various guises pottered on the street outside beneath a multitude of coloured umbrellas. Cars parked bumper-to-bumper against the curbs on both sides of the road, and smoke belched from under the canopy of a hotdog vendor on the pavement directly outside. I squinted through the rain-splattered window, seeing nothing out of the ordinary.

"What? What am I looking for?" I asked, turning back to Belinda.

"Look outside the men's suit shop on the corner." Belinda's lips quirked into a smug smile, and she cocked her head. "Hurry up. Stop staring at *me* and look at *him*."

I shifted my gaze outside again. An old, slim-built man leant forward to afford a closer study of the shop's window display. His grey wool coat hung from bony shoulders, and the hems of his black trousers kissed the wet pavement, obliterating sight of his shoes. A black fedora rested on the back of his head, as if he'd pushed it away from his brow to see better. He brought his leather-gloved hands out of his pockets and turned, his left profile towards me. A straggly grey beard bushed inches below his jaw line, his moustache so thick that I wondered how he breathed through his nostrils.

"See him now?"

I frowned. "What, the old duffer with the beard?"

Belinda laughed, a sanctimonious jingle. "Yes, the old duffer with the beard. Ring any bells, does he?"

My frown deepened. "No. Should he?"

*Look really hard, Carmel. Think.*

I moved closer to the window. The old man now held a wallet. With head bent low, he pulled out some money and flicked through the notes. Counting his cash?

"Oh," said Belinda. "Silly me. *This* man doesn't ring any bells—it was the *other one* who did that."

My heart slammed painfully. Air hitched in my throat, and I swallowed, though not fast enough. The acid taste of bile burned the back of my tongue, and I palmed my mouth.

*See him, Carmel?*

I nodded.

"Ah, it's a wonderful thing to see you so fucked up by the sight of someone. Bet your emotions are all over the shop now, aren't they?

Pun intended." Belinda prodded me on the arm. "Oi, I'm talking to you."

I ignored her, and she sighed. My eyes widened as the years were stripped away.

*Remember him, Carmel? Remember what he said? "And isn't that a big girl you are now? And Nelson. What a lovely name for such a beautiful dolly... There's upset I am then, Carmel. Mr Lawton's money bought the sherbet and lolly, and my present was the sweets..."*

Oh, Jesus. Oh, no...

"Don't make out this isn't what you wanted, Carmel. You're such a bloody drama queen." Belinda giggled. "What are you going to do? Take an early lunch? That's all well and good, but by the time you go and ask your boss, Mr Hemmings will be gone. *Then* what will you do? Who knows when the opportunity will arrive again for you to go over to him and—"

I didn't hear the rest of what she said. The rain lashed down on my face, and the door of the shop had already closed behind me.

The smell of new suits and rain-damp coats assaulted me. I blinked away moisture and searched the small outlet. A young brown-haired man stood behind the counter to my right, his head bent over a ledger, the end of a pen in his mouth. Racks of suit jackets lined the top half of the walls, their trouser companions on the rows beneath. To the rear of the shop, one shoe of each pair sat on transparent plastic shelves. Black or brown brogues, tan Hush Puppies, hiking boots.

*He* browsed a rack situated beside the shoes, his naked fingers caressing a burgundy silk tie spotted with yellow. Where had all his weight gone? And his height appeared diminished—or was that because I had grown since the last time I'd seen him? I stepped forward.

"Can I help you?"

I turned to the man behind the counter. He stood upright now, the ledger closed, the pen beside it on the counter.

"Ummm, no. No, thank you. I'm just browsing. I need to buy my dad a tie. I see them up there so I'll…"

I walked to the back of the shop, my strides sure, my heart thumping. The speed of the pulse in my neck quickened, and I reckoned the vein bulged my skin. Swallowing to banish the dryness in my throat, I reached out and smoothed my fingers down a dark blue tie with gold diamonds. The smell of *him* burned my nostrils—his damp coat, fusty aftershave, and something else...cigar smoke?

"Nice, aren't they?" he said.

I faced him and recognised his eyes—the only thing that remained the same. His sallow cheeks and spindly nose was nothing like the old Mr Hemmings, and I struggled to accept this man as him.

"Do I know you?" I asked and looked at his hands still caressing the burgundy tie. His slim fingers—I couldn't imagine them reaching inside a lollipop jar.

He frowned and narrowed his eyes. "I don't think so."

"I'm sure I do," I said. "Didn't you used to run a shop?"

His cheeks above the beard reddened. "I...uh...I..."

"Yes, I'm sure you did," I pressed, "the one that had lots of sweets behind the counter in jars. And you gave me a handkerchief once. I still have it, in fact. And my mam used to send me to the shop with a brown envelope for you, and you'd give me boxes of cigarettes in return. I'm *sure* that was you." I fingered my chin.

He let the tie fall from his grasp, cleared his throat, and patted his chest. "I, well, I... Yes. I did."

"I can't *believe* it. That it's *really* you. I've thought about you for such a long time. You know, wondered where you'd gone. I mean, one day you're in the shop letting me sit behind the counter and everything, and the next…well, you just weren't there anymore. No one told me where you'd gone, either, and I was *so* disappointed. I'm so glad that I've bumped into you again."

Relief crawled into his eyes, and the blood sucked out of his cheeks, leaving them bleached.

"Carmel Wickens?" he asked.

*Like he doesn't bloody know.*

"Yes, that's me. How *are* you? Where have you *been*?" I touched his arm, his prickly coat material biting my fingertips.

He patted my hand—*Doesn't that make you cringe, Carmel, knowing what he may have done with that ha*—and said, "Well, dear, I've been away, that's all. And I'm fine. More to the point, how are *you*?"

Belinda's giggle permeated the shop. "Wouldn't he like to know? Fucking old pervert."

His clammy skin against mine brought stomach acid surging into my throat again. I moved my fingers and placed both hands in my jeans pockets.

"Oh, I'm all right. Grown up now, you know."

He nodded, his beard rustling against his coat collar. "I see that, yes, I see that." His wide smile broke through the facial hair.

"I bet you bloody do and all," sniped Belinda. "Bet she doesn't tickle your pickle now, does she? Older girls don't do it for you, do they?"

I glared at Belinda then returned my attention to Mr Hemmings. "Are you in town for long? Shopping, I mean." I smiled, despite my guts twisting.

He cocked his head and stared at me.

*Reckon he can see right inside your eyes—right inside your head. Blink. Blink…*

"Oh, I'm just browsing, really," he said. "Umm, why do you ask?"

"I just wondered what you were doing for lunch. Whether you'd like to catch up or something?" I scrunched my hands inside my pockets. "Or would an evening be better?"

He didn't answer, just stared at me for long moments. A shiver crept up my spine.

*What is he thinking, Carmel? Is he recalling the pictures and what he did when looking—?*

"Or maybe you wouldn't want to spend any time with me. I mean, I wouldn't if I were you. You know, I wouldn't want to spend time with a youngster that I hardly recall. Why would you remember me, after all?"

He threw his head back and laughed. Yellow teeth decorated his mouth, and silver-coloured fillings graced every other molar. "Of *course* I remember you. I've thought of you often."

*I bet he bloody has—filthy bugger.*

I smiled, my jaw clenched. "So, would you like to meet up? Only, I've got to get back to work. I nipped out when I saw you in the street, and my boss won't be happy if I stay out too long."

"This evening," he said and fumbled inside his coat. He held out a business card. "Here." He pointed to an address on the card, his fingernail brown and brittle. "Tonight at seven o'clock."

"Okay," I said. "I must dash. Lovely to see you again, Mr Hemmings." I backed away from him towards the shop door.

"Lovely to see *you*, too," he said.

"Is it just my imagination, or is he leering at you?" Belinda popped her head out from behind a rack of trousers.

I jumped and squealed.

Turning, I smiled at the man behind the counter and left the shop, racing over the road. With burning cheeks, I scooted into work and glanced around the shop. No one seemed to have noticed my disappearance, so I continued with what I'd been doing before the interruption, my mind as busy as my hands.

# Chapter Thirty-One

A dirty grey tower block loomed above me on the estate where I'd grown up. Dark purple clouds scudded behind it in a pitch black sky, their destination somewhere to the west. Mr Moon peeked round the left side of the building, one eye and half a smiling mouth visible. Trees dotted a grassed area around the tower, their branches empty of leaves as if the wind had snatched them away in fury. Streetlamps cast their fuggy orange glow on the rain-slicked pavement, and I shucked up my shoulders, buried my chin inside the neckline of my coat, and lifted my hood.

Flat twenty, level six.

An uneven paving slab walkway led to the main doors of the building, and I stepped onto it, cautious of my footing. At the door, I took a deep breath and pushed it open, the peeling blue paint rough on my palm. The odour of dried piss and spilled beer prevailed, and I stifled a gag. A typical tower block, then. I supposed the lifts wouldn't work, either.

I jabbed the elevator button, surprised at the low hum and the level indicator window lighting up. The green numbers changed from eight to seven to six. A loud ping issued, and the lift door glided open. I stepped inside a relatively clean cubicle, pressed for level eight, and waited for the doors to close. The main tower door flung open and bashed against the inside wall. A guy on a skateboard rolled towards me and entered the lift, the smell of the outdoors radiating from his jeans, black bomber jacket, and red knitted hat. Red cheeks stood out against his super-white skin.

"Level you garn on?" he asked then sniffed.

"Eight," I said and nodded at the buttons.

"Right. Garn see Teddy, are you?" He winked.

"No. Not tonight." I settled farther into my coat hood.

"Not need nothin' tonight, then, eh?"

"No. Maybe tomorrow?"

"Okay. I lettim know you be round. Get the stuff you need, know what I mean?"

"Thanks."

I buried my chin again. Maybe this kid thought I was someone else? The doors closed, and the lift trundled upwards.

"Hear about Meeta? About how she garn? Sad shit, man, sad shit. Miss her."

I frowned, willing the level to reach eight. "No, I didn't."

"Well, me tell you about it tomorrow when you pops in Teddy's, right?"

"Right," I said.

The door slid open with a sigh that matched my one of relief. The guy scooted out, flipped his skateboard and jumped, landing back on it with ease. He rode down a concrete corridor, his hand raised in farewell. While his back turned, I stepped away from the elevator and descended two flights of stairs to level six.

The silver two of number twenty hung askew, one nail attaching it to the door; the zero veered off centre. A recent coat of red paint shone on the door, and a white net curtain covered a square of glass in the top. Light glowed inside as if down a hallway, and the window to my right yielded nothing but blackness. I rapped on the door. A figure shuffled towards it, and a shadowed arm reached for the handle and opened the door.

His knitted beige cardigan looked homemade.

*Maybe he got back with his wife after his release? You hadn't thought about her, had you, Carmel?*

Shit. I lowered my gaze from his beaming face and stared at his slippers. Dark brown faux leather with cream elastic side panels.

"Attractive!" said Belinda.

I looked up. She stood behind him, peeking round his waist, the smile on her life-face elfin. I frowned at her and gave Mr Hemmings my attention.

"Hello," I said.

"Carmel! Come in, come in." He moved to the left and waved to usher me inside.

I stepped over the threshold. Warmth enveloped me much like the heater in his old shop, and a pang of nostalgia prodded the backs of my eyes. Smiling, I stood next to a room on my right.

He closed the front door, tethered the chain, and shuffled towards me. His grey hair flopped forwards to rest against his forehead, and he swiped it away.

"Would you like a cup of tea?" he asked. "Or perhaps some pop? Do you like pop? I have some cola in the fridge. Or maybe lemonade?"

He smiled and came closer, his arm brushing mine as he reached for the door handle. Once switched on, the light revealed a kitchen, and he walked over to a small white fridge sitting beneath a worktop. He plunked a bottle of cola on the counter and stood on tiptoes to open a cupboard above the cooker. Clutching two glasses, he set them down and began to pour, the popping soda bubbles loud in the quiet.

"How's your mam?" he asked, his back to me.

"Oh, I don't see her these days. Moved out some time ago. How's Mrs Hemmings?"

He stiffened—his shoulders a rigid line—and sucked in a breath. "Oh, I haven't seen her for a long time, either. Seems we're both alone, eh?" He picked up the drinks and turned to face me. "Come along into the living room where it's warmer." He stood in the doorway and dipped his head to the right. "Would you mind closing this door behind me? It gets quite cold of a night if I leave it open."

I closed the door by hooking my foot around it then followed him down a short hallway.

"Damn council were meant to fix my window latches. They don't shut properly, let the cold in, you know. Dreadful when you think of my age, really. I could get ill, couldn't I?"

*Nothing that you don't deserve, you old nonce.*

In the living room, an electric fire boasted two lit elements, their orange glow like monster's lips. A moss green, velvet three-piece suite surrounded a Chinese-patterned rug in greens, creams, and blues.

Mr Hemmings placed our drinks on a glass-topped coffee table and tsked. "I keep forgetting to use coasters," he said and bustled over to the mantelpiece and selected two. His foot nudged a fire companion set sitting on the hearth. The brass tools tinkled against one another.

*Quite a posh place, eh?*

"Yeah," said Belinda. "Seems that even if you commit a despicable crime the government thinks nothing of housing you and giving you money to furnish it. Disgusting, if you ask me." Belinda sat on one of the armchairs farthest away from the door, her legs dangling, not quite reaching the floor. She sniffed. "Still, that's handy to know, isn't it, Carmel?"

From the doorway, I stared at her and frowned.

"At least you'll have the peace of mind knowing you'll get somewhere to live once you've done your time for the crimes you've committed in your life." She smirked.

I tuned her out and sat in the other armchair beside the door. Finished with the drinks, Mr Hemmings sat on Belinda. Her stifled, indignant scream hurt my ears, but I smiled and fought the urge to laugh. Belinda zipped out from beneath him, and Mr Hemmings shivered.

"Someone walked over my grave," he said, chuckling.

Belinda stood in front of him and leant forward, her face inches from his. "I'll fucking put you in it if you do that again."

I smiled at Mr Hemmings then turned to look at the TV.

A picture of me as a child sat on top of it.

"Oh, how sweet. You have a picture of me," I said, my tummy flip-flopping.

He glanced towards the TV, smiled, his eyes glassy. "Yes. It's the only one I have of anyone I knew back then."

"Have you lived here long?" I asked.

*Nice frame, that. Looks real silver to me. Glad to see you've got your clothes on in the picture.*

"About two weeks," he said.

*Didn't Bob only take pictures of you in the pretty dress or that…that thing?*

"Oh, right. Where did you live before that?" I picked up a glass of cola, drinking deeply.

Mr Hemmings' cheeks changed shade—a hue bordering purple.

*You've got normal clothes on in that picture. Even got that blue coat on that you pinched from school.*

"I lived near the moors," he said. "Fancied a change of scenery once the wife announced she wanted a divorce. You know how it is, I'm sure." He picked up his own drink, quaffed half, and panted for breath.

Belinda lounged on the sofa, picking her nose. "Yeah, she knows how it is. The moors, eh? Funny that. There's a prison near a set of them moors. Up north somewhere."

"Oh, right," I said and finished my own drink, the heat from the fire drying my throat.

*Reckon he must have taken that picture himself, Carmel.*

"So where do you live, then?" he asked. "And what have you been up to since I last saw you?" He cleared his throat and sipped the rest of his drink.

*Spying on you, he was. Filthy, nasty, perverted, bast—*

"I live on the other side of town. I needed to get away from…here. And I've got a job, sorting myself out slowly. Left home about three years ago now."

Mr Hemmings narrowed his eyes, peering at me. "Have a falling out with your mam, did you?"

*Wonder how he got to keep that photo? Considering what he was put away for…*

"Something like that," I said.

"That's sad." He drummed his fingertips on the chair arm. "And you don't see her, you say?"

"No, no, I don't." Tight smile.

Was his sigh one of relief?

"Have you seen anyone you know since you came back?" I asked, moving forward to perch on the edge of my seat. "You know, anyone from the old days?"

His eyes widened, and he rubbed the end of his nose. "No. If I'm honest, I'm not sure why I came back here."

Belinda guffawed. "Not sure, my arse. You're hoping to reacquaint yourself with Annette and get some more pictures, aren't you? Dirty old fucker. Did you hear that, Carmel? He's a dirty, disgusting old nonce who—"

"Your mam still live in the same place, then?" He inhaled deeply, his exhale a shudder.

"She does as far as I know. Why?"

"Oh, no reason. Anyway, let's talk about you. I want to hear all about you."

I laughed quietly and laced my fingers, hugging my knees. "*All* about me? Are you *sure*?"

"Why, yes," he said. "You were my favourite customer, weren't you? Why wouldn't I want to know how you've fared?"

His eyes focused on me, seemed to bore into mine, and I disguised a squirm.

"Well, I was sexually abused as a child, but then you knew that, didn't you? You saw enough of the pictures." I paused and took in the unbridled shock on his face. His beard and moustache parted, and an open gash gaped slack and wet. My guts lurched, but I pressed on, "And Mam, she didn't see fit to feed me, clothe me, love me. She lived for heroin, Mr Hemmings, and I was the result of a teenage sexual assault. Blamed me for it my whole life, she did."

His jaw hung slacker, and the skin around his eyes appeared to slough away from his eye sockets. "Sexual assualt? But I...I didn't..."

"You didn't *what*, Mr Hemmings?" My heart thudded, wild, painful.

"I didn't...she didn't..." He fiddled in his trouser pocket and produced a crisp, white handkerchief. Snapped it open, mopped his brow. "She didn't...didn't say no. She didn't tell me she'd got pregnant by me. I..."

I clamped my jaw closed and swallowed.

Blinked. Closed my eyes for a time.

"Uh-oh. Now look what you've gone and done," Belinda whispered.

*Oh, shit, Carmel.*

I opened my eyes.

An iron poker protruded from his forehead. Still seated, his arms splayed to the sides, Mr Hemmings stared up at the instrument in his head. His chest rose and fell in sporadic bursts. Blood seeped from his ears, nose, and mouth, dribbled down his chin, and pooled against the collar of his cardigan.

My heart thundered, and I glanced down at my hands.

They didn't tremble.

I stared at Mr Hemmings again.

"You'll need to wipe that poker, you know." Belinda.

"I know."

A gargle escaped Mr Hemmings' mouth along with bubbles of blood that popped upon meeting the strands of his beard.

"I'd suggest taking that glass with you. The one you drank from." Belinda again.

"Okay."

He coughed, spluttered, tried to form words.

"And wipe everything you've touched, including before you came into this flat."

"Right."

His body jerked then came to rest, his chest no longer moving.

"Give him five minutes to, you know, climb the star-steps, pass over, then get a cloth for the poker," she suggested.

"Okay."

"And take the cloth with you too."

"Yes."

I continued to stare, shocked at the sight of him.

"Oh, and Carmel?"

"Yes?"

"You'll be wanting to take that picture of you on top of the TV as well, won't you?"

The door closed. Expecting the lift to lurch downwards, surprise gripped me when it moved upwards. Shit, shit, shit.

*Should have taken the stairs, Carmel… Put your coat hood up. Quickly.*

Two floors higher, the lift stopped, and the door slid open. I squeezed my eyes shut.

"All right? You garn home now?" The teenage boy minus his skateboard.

Relief wiggled through my veins. "Yeah," I said, my voice muffled against my coat collar, the cola glass stiff in my coat sleeve.

The door closed, and the lift dropped downwards.

"Tole Teddy you be round tomorrow, yeah? He get you some good shit." He stared at his trainers—white Nikes.

"Okay, thanks."

"What time?"

Level seven…

"Oh, about eight?"

"Eight be good. He get deliveries at seven, so it a bit hectic round about that time, you know what I'm sayin'?"

Level six…

"Yeah."

"So, what be your poison, then? See, I makes sure Teddy got what you needs before you arrive, yeah?"

"Oh, I don't mind." I smiled. "Anything."

Level five…four…

"Anything?" His laugh rumbled in the small enclosure. "You is up for tekkin anything?" He snapped his fingers together and jigged on elasticised legs. "My kinda gal, man. Whooo wee. Funny shit. Yeah, you're funny." He sucked on his bottom lip and nodded to a beat only he could hear.

Level three…two…

The lift stopped.

Shit! SHIT!

The door opened.

"Going somewhere without me?" Belinda asked and stepped inside the lift.

The teenager stuck his head out, looked left then right. "Fucking damn kids, man. Pissin' about with the buttons, innit?" He sucked his teeth, stepped back inside, and jabbed the ground floor button with his thumb. "Where you off to now, then?"

Belinda stood behind him and pulled faces, sticking out her tongue.

"Home," I said.

"Where is home?" he asked, glancing at me.

My stomach rolled as the lift reached the ground floor. The doors opened.

"Where I'm safe," I said and stepped out into the piss-addled lobby.

"So, I see you at Teddy's tomorrow, all right?" he said, walking through the main door with me.

"Okay." I drew my hands up into my coat sleeves. Leaned on the door, rubbing where I'd touched it earlier.

"So, umm, yeah. I'll see you tomorrow." He lurched from one foot to the other.

Embarrassed?

*I think he fancies you, Carmel.*

Horror bloomed in my guts.

"Yeah," I said and ran up the paved path and away.

# Chapter Thirty-Two

Months shot by without seeing Belinda. Another birthday came. Funny that I woke up and automatically looked at the bottom of my bed for a present. Finding nothing, I resorted to filching through the rubbish bin down the alley at the end of the row of Victorian houses, knowing there wouldn't be anything there either. Old habits died hard. Gary nipped round that day bearing a wilted poinsettia, a probable remnant from Christmas, but I didn't mind. The thought counted.

One Friday, not long after my twentieth, I stopped at the chemist before going home. The skin of my hands had dried out and they itched. My boss, one with a remedy for almost anything, suggested I buy some intensive hand cream.

"After rubbing it on your hands before bed, put on some latex gloves. That'll keep the moisture in. When you wake up in the morning, your hands will be soft," she'd said.

I took her advice. Once purchased, I placed the items in my handbag and popped into the supermarket. Late Friday evenings saw me stocking up on food—got some cut-priced stuff, then. Sometimes Gary visited, and we'd watch a video while scoffing pizza until our tummies grew bloated and hard. Nice evenings, those. However, by nine o'clock, I realised Gary wouldn't call round. Bored, with nothing of interest on TV, I bustled round my bedsit, cleaning. The fresh smell of bleach and Mr Sheen revived my slacking senses, and by ten o'clock I stood and looked out of the window, wide awake.

A young man leaned against the streetlamp below my window, his breaths white puffs in the cold air. He threw a glowing cigarette into the road and ground it out beneath his heel. Shoving his hands in his coat pockets, he glanced up at my window, pushed away from the lamppost, and loped down the street. Was that the bloody teenage boy with the skateboard? The urge to follow him was strong, and I raced over to my wardrobe and wrenched on my coat. Winding a scarf round my neck, I pulled on my boots and swiped up my keys.

*You've forgotten something, Carmel.*

"Oh, yes. Shit."

I grabbed a box and stuffed it into my bag, slinging the bag's handle over my head. Keys in pocket, I opened the door, my breaths forming moisture on the scarf near my chin.

*You'll be careful, won't you?*

"Yeah, yeah."

The cold air smacked me in the face, stung my eyes, and nipped my ear tops. I glanced down the road. The man had reached the end of the street, his bobbing frame growing smaller, his breaths a train's steam. Had he followed me the last time I'd seen him to find out where I lived? It was ages ago, so why appear now?

I'd convinced myself that he wouldn't put two and two together and tie me to the occurrence in flat twenty, level six.

*Told yourself enough times that it didn't happen, and you now believe it's true.*

I quickened my pace. Why did I want to catch up to him?

*You know why.*

The path glistened with frost, and the hedges bordering the gardens bore white evidence that winter's chill would linger for some time to come. The frigid air chilled my lungs, so I buried my chin in my scarf, bringing it over my nose. The young man reached the end of the street and turned right, leaving another puff of breath as proof of his existence. I ran, despite the icy glimmer underfoot, praying the tread on my boot soles would grip the frozen tarmac.

Upon reaching the corner, I peered down another long road. He bounced along, head low, shoulders hunched. Maybe fifty metres ahead of me now, he veered across the street without looking, jeans baggy, his white Adidas sports coat too big for his skinny body. A car screeched to a halt, horn blaring, and he flipped the driver the bird. I smiled.

On the other side of the street, another road led west, a small convenience store dominating the corner. He disappeared into the shop. I followed. Inside, I didn't see him at first, but his voice sailed back to me.

"All right? Twenty Benson and Hedges and a box of matches."

"Do you have ID?" asked a woman.

"ID? You tekkin the fucking piss? I don't need no ID. I'm twenty-one, man. You *know* this." He clicked his tongue.

I smiled again and walked to the back of the shop. A counter spanned the width. Staggered plastic shelves sat on top of it, holding various chocolate bars. Cigarettes lined the back wall, and the middle-aged female shop assistant stood poised, her hand midway to the cigarettes the man had asked for.

"You should be flattered I'm asking for ID," she said and picked out a gold packet of Benson and Hedges.

"Flattered? Man, you *is* tekkin the piss. You know how old I am—been comin' here on and off for a long time."

She laughed and held out her hand for payment. Sale completed, she said, "Just let me serve this young lady, and we'll have a natter." She turned to me. "What would you like, love?"

I pulled my scarf away from my face. "Oh, I'll have what he had, thanks."

The young guy leaned towards me, eyes narrowed, his black beanie bearing the Puma logo. "Is that you?"

I faced him fully. "Me?"

"You don't remember me, right? Story of my life." His mock-offended expression drew the urge to giggle.

I frowned. "Umm, *should* I remember you?"

His brown eyes widened, and his rugged, good-looking features made my stomach clench. "I'da hoped so, but it don't matter." He rested an elbow on the counter, looked at the woman and said, "I been thinkin' of this woman for a long time, you know, and when I finally see her again, she don't know who I am. Mortified ain't the word, man."

I smiled and paid for the cigarettes.

"Got an easily forgettable face, Richie, that's your problem." The woman handed me some change and winked.

"What? You sayin' I'm forgettable now? Tsk. I should tek my business elsewhere, you know."

I shoved the cigarettes in my pocket and turned to walk away. "Well, umm, nice to have met you both, anyway. Bye now."

By the time I reached the shop door, he stood behind me and held it open. "You *sure* you don't remember me?"

I stepped through the doorway and turned left, looking up at him. "Yeah, I remember you. You're the kid with the skateboard in the lift."

We walked, him bouncing beside me. His smile brightened his face, and his lips revealed a gold tooth at the front. "Kid? Tsk. And you didn't come back to Teddy's either, man. I waited for you."

"You did?"

"Yeah, though I wondered what a girl like you would be doin' getting gear from Teddy, know what I mean?" He sniffed and opened his cigarettes, offering one to me.

"No thanks," I said. "What were you doing back there in Pointer Street?"

He paused in lighting his cigarette. It dangled from his lips, and the match rested against the strike strip on the side of its box. "Waitin' for someone, you diggin' me? Fucker didn't show up." He struck the match, the sizzle loud as the flame bounced to life.

A drug related meeting? Relieved that his hanging around my place had been a coincidence, I lightened my steps.

"I see," I said and slid my hands into my pockets.

We walked faster without talking, and my bag smacked against my backside. I glanced at him, took in his profile. He sucked on his cigarette; the end glowed the colour of Mr Hemmings' electric fire bars.

"You hear about that murder near Teddy's?" he asked. "Night I met you? Some fucker topped an old geezer."

I widened my eyes. "Really? Sounds nasty. What happened?" I blinked, sniffed, and wetted my lips.

He spat a bubbly glob of spittle on the pavement then sucked on his cigarette again. Exhaling, he said, "The old bloke, he got a poker in the head, know what I'm sayin'? Right in the middle of his forehead, man."

"Ouch."

We turned left at the end of the street and headed towards the estate of my youth. Blue-tinged clouds scarfed in front of the cheese ball Mr Moon, and a light smattering of rain began to fall.

"Ouch is right. He musta royally pissed someone off. Rumour went round he was a nonce. If that be the case, serves himself right, eh?"

Misty-looking rain settled on my cheeks, and the cold air froze it. I swiped my face, quickly putting my hand back in my pocket.

"Yeah, I suppose. Did they catch who did it?" I swallowed.

"Word on the street is that because of what he was, the police weren't really interested in finding no killer. That's one less kiddie fiddler to be worryin' about, see?" He flicked his cigarette butt into the road. It bounced; orange sparks showered then disappeared into darkness. "Still, it gave me the heebie-jeebies at the time. Mind you, all kinds of shit goes down round there, innit. Goes with the territory."

The territory stood before us now, a waste of space, an estate housing drug addicts, sellers, prostitutes, nonces, the dregs of society. Smattered among them lived ordinary people trying to eke an existence among the criminals.

*But you've made it out of there, Carmel. All on your own.*

Upon nearing the grey tower block, he said, "You comin' to visit Teddy tonight?" He laughed. "Or you goin' to visit whoever it was you visited last time?"

I blinked. "No. My friend doesn't live there anymore."

"Who was that, then?" He frowned and stared at the black, cloud-scudded sky. "Ah, mebbe that blonde bird, innit? The one with the twins? She hardly spoke to anyone, man."

"That's her," I said. "She moved out."

"Yeah." He shuffled from foot to foot, stared at his trainers, another pair of Nikes. "Umm, like, I wasn't jokin' in the shop when I said I'd thought about you."

I raised my eyebrows. Smiled. He looked up, his face reddening.

"What you doin' tonight?" he asked, toeing the tarmac.

"Going to visit someone and then going home. Why?" I cocked my head, made eye contact.

"Wanna meet me for a drink in a bit? We could nip into The Shackle. Stays open until two."

"Yeah," I said. "Why not? Shall we meet back here in say…" I glanced at my watch. Ten forty-five. "Two hours?"

"Yeah," he said. "Yeah, and don't you be lettin' me down now, else I got another lonely stretch of thinkin' about you, innit?" He smiled, his gold tooth glinting from a nearby streetlamp.

The quiet of the street hummed around me, and I stood and surveyed my old home from the darkness of the alleyway. The front of Mam's house sat in darkness, the windows empty eye sockets. With my scarf over the lower half of my face, I shrugged my hood over my head and walked, head down, to Mam's front door. The handle, dull silver, still dangled as if broken. With my hand inside my sleeve, I pushed the handle farther down. The still-scarred door swung open on silent hinges, and the odour of my younger years gusted out to greet me once again. My stomach churned, and I stepped inside, biting back a retch. Bare concrete beneath my feet—was Mam getting a new carpet at last?—echoed from my tread. Closing the front door, I stepped into the hallway.

The door to the cupboard under the stairs stood ajar, the shape of a shoe visible in the open crack. Memories of the night I'd dropped the fifty pence slashed through my mind, and the little girl I once was resurfaced. Sorrow rendered my legs weak and, shoving the images of that beating away, I stumbled into the darkened living room.

Familiar shapes: the decrepit sofa, my old chair beside the window, the coffee table holding the usual bric-a-brac. I squinted, peering through to the kitchen, seeking out the door to the back room. A line of stark light shone from beneath, showcasing a section of the dirty kitchen floor. Muffled grunts sounded, and a female said, "Finished?"

Mam.

I flattened myself against the living room wall beside the door adjacent to the kitchen, my breaths heavy, my heart ticking hard. The wall cold beneath my palms, I rested the back of my head against it and closed my eyes, immediately snapping them open again. The door to the back room opened—I'd recognise that sound anywhere—and the light spilled out, reaching the fusty carpet beside my feet.

"You know the drill," Mam said. "Flick the door latch up on your way out. Thank fuck you're the last one of the night." She cackled then snorted.

*Big old scary dragon.*

"Same time next week?" a man asked.

"Yeah. Yeah, see you then."

The kettle switch flicked, Mam's lighter clicked, and the man breezed past me towards the living room door. I held my breath, and my pulse quickened, its throb painful in my neck. After releasing my breath, I inhaled once more. The scent of recent sex wafted in his wake, and I swallowed the rising vomit. He exited the living room and walked through the hallway, his shoes scuffing on the concrete. Then he fiddled with the door latch, stepped outside and slammed the door.

I stared around the gloom-filled room. The shabby net curtains seemed to glow, a square of dirty cream in an otherwise grey house. The switch on the other side of the wall snapped, and I jumped, my breath hitching. Stutters of light flashed on the carpet and the wall to my left as the kitchen strip light burst to life. Water sploshed, the sound of it filling a cup loud.

"Ow! Burnt myself. Fucking hell, that water's hot," Mam grumbled.

*It would be. You just boiled it, you thick bitch.*

I inhaled deeply, steeled myself.

Pushing off the wall, I turned and stood in the kitchen doorway. Mam swung round, her mouth an O, eyes wide in sunken sockets, hair greasy and lank, as usual. She stared at me. Screeched.

"Hello again, Mam."

# Chapter Thirty-Three

❦

She sloshed the teabag against the side of her cup, squeezed it, then plopped it on the worktop. Steam rose from it, and I thought about picking it up and pressing it against her face.

"What the fuck are you doing here?" she said, spooning sugar into her tea. "And why the hell am I making this tea when you *are* here? Get the milk out, kid."

I did—but not from fear or habit. She left her cup on the worktop and slouched to the table, bare feet slapping on the lino. I poured milk into her tea, stirred the brew, and listened to the sounds of her shuffling into a comfortable position.

Her lighter clicked again, her previous cigarette still burning on a saucer by the kettle. I left it smouldering, the grey smoke rising into the air. Then I turned and walked to the table, placing her cup down.

Mam stared at the window in the back door—at her image reflected there?—and puffed on her cigarette. Wrinkles lined her red, lipstick-smeared mouth now. She'd aged quite a bit. Her greasy hair hung limper than I remembered, resting in slug-like strips on her shoulders. She'd acquired a new working dress—red with fake diamonds on the neckline. The skin on her slim body sagged around her waist, three rolls laying one on top of the other. Why did men go with her? Desperation? Any hole would do? You didn't need to look at the fire when poking the coals?

"So, like I asked just now. What are you doing here?" She exhaled smoke, sipped some tea, and winced at the heat of it.

"I saw Bob last year, he—"

"Yeah, I know. He said you'd popped round." She sniffed, and her arms jerked. "Well, it took you long enough to come back again. Happens I don't want to see you anymore now.

Had a lapse of sanity back then, I reckon." Still staring at the window, she huffed, dumped her cup down, and crossed her arms over her stomach. A tic in her eye flickered, and she blinked, making it worse.

"I'll just go, then, shall I?" I moved to walk away.

"Nah. Nah, you may as well stay for five minutes now you're here. So, what you been up to?" Still staring at the window. Tic still flicking.

"Nothing much. Working mainly." I stared at her reflection in the window. Her gaze met mine.

"Like your job, do you?"

"No. I'm going to go to college next year."

She barked a laugh—harsh, hurtful—her black teeth rendered invisible in the blackness outside. "You? Go to college? Got ideas above your fucking station, you have. What the fuck would *you* do at college?"

I bit back a vile retort, said instead, "I don't know yet. It's something I need to think about. Maybe I could be a doctor, something like that. I want to—"

"Be better than me?" She harrumphed out a sigh and nodded absently, gaze moving from me to her own face. "Yeah, actually, I should give you some credit. You do that. You make something of yourself. Make the whole…*thing* worth it."

"What do you mean, *thing*?"

"Never you mind. Just make your existence worth the hassle, that's all." She stubbed out her cigarette, reached for another. Click. Deep breath. Exhale.

"Don't you ever want to change your life, Mam?"

She laughed again, harder this time, close to choking. Her cheeks reddened, and spittle flew from her mouth and landed on an edition of *Chat!* magazine. She gulped some tea, steadied herself. "And how am I meant to do that, kid? Doing *this* is all I've ever known."

"I don't mean your job, Mam, but your habit."

"Oh, that. I couldn't give it up if I tried. Got too much of a hold on me. And talking of my habit, I need a dose. You're winding me up, getting on my nerves." She scraped the chair back and trudged to the living room.

I followed and sat on my old chair by the window.

"Why didn't you give me up for adoption, Mam?"

She stared at me, momentarily perplexed. Her brow furrowed—was her mind that confused that she had to search her memory to remember how to answer a simple question?

"That's a bit personal, kid. Maybe I don't want to answer that." She sniffed, cuffed the end of her nose.

"Well, maybe I need an answer to that question."

She sighed, stared at the coffee table. "I wanted…wanted something that belonged just to me, if you must know. Even when me parents kicked me out for being pregnant, even knowing how you got to be in my belly in the first place, I thought…" She stared out of the window.

"Thought what?"

"Thought everything would be okay. Then you were born and…and you looked just like him, and—"

"Like Mr Hemmings, you mean?"

Her mouth hung slack, and she blinked several times—trying to erase images of him forcing himself on her? "How did you…?"

She began preparing her medicine, and I said, "What's it like taking that?"

Her nose scrunched, and she opened and closed her mouth—a bizarre display. "Gotta have it else I get twitchy, you know that, Dumbo."

"No," I said, leaning forward in my seat. "What's it like? D'you get a rush, or what?"

She sighed, flicking the needle. "Not anymore, no. Why, you thinking of taking up the habit?" That cackle again.

"No, just that I read somewhere that you only get a good rush the first time, maybe the second, and that if you want that rush again, you've got to inject it in your neck."

She shrugged, frowned, and relaxed her shoulders. "Is that right?" The needle sat slack in her palm. "Not heard that one before." Mam stared at the net curtains, her gaze darting left to right. "Fucking dark in here. Stick the light on, will you?"

*Don't, Carmel. Someone might pass the window, see inside.*

"You do it," I said, and despite the bravado in my voice, my stomach betrayed me and flipped over.

Her eyes widened in the gloom, and she settled back against the sofa. "I'll let that slide—the rudeness—because I can't be arsed to argue." She put the needle on the cushion beside her and tied a nylon stocking round her arm, slapping at a vein. Moved so close to it that her nose almost touched her skin. "Fucking bastard. Come on, rise."

"Probably buggered, Mam. Try another." I gripped my knees, my heart pounding.

"Yeah, maybe you're right, kid. Not so thick, really, are you? Sod it, I'll do what you said. Need a good rush, me."

Mam jabbed the needle into her neck.

I stood, my knees wobbling. Walked to the kitchen and emptied her tea into the sink. Shoved her cup into my bag. Wiped the milk carton. Stole the spoon.

In the living room, I picked up some of Mam's medicine and a needle, slipped them in my pocket, and took one last look at her.

*Dead to the world.*

"Goodbye, Mam."

*   *   *

The trees lining the alleyway enveloped me. Safe… Chin dropped to chest, hood up, scarf over my face, I walked away—away from the street that held the secrets of my childhood, from the house where the walls had watched my torment and stood to see me fight another day.

I turned into the park. The frosted grass crunched underfoot, and the damp wetted my shoes. Mr Moon peeked from behind thick clouds, his face yellowed and aged. The firs, oaks, and birches that witnessed Belinda's accident swayed in the breeze, their branches waving hello.

"Hello to you, too," I murmured.

"Talking to fucking trees now, are we?" Belinda called. She hung from the monkey bars up ahead, her arms elongated—a primate at play.

"Piss off," I said and walked towards the swings, hands in my pockets.

The swing seat chilled my backside through my coat, and I shivered. The skin around my eyes tightened in the icy air, and I gripped the swing chains, cold against my palms. Scuffing my feet on the tarmac, I pushed off, relishing the wind freezing the tears on my face. My hood blew backwards, and the hair on the back of my neck stood up as coldness seeped through the previous warmth.

Belinda sat on the swing beside me, zipped from being static to sky-flying in a second. Our swings moved in the same direction.

"Crying, are we?" she asked.

I turned to her. Belinda's wind-dried, eye-socket face resembled a raisin. Her chubby fingers gripped the swing chains, and her burial dress flapped up and down, her meaty knees and calves playing peek-a-boo.

Her presence rankled, and ire gathered on my tongue and broke free. "No, I'm fucking not.

And if I was, so what? What the hell has it got to do with you? What do you care? You don't understand—never have."

I faced forward, focused on propelling myself higher, and stifled the need to kick Mr Moon's head in. He smiled his thanks, staring at me with his sad, half-lidded eyes.

"Oh, I understand, all right. You're nuts, aren't you? A twisted, freaky little nutter who insists on retribution. There are other kids in this world who've suffered like you, and you don't see them going round bumping people off, do you?"

My jaw clenched, and my stomach tightened. Rage built. If Belinda could die again, I'd have gladly killed her a second time. "I haven't *bumped* anyone off. Those people had *accidents*."

"Yeah, yeah, whatever you say. Killer."

My nostrils flared, and I inhaled. The cold air stung my nose, and tears pricked my eyes again. "I'm not a killer," I said, so low I barely heard myself.

"So you say. Anyway, how do you feel now? Better?"

I paused, examined my emotions. Though a sense of freedom blossomed, a part of me was hollow. An empty void remained, slowly filling with the sadness of childhood memories. Would the void close over once all the hurt had been sucked inside? Could I seal it and move on?

"No," I said. "I don't feel better. I won't until they're *all* gone."

Yes, sure that inner peace would claim me once *he'd* been sorted, I slowed the swing. Determination settled on my shoulders, snapping them straighter.

"You're fooling yourself, d'you know that?"

I stopped the swing and stood. Belinda swung so high I hoped she'd flip right over the top bar and fall off.

Sighing, I stared at her. "Like I said just now, piss off."

I lifted my hood and left the park, intent on meeting with Richie and having a stiff drink or two in The Shackle. Belinda's voice followed me, an eerie, melancholy wail that sent shivers up and down my spine. Tuning it out, I thought of other, more pressing things.

The languid walk to the grey tower block did me good. Refreshed, my emotions sewn tightly into the recesses of my mind, I stood outside the entrance. Would Richie show up? What did I want to meet him for anyway?

*An alibi, maybe?*

That wouldn't work, Nelson. The timing isn't right.

*But it's something, isn't it? Besides, I'd bet your mam's accident would look like an overdose. Suicide, even.*

Hopefully. I wonder who'll find her?

*You left the door on the latch, didn't you, so I'd say Bob.*

Yeah. Probably when he drops her next batch of medicine off. In the morning.

*He'll have to sell it to someone else now, won't he?*

I nodded and stamped my feet to keep warm. Moisture from my scarf wetted my lips.

I wonder if he'll miss her? They've known each other a long time.

*Miss the money she brings in, I'd say. And he won't have a venue for Thursday nights now, will he?*

No.

The door behind me swung open, and I jumped, turned. Richie stood smiling, his gold tooth an oddity beside its white companions.

"You came, then. Didn't think you would." He nudged my arm and shuffled from foot to foot.

I smiled. "Yeah, I came. So, does The Shackle get busy at this time of night?"

"Yeah. People round here like a drink, innit."

We walked across the grass until we reached the pavement. Scant traffic occupied the roads, and the windows in houses and flats stared darkly, their occupants in bed. Our mouths silent on the walk to the pub, I wondered if Richie felt awkward. Tongue-tied. I glanced at him. He didn't appear uncomfortable. A slight smile tweaked his lips, and he walk-bounced with more assurance than he had previously.

The low throb of music sounded, and we turned a corner. Ahead, a car park to the front, The Shackle stood, lights beaming from the windows, occasional laughter filtering into the night air.

"You ready for a drink, then?" Richie asked.

"Yeah. I need one after the day I've had."

"Bad one, was it?" He pushed the door open, and chattering voices and music swallowed my reply. Air thick with cigarette smoke and the strong scent of hops caressed my face. I took my hood down, pushed my scarf from my face. I ran my fingers through my hair to tidy it and followed Richie, nudging through patrons to reach the bar.

"What you havin'?" he asked.

"Bacardi and Coke. A double." I reached for my bag, remembered the cup from Mam's. My stomach clenched.

"I'll pay," he said.

Settled at a corner table, we chatted like old friends. The subject matter took a sinister slant, surprising me. Why did I attract people like him? Gary was just the same—loved talking about weird stuff.

"I reckon," Richie said, sipping his beer, "that all nonces ought to have their balls cut off. I mean, them kiddie fiddlers—think they should be hung, innit?"

I nodded. "Yeah. What do you think about people who go after them, then? You know, those abused kids growing up and bumping off their abusers?"

He laughed. "Bumping them off? I ain't heard that expression in a long time. Well, it's all right, yeah. Them perverts is getting what they deserve. Bastards. Reckon those that kill them are justified. Like, wouldn't *you* want to kill someone who did that to you? I would."

"I suppose."

We yammered on, finishing several drinks. A sense of righteousness stole over me, and the alcohol loosened my taut muscles and nerves. The bar's bell rang, signalling last orders. A ribald cheer went up, and customers scrabbled to the bar, their outstretched arms waving ten- and twenty-pound notes.

"D'you want another?" Richie asked, nodding at the bar.

"No. I think I've had enough. The air outside will hit me like a sack of shit, I bet. I've got to walk home yet."

We rose, and my knees sagged. Head spinning, I took a moment to regain my senses. I'd never drunk so much before.

"Where d'you live?"

I followed him through the crowd and out into the night. "Not far."

Retracing our steps, we walked in silence. Thoughts bombarded my mind. Who would bury Mam? Would Bob tell the police about me, and would they try to find me? Who would live in her house now?

*The council will have to clean it out before anyone else can have it. They can't give it to anyone yet, the shit state it's in.*

Hmm.

*Reckon old snooty next door will be pleased. Did her a service, didn't you?*

I sniffed.

*I hope you don't feel bad. Your mam only did what she'd have done another time. It just happened sooner, that's all.*

Bad? I stifled a laugh. What was there to feel bad about?

*Well, this kind of thing gets to people. They think it's what they want, and then when it happens—it isn't.*

We stood outside the tower block.

"Do you live here?" I asked.

"Yeah, with me mam and Teddy. Gonna get a place of my own soon." At the entrance, Richie leaned against the door. "Wanna meet up again some time?"

"Yeah. That'd be okay. Nice, I mean."

"You got a bloke?" He stared at the ground and kicked a loose pebble.

"Not as such, no. I've got a close friend. Male. He's cool." I thought of Gary and how he'd react if he knew the truth about what had happened in the past few hours. Would he change towards me if I confessed certain things? Would he be jealous that I'd been out with Richie? Did I want him to be? Confused by this sudden turn of thought, I frowned.

"Ah, right. We could be mates, though, innit?" He looked up, stared at me. "Like, we could meet every now and then. Have a few drinks."

"Yeah. That'd be cool."

"When?" His cheeks reddened.

I smiled. "I'm not sure when I'm over this way again."

"Well, I live in flat twenty-seven. Level eight. Stop by when you're free." He pushed away from the door, turned to open it, and glanced back. "See you around, innit?" he said and walked into the foyer.

The door thudded closed behind him.

# Chapter Thirty-Four

Sunlight filtered through the curtains. I was in bed, my mind sharp on the future, the pillow hot beneath my head. I turned it over and rested my cheek against the cold material. It was Saturday, the day I usually cleaned and took my washing to the laundrette over the road. I'd cleaned last night, so that left enough time for me to laze around. To think.

The morning passed in a haze. On my own—Belinda didn't show, and Nelson sat quietly on top of the wardrobe—I struggled to bat away the uncomfortable emotions jostling inside me.

Questions played tag with one another, unrelenting in their search for answers. Some tumbled in before I had the chance to respond, tripping and falling in an untidy heap in my mind.

Is this what you want? Even though your mam treated you badly, don't you feel remorse? What's it like to be the catalyst for so many accidents? Are you tainted, is that it? Were you infected with badness from the moment Mr Hemmings fucked your mam? Are you bad to the bone, destined to wreak havoc in others' lives?

On and on they chattered, strangers' voices inside a troubled skull. My answers inadequate, I grew more confused as time wore on. Anger, bitterness, and the feeling of being attacked stomped through me. Questions of my own formed.

Why should I be the one to feel bad? Didn't I suffer enough to justify the accidents? Didn't those people—like Richie said—deserve all they'd got? How come *I'm* the one left feeling bad—again? Life isn't fucking *fair*! It isn't right that I'm here all twisted up and confused. I've had enough of that in my life already. Stop. Just stop.

I threw the quilt from my body and darted out of bed. With a cold can of Coke from the fridge in my hand, I opened the curtains and stared at the street below. People scuttled like spiders, dodging past one another in their tasks to buy their shopping, go home again, home to warmth. To their nice families, caring people, who hugged their children, laughed, and never spoke a cross word.

Mothers pushed prams, the children in them well nourished, smiles on all their faces. Men on DIY duty entered the tool shop and emerged bearing saws, hammers, bags of screws. Off home then to put up the shelves, the new doors, fix the leaking tap. Children skipped, their eager hands shoving the convenience shop door open. Sweets. They'd be buying sweets. Spending their pocket money.

Why hadn't my life been like that? How come I'd been chosen to suffer?

A tear plopped onto the windowsill. I clamped my jaw and blinked away the wetness.

*You've got washing to do, Carmel.*

"I know."

*Best be getting on with it, then.*

"Yeah." I sighed. "Yeah, best I do that."

I loved the smell of the laundrette. So clean. A mixture of different washing detergents slammed into me, and I inhaled deeply, a sense of calm hugging me tight. Empty and quiet most days, this place always gave me happiness. A couple of washers threw clothing around inside them, the owners of the laundry absent.

Mam's washing machine rarely washed anything. So old, it clanked on the spin cycle and burped out water from the filter at the bottom.

*Stop thinking about things like that. Just…stop.*

I hefted my laundry bag onto the bench in the centre of the room and walked over to the soap powder machine. Four different brands showed through the glass panels on the front. Daz, Bold, Ariel, Surf. Which one today? My coins jingled inside the machine's belly, and the electricity meter under the stairs flashed through my mind. I shuddered and pushed the Daz button. A box big enough for my two wash loads clattered into a tray. I picked it up and sniffed its aroma through the box.

Finished sorting my washing into two machines, I sat on the bench to wait. Forty minutes for the washes, and an hour for the dryers gave me time to read. I opened my bag.

The cup was there.

I patted my pocket; the solid shapes of the spoon and needle inside.

I swallowed, fished out my book—an Agatha Christie—and zipped up my bag.

*What are you going to do with the cup and spoon, Carmel?*

I don't know.

*That spoon's all black. The medicine did it.*

I nodded.

*You could smash the cup into pieces and put it in one of the bins in town.*

I opened my book and lost myself in the pages for a time. Machines whirred, the sound of water soothing. The air seemed thickened with scents, heat, and comfort. The laundrette door swooshed open, and a blast of cold air nipped through my jeans. I looked up.

"Carmel! I thought you'd be in here. Thank God I've found you." The door closed behind a flush-faced Gary. He breathed as if he'd been running. Sweat beaded his forehead below the peak of his green baseball cap. "You've got to come, quickly." He waved an arm towards the door, the sleeve of his coat crackling.

"Hello to you too. What's the rush?" I closed my book and slid it into the side pocket on my bag. "Won a bet on the horses and need help spending the winnings?"

"It's your mam. Something's happened." He stepped closer to me, eyes wide, mouth downturned.

I sighed. "Gary, you know I don't have anything to do with her. I don't give a shit what's—"

"She overdosed again, Carmel." He sat beside me, hands dangling between his open legs. He bit his lower lip and swiped his forefinger beneath his nose.

"Wouldn't be the first time." I shrugged. "Won't be the bloody last, either."

My washing swam round in the rinse cycle. So clean.

*Bet it smells nice.*

He turned and looked at me. "You really *don't* give a shit, do you?"

"Gary," I cleared my throat, "if you'd been brought up by her, you wouldn't give a shit either. You're basing this on how *you'd* feel if it was *your* mam. Mine isn't like yours, is she."

"Wasn't, Carmel."

"What?"

"Your mam *was*n't like my mam. Your mam's, umm…" He took a deep breath. "Your mam's dead."

I moved the sleeve of my coat, checked the time. "Washing'll be done in a minute. It's spinning, look."

"Bob told me about it in the pub just now. He wants you to meet up with him. Discuss things."

"I reckon I'll do my ironing this afternoon, Gary. Saves me doing it tomorrow. What do you reckon?"

He frowned. "You're her next of kin. There are things you need to sort out."

"Yeah, I'll have a nice lazy day tomorrow. Might try and bake some biscuits in my little oven. Do you reckon they'd cook all right in there, seeing as it's really only a grill? Or we could even go out for a pub lunch. D'you fancy that?"

He gripped my arm and stood, pulling me up with him. "Stop going on about stupid shit, will you? Your mam's dead, and all you can think about is washing, ironing, and what you'll be doing tomorrow?"

I yanked my arm away and plunked my hands on my hips. "You want to know the truth? Yes." Spittle flew from my mouth. "That's *all* I'm thinking about. Bob can deal with it by himself, fucked if I care. You don't understand, okay? And you never will because you've been brought up proper. I, my friend, have been tainted since the day I was born." I laughed, opened one of the washing machines, and transferred the laundry from it to a dryer. The aroma wafted up my nose, and I smiled. "So, nice of you to come and tell me and all that, but really, you wasted your time. I thought you'd have *known* that after all our discussions."

Gary leaned against a washer. It danced through a spin cycle, juddering his body. His cheeks wobbled. "Yeah. I do. I just...I just thought that if it happened for real, that you'd want to know."

"Well, I don't. I might well go and see Bob, but I won't go to that woman's funeral. She can be buried alone and unloved, just like I've been all my damn life." I slammed the dryer shut and fed coins into the slot at the top. "Anyway, a change of subject, yeah?"

He sighed, nodded.

"Pub lunch tomorrow?"

<hr />

The Cross Keys housed few customers. A middle-aged pair nestled in one corner, their noses close, and two old men propped up the bar exercising their elbows and jaws. Gary ordered our drinks—Guinness for him, Coke for me—and we chose a table in the opposite corner to the couple. The table I'd last sat at with Bob.

Gary's gaze darted from side to side. He sat with his back to the wall so he faced the door. "Sit down there," he said, pointing to the chair opposite him.

I frowned at his forwardness but did as he'd asked. "So, are we eating lunch in here, then?" I picked up a tatty menu from the table and opened it. Lasagne and chips? Chicken and baked potato? My mouth watered. "I'm going to have lasagne, chips, and a side order of garlic bread. What are you having?"

Gary focused on the door. I nudged his foot under the table.

"Are you with it today, or what?" I asked.

"Hmm?" He looked at me and picked up his glass. "What did you say?"

I sighed. "What are you having for *lunch*?" Irritation tinged my words.

"Oh, you order. I'm not fussed." He gulped his Guinness and stared at the door again.

"Am I cramping your style? Or are you expecting someone? Only, you seem distracted. Like my company isn't stimulating enough. Shit, talk about rude." I snapped the menu shut and stood, walked away from him to the bar, and ordered our meals.

Back at the table, I said, "Lunch will be fifteen minutes. I got you the same as me. Tough shit if you don't like it."

"Oh, right," he said, craning his neck to see around me. "What are we having?"

Spite narrowed my eyes.

*I bet Richie wouldn't treat you like this…*

"You'll have to wait and see, won't you? Seeing as I've already told you what I'm having, and you weren't listening…"

He sat upright, looked at me, and said, "Sorry. Sorry, Carmel. I'm just—"

"Rude. Yeah, I know."

We sipped our drinks, an awkward air swirling around us. Gary didn't seem the same. Was it because he'd brought me the news about Mam and appeared to feel *sorry* for the old cow? Did I suffer from an immature burst of *he's my friend, not yours, Mam*? Did I expect him to side with me at all times, regardless of what I did or said?

Yes, I supposed I did. He always had in the past, hadn't he?

The scarred tabletop drew my attention. Whitened circles of previously spilled beer and cigarette burns decorated the wood. Chips and dents gave the table a weathered finish. No wonder they used beer mats. I picked one up and began to strip away the picture layer, disposing of the curly remnants in a large blue Fosters ashtray. Was my life like that beer mat? Was everything going to be stripped away, encouraging the inside outside? I blinked away tears. I didn't need them falling here. Gary would think I'd finally softened about Mam and keep on and on until…

Our meals arrived. We ate in silence. I didn't care—too hungry to be bothered about a little tension. If Gary wanted to act weirdly, that was his problem. Snotty sod.

My lasagne finished, I picked up a slice of garlic bread and took a bite. "Want some?" I asked, my mouth full.

Gary jumped. "Oh, uh, yeah. Please."

"What the fucking hell is *wrong* with you, Gary?" My brows hurt from frowning. "You're not with it at all. I may as well have gone out for lunch on my own. Some company you are."

His eyes widened, their whites bloodshot. He cleared his throat, twitched, and dropped his knife and fork on his plate. "Uh, um…"

"What? What's wrong? If you've got something to tell me then spit it out. You're pissing me off, you are." I gulped my Coke then slammed the glass on the table. "Can't be doing with this awkward atmosphere shit." My head throbbed.

"Um, Carmel?" He picked at a hangnail, ripped the skin so hard it started bleeding. Finger in his mouth now, he smiled and blushed.

"Yes?" I glared at him, my anger growing.

"There's someone," he nodded, "behind you. I uh...I..."

I turned.

Bob, his face lined and haggard, gave a watery smile. His moustache needed trimming, as did his beard. Grey hairs interspersed with the dirty brown, and the brief thought of him finally ageing zipped through my mind.

"It's my fault, Carmel. I made Gary bring you here."

I whipped back round to face Gary. "You fucking b—"

My lunch swirled in my stomach and threatened to reappear. I swallowed the lump of treachery in my throat, swallowed the disbelief that Gary would do this to me.

"Don't, Carmel," Bob said and sat beside me. "I wanted to see you. About your mam."

Bob's stale odour was disgusting. I wanted to run, run the hell away from these two men and never see them again. Remaining seated, I narrowed my eyes at Gary. His blush deepened, and he sucked on his finger—hard.

Turning back to Bob, I said, "What is there to see me *about*? The silly cow topped herself, as we knew she would one day. Good riddance, all right? I don't want anything to do with it all. I cut her out of my life ages ago."

Bob placed his hand on my thigh.

I tensed and flicked his touch away. "Get your hand off me," I said through clenched teeth. My gums ached.

Startled, Bob leant back in his seat. His slack lips worked for a while before any sound emerged. "Carmel. Please, just calm down." Bob's head shook as if he needed a fix, his greasy hair flicking into his eyes. "Take a walk with me, yeah? Cool down outside. Just let me explain a few things. I need to—"

"All right," I said, the pressure too much. "Half an hour." I turned to Gary. "You needn't wait for me. I'll make my own bloody way home, thanks."

I turned and stalked from the pub, the sound of Gary's sharp intake of breath and Bob's unsteady footsteps behind me.

# Chapter Thirty-Five

❧

We walked away from my old territory, through an industrial estate, and down to the canal before speaking. The pebbled tow path glistened with moisture—rain had fallen while Gary and I had eaten lunch. A couple of barges lined the canal, as did thick clusters of trees, their branches static in the still air. A tunnel sat in the near distance; four people stood on top of it watching the calm water below.

"So, what did you want to talk to me about?" I asked, hands bunched in pockets, gaze focused on the arch of bricks ahead. His elbow brushed against my arm, and I cringed, tuning out the contact.

"I've been thinking a lot lately. Like," he cleared his throat, "as I've got older. Looked back on the stuff I've done. Not done. Then this with your mam…"

I glanced out of the corner of my eye. Bob's face twitched, his nose wrinkling. His eyes bulged.

"Yes?" I prompted.

"I've done some bad shit, kid. I know it now and I knew it at the time, but it didn't…doesn't seem to matter."

The pebbles crunched under our tread, and the air shuddered as though sighing with me. The tunnel drew closer, and a barge chundered through it, the echo of its engine loud.

"Doesn't matter?" Anger pinched my cheeks, raised a heated blush. "The fact that you used me as a kid, took *pictures* of me and *sold* them, for fuck's sake. That doesn't *matter*?" I walked faster, my legs stiff, my arms clamped to my sides. My nails dug into my palms.

Bob quickened his pace, trotting alongside me. His foul breath soiled the air, blew in my face. The barge from under the tunnel cruised past, leaving beige, frothy water in its wake.

"No, no, that's not how I meant it. I meant—"

"What *did* you bloody mean, Bob? Come on, tell me. I'm intrigued as to whether you're going to be blatantly honest like Mam always was, or give me some bullshit excuse as to why you fiddled with kids, fucked up mine and their lives, peddled drugs, prostitution—"

"All right. All *right*! Stop. Just…*stop*, yeah? Shit." He looked around, body jerking. "Is there somewhere we can go for some privacy round here?"

My heart thudded. If he thought for *one minute*… "Privacy? Get your *filthy* mind out of the gutter. I'm not the young, stupid, trusting little girl I once was." I took a deep breath. "I'm going to turn around now and walk back the way we came. Away from you. And if you follow, I swear I'll tell the police all about you. Dirty, nasty, blo—"

"No. *No*, Carmel. I didn't *mean* it like that. *Listen* to me, will you?"

We stopped walking just before entering the tunnel and stared at one another, our breaths heavy. Anger ticked through my blood, heated it, made me want to reach out my hands and push the filthy little bastard standing in front of me into the canal.

"Bob, you have thirty seconds to say what you have to say then I'm gone."

His face paled, and he sniffed, hawked phlegm, and spat it into the water. "I meant that I needed the privacy for a fix."

Inwardly smiling, I kept my face composed. "Oh. Well. That's all right, then." I peered through the tunnel at the landscape beyond. "There's a field a little way ahead. I doubt anyone will see what you're doing there. Will that do?"

"Yeah," he said and sighed a sigh of the vastly relieved. "Yeah. That'll do nicely."

We ambled through the tunnel in single file, Bob in front of me. The dank air reeked of mould and dirty water, intensified in such close quarters. The sound of our footsteps crackled like Rice Krispies in freshly poured milk, and a steady drip of water from the tunnel ceiling plopped into the canal. Once we were through to the other side, the daylight, though meek, bombarded my eyes, and I blinked to refocus. Light rain began falling, misting my face, and I followed Bob along the tow path again, neither of us speaking.

Bordered by hedges, the field emerged on our left. I wasn't sure how we would gain entrance. "Keep walking," I said. "Maybe there'll be a gap in the hedge a bit farther along."

Bob raised a shaking hand—*he must really need a fix*—and bent his head as the rain fell harder. I lifted my hood and looked to the other side of the canal. Farm fields stretched for miles, and the bell tower of the church where Mr Lawton had…where he'd… Well, it stood in the distance. Serenity reigned. The sound of rain on the canal surface, birds twittering, and our feet on the path created a pleasing melody, and I wondered if Mam watched us from the top of the star-steps.

*She's more likely looking up from the flames of Hell.*

I moved my gaze to our side of the path. A slight dip in the hedge caught my attention. "Here, Bob. This is low enough to climb over."

We scrambled over the hedge and stood in a field full of high grass that whispered as a sudden wind picked up. Three large stones jutted through the grass, and I pushed towards them.

Sitting on one, I patted another. "Take a seat. Do your thing."

Bob crouched and set his gear out on the stone. "Shit. No spoon. No—"

"Needle? Here, I have both."

Bob gaped at me and ran calloused fingers through his soaking hair. Drool from the corner of his mouth dripped into his beard. "What? You on the gear now?"

I smiled and dug into my pocket, bringing out the needle and spoon. Handing them to Bob, I said, "Something like that."

He snatched them, dropping the spoon into the grass in his haste to prepare his ambrosia and inject. "Fuck. Shit." He ruffled the grass, eyes widening, hair falling forwards, obscuring his face.

I smirked and fought the need to laugh at the pathetic specimen beside me. "Bob, calm down. It's just there, right by your foot."

He sighed and snatched it up. "This shit has got a hold on me, kid. Like a demon, it is. You ought to be glad you haven't got any demons chasing through your blood."

"But I do. Still, we're not here to talk about me, are we? You wanted to tell me something, didn't you? Well, get your gear inside you and spill. I want to get home, and you've already had the half an hour I promised."

I turned away from him, stood, and surveyed the surroundings. The people on the bridge had moved elsewhere. A large patch of trampled grass jostled to our right, seemingly a bargee's dumping ground. While Bob busied himself, I traipsed over and inspected the rubbish. Black sacks and carrier bags full of refuse spilled their contents. A thick metal pole—from a tent?— and some sort of engine sat to the side nearest the hedge. A boot, a mobile phone with the screen smashed, and a wet, black T-shirt lay closest to my feet. I picked up the pole, using it as a cane on my way back to Bob. It sunk into the ground with each step, its end muddied.

Bob sat on a stone, his head hanging low, hands on his knees.

"Better?" I asked.

He nodded, lifted his head, and stared at me, his eyes glassy. "Look at this," he slurred and reached into an inside pocket of his coat. "My notes. Don't read them until you get home." He held out a small, red-spined book, its black cover veined with a grey marble effect. Rain plopped onto it, and I took it, slipping it into my pocket before it got too wet. "It's all in there. Everything you need to know."

Had he written things down that related to Mam? Were there things in that book that would help me understand? Forgive?

He stared at me still, his gaze penetrating now, and I recalled my pleasure at him noticing me, calling me his favourite girl. The years zipped backwards, and I saw the old Bob, the clean-shaven man with the bulging pockets, his short-spoken sentences. And Mam, pandering to his every whim.

*Yeah, right down to selling her own daughter…*

"I took too much, Carmel."

I blinked, shrugged off the past. "Pardon?"

"I took too much gear. Just now. On purpose. Nothing left for me without your mam." He gazed at the overcast sky, tears in his eyes. "She was the best, you know? The fucking best."

My eyes widened, and I sucked in a breath. "Was she? Was she *really*? I must have missed that, then. Must have slipped me by. See, I was under the impression that she was an uncaring, heroin-loving bitch who thought nothing of using me for her own ends. And you," I said, anger building, "*you* partnered her along the way. The pair of you—sick fucks. How the hell you can say that bitch was the fucking best I'll—"

Bob lurched to his feet and swayed. He raised his pointer finger and jabbed it towards me. "Don't say it. Don't say nothing bad about my Annette. I won't bloody have it. If it wasn't for you…" He spat, phlegm landing on the toe of my shoe. "Well, let's just say that my parting gift to you is in that book. You'll see. You'll fucking see."

He threw his head back and laughed, great bellows that ripped into my soul and roused the red mist within, shattering my illusion that he had given me the gift of freedom in his notebook. Bob swayed, and his laughter and too much heroin sent him reeling backwards.

He plunked down on the stone, closed his eyes, and said, "Ow. That hurt, that did." He rubbed his tail bone with one hand and his nose with the fingers of the other. His nose gristle clicked, turning my stomach. "Annette. Annette," he yelled, face upturned. "Wait for me, darlin'. I'm on my way." Roaring with laughter, he rocked back and forth, each movement intensifying my anger.

I clamped my jaw tight, clamped the pole tight, and swung it, hitting that good-for-nothing whore lover in the face. Mud flew from the pole's end, and blood spurted from the vein in his temple, squirting with each beat of his heart. He registered the contact and flopped sideways to the ground. In the foetal position, he closed his eyes, blood dribbling over their lids, the bridge of his nose. His red life continued to spurt, high arcs from the wound, splattering the grass around him. Static, clearly with no urge to fight, he smiled.

"I'm coming, lover," he shouted at the sky. "Won't be long. And that bitch kid of yours…" He panted, lips paling. "She'll not rest easy, even after I'm gone." He opened his eyes, moved his head to look at me. "You think…you're done…don't you? You think…with us gone…it'll all go with us."

I stared at him, hatred in my heart.

"Well think again, Carmel."

I raised the pole high in the air over me.

And brought it down on his head.

Hard.

A prickle from the hedge dug through my jeans and into my leg. I pulled it out, winced, and picked up the spoon and needle. I cleaned it on my jacket then walked back along the tow path. Under the tunnel, the dripping water sounded louder, heavier. I stared ahead and glanced back once. No barges occupied the canal. Nobody stood on top of the tunnel or on the tow path. I tossed the spoon and needle into the water. Wiped off the end of the pole and tossed that in, too. Hands in pockets, head down, I walked home, my fingers rubbing against the front of the notebook. The need to read it now wreaked havoc with my willpower. No, I wouldn't read it yet. I wouldn't.

# Chapter Thirty-Six

The next day, my footsteps once again took me back to the street of my youth. I entered from the top end of the road. Mr Lawton's old house boasted white netted curtains at the windows. A woman and her two little girls sat on a bench out front—waiting for Daddy to come home and take them shopping? The children's faces bore smiles, their cheeks reddened by the cold snap in the air. I envied them their innocence and their mother, who hugged them to either side of her. I turned away, the scene too painful to linger over.

The alleyway where I'd escaped home so often beckoned from the other end of the street, silently asking me to tread its path. To not loiter outside Mam's house. Too late. I stood in front of it now, the nets in the window barking their filth like an angry, starving dog.

The door of the spiteful, nasty next-door neighbour opened. Snotty stepped out onto her path, black patent court shoes covering grey stockings, her head bent low over her brown leather handbag as she checked its contents. A multi-coloured headscarf, knotted beneath her chin, protected her tight perm.

*That knot should be round her throat, shouldn't it?*

She closed her door, turned, and jumped upon spotting me, her rain mac crackling as her arms flapped away from her body and back down again.

"Oh," she said. "It's you. I'm…" She flicked her gaze towards Mam's house, and her cheeks grew ruddy. "I'm sorry to hear about your mother."

I chuckled under my breath. "Are you? Are you *really*?"

She blinked and gripped the handles of her bag, her knuckles purple against the white of the surrounding skin. "Well, yes...yes, I am. It would be un-Christian of me to feel otherwise."

I stared at her, spite infusing my tongue. "Like it was un-Christian of you to ignore my childhood? To listen through the walls and know what was happening, yet live in your secluded bubble as if I didn't exist? Except when you chose to send your looks of hatred my way."

Flustered, she said, "Yes, well...I can't undo the past, but I can apologise for turning the other cheek now. I feel dreadful...just *dread*ful..."

*I think she means it, Carmel.*

Do you?

*Yes. So she's safe, then?*

I thought about it for the tick of ten heartbeats, locking gazes with the woman who could have freed me from a life of abuse. Her eyes watered, and her bottom lip wobbled. She held her bag in front of her, its belly resting against hers, a shield against my wrath.

She stepped onto the grass, soiling her posh shoes, wet earth swallowing the three-inch heels. One hand reached out, touched my arm, fingers squeezing, the skin as wrinkled and leathery as her bag.

"I'm so sorry, my dear," she said, eyes beseeching me, begging for forgiveness.

I swallowed the lump in my throat, my body betraying me by revealing my emotions.

Yes. She's safe.

She skittered away, glancing back once, and I stared at her shoes, dirtied by the patch of grass that served as a front garden to both her house and Mam's. I fancied my dirt had sullied her—and not just the mud, either—perhaps even giving her nightmares, nights of restlessness in not knowing what to do. Had she batted away her sorrow for me as a child by putting me and Mam in a socially unacceptable box?

*Yes, I think she did.*

With one last look at Mam's dirty windows, one last peek into the memories that hovered behind the bricks and glass, I turned and walked down the street for the last time, down that alleyway, across the park, smiling at the swings, the trees, and the many memories they held.

I sat on a swing, the seat the same one I'd occupied back then. The swing's rusted chains dirtied my palms, leaving orange streaks on the undersides of my fingers, but I didn't care. It would wash off—one stain I could banish with water, unlike the many others inside me.

Gary came to mind. Would I stay friends with him forever, despite what he'd done? I hoped so. Could I confess everything to him?

Unsure of the answer, I swung high, the dampened air whipping my hair in all directions. And what about Richie? How did I feel about him? I mean, he liked me, that much was obvious, but did I feel anything for him? No. He'd been useful, but now that it was over, I didn't need him anymore. I swung higher, higher, wishing Mr Moon hung in the sky so I could kick him in the head once more.

Liberation flew through me. I was free, free at last.

The swing slowed, and I waited until it stopped completely before getting off. Swiping my rust-coated hands against my coat, my palms brushed the bulge of the notebook in my pocket. I ignored its presence and jogged past the site of Belinda's accident. And smiled. Rain fell, sheets of it battering the top of my head, cleansing the dirt. I smiled again, laughed.

I was going home.

"You took your time." Belinda was on my sofa, yellow pus dripping onto one of the cushions. She chanted, "I know what you've been doing!" over and over, getting on my nerves. I ground my teeth and inhaled through my nose, the air drying my throat.

*Don't let her rile you, Carmel.*

A sense of despondency crept over me. Would Belinda ever go away? Would she always be there, dogging my thoughts, my steps?

"Yes, I will. Already told you that before." She sniffed, the liquid from her eye-socket face disappearing. "That's the price you pay for bumping off your best friend."

I closed my eyes, wished my heart rate would slow, and took off my coat. Nelson smiled from the top of the wardrobe, wobbled on her perch as I opened the door and hung my coat on a hanger. The fleeting thought that my rain-soaked coat would taint my posh silk-covered hanger poked at me, and I removed it, placing it on a metal one.

"You going to open the book, then? Come on, I want to know what it says. You've had it since yesterday." Belinda's life-face appeared, and she smirked, her top lip curling.

I wanted to slice it off.

"Actually," she said, "I already know what it says, but I want to see your face when you—"

"Piss off, Belinda. I don't want you here. Go and haunt some other poor fucker for a change." I closed the wardrobe door, walked to the fridge, and picked up a Coke.

She cocked her head in contemplation. "Hmm. I could do. But d'you know what?"

I sighed, already knowing her answer. "What?"

"I'm not going to."

Her sarcastic smile needed wiping from her face. I stepped forward, intent on gripping her throat, choking her words, killing her all over again.

"So you admit it, then?" she asked.

I frowned. "Admit what?"

"That you killed me." She twirled her hair round her fingers, fingers muddied with the dirt of her death site.

"I admit no such thing. Leave me alone."

The snap of the Coke can tab made her jump. She stood and then sat cross-legged on the floor. I drank, easing my dry throat, and plopped down on the other end of the sofa that Belinda had occupied. A film had formed on the glob of yellow pus on the cushion, and my stomach churned with disgust and anger. I leaned my head back, closed my eyes, and thought through my feelings.

*You've got them all, Carmel. All the people who affected you. Will you be okay now? Has it all gone away?*

My eyes closed again. Condensation from the Coke can dribbled beneath my fingers, pooling on my leg. A shiver trundled through me. Elation? Or a reaction to the wetness? Childhood visited, images of me as a kid darting against my closed eyelids, the pictures tinted red-yellow from the sunlight filtering through the window. It had stopped raining. Was that a sign? Did the sun's rays *mean* something?

"Oh, stop it. You're over analysing. The sun has come out because it does, that's all. There isn't a divine meaning to why it's heating your face. Get your head out of your arse and face some facts. You're a bad girl, committing those so-called accidents. You can deny it all you like, but you intended for all this to happen. You did." Belinda languished on the floor, her stretch resembling a food-sated cat.

My nostrils flared.

"Open the damn book and be done with it. There isn't time to think about the past and try to justify your actions. To relax now would be silly."

I snapped my eyes open, my heart thumping an erratic beat. "What do you mean?" I asked, sitting upright, holding the Coke can so tightly my fingertips hurt, whitened. The can dented.

"Just open the fucking book."

I stood on quivering legs, placed my Coke on the table, and staggered to the wardrobe, fumbling inside my coat pocket, fingers unable to grasp the notebook.

*Take a deep breath, Carmel. It'll be all right. It will.*

The book snagged against the pocket opening, and I yanked, my frustration hindering its exit. I stamped my foot, tears burning the backs of my eyes, insecurity engulfing me, rendering me five years old again. Freeing the book, I took it to the sofa and placed it on my lap, unable to touch it.

*He'd* touched it. *He'd* written in it. Had *she* touched it too? Had *she* scrawled on the pages with her illegible handwriting? Did her uneducated words fill the pages? I stared at it, the book that possibly held the key to end my suffering. The page edges, cream with age, mocked me from beneath the cover. A yellow sticker decorated the top right corner, a smiling face within a circle, the universal graphic for acid, its edges tatty, dirty.

*Dirty like him.*

I glanced at Belinda, who now sat upright, hands clasped in her lap, eyes wide in her life-face. "Open it."

The first page showed a list of names, the title of NETTIE'S CUSTOMERS underlined. I recognised some first names, recalled their faces, the way they had spoken to me. Or not. The policeman—the old one who had visited that night so long ago—his name featured near the bottom of the page, as did Mr Lawton's. When had he visited?

*Must have been while you were at school, Carmel.*

Yes.

Three more pages of Mam's customers followed the first. None of them had harmed or touched me, not that I could recall, anyway. Except Lawton, who had *seen* me...

*They're safe, then.*

Yes.

The next heading, SMACKHEADS, told its own tale, many pages of the book dedicated to them. And the next, PIC CUSTOMERS, had my stomach lurching and my heart thumping so hard it hurt. *How can my legs go to jelly when I'm sitting down? How can they feel full of fluid when bones and muscles fill them?*

Names. *And* addresses.

*Is it over, Carmel? Please say it's over. Please...*

I swallowed, turned to look at Nelson, my beautiful dolly. She stared blankly ahead, her one eye releasing a single tear. It plopped down onto her dress, the same tear plopping from my eye and settling onto my T-shirt.

"Over, my arse," said Belinda, standing now, her eye-socket head bleeding, her fingers dancing against one another like spiders' legs.

My mind raced, and my throat throbbed with unshed tears—tears I couldn't set free. Not yet. Not just yet.

"No," Belinda said, hands on pudgy hips. "Not just yet. Time for that later. Now, you've got work to do."

# Chapter Thirty-Seven

❦

This is serious now. Like I keep telling you, I can't just go up to them and do it. It has to be right. If you want me to get all of them, I have to be careful. Can't go round being lax now, can I? If I get caught, that leaves some still out there, out there to perv on someone else. So stop pushing and shoving, will you?

Pardon? You just want it to be over? Well, hello? Like I don't? Do you think I like living this way, on the edge, wondering if this time, this time I'll get caught? I assure you, I don't. I dread hearing the knock on my door. I dread opening it. The relief when it's only Gary standing on the other side is massive. But you know *that, don't you? You watch me from the top of the wardrobe every time.*

*You've changed. Changed since the day I opened that damn book. Everything has to be done now, each of them suffering accidents as quickly as possible, their death one after the other like a snake of dominos falling.*

*Well, tough. It can't be that way. You'll have to be satisfied with how I've chosen to do it, as will Belinda. I can't stand the pair of you going on and on and on at me anymore.*

*What? Why are you gabbling about Richie now? What's he got to do with it?*

*Ah, I see. An alibi. That's a good point, but I'm telling you, if you push at me any more today I'm likely to snap.*

*Leave me be. Let me dispatch them in my own time. After all, they're not going anywhere. They're like Mam's medicine. My drug.*

*They're in my veins.*

Printed in Great Britain
by Amazon

17589428R00246